James Maw was born  Home, Kent, now a brief period as a hym so bleak?' (1962–3), J *not the King, Went* moments of Charles I, off in particular. After ~~~~~~~~~~~~~~ ~~~~~ obscurity at a state junior school at which he wrote *Have Them All Out*, documenting the long-running battle with his teeth, his second play, *Bedlam*, was produced at the Edinburgh Festival by his classmates in 1975. In 1980 *Milktrane*, a musical drama, was produced at the Old Vic in London.

1981 saw Maw receive a third-class degree in English from the University of York. A career as actor and TV presenter followed but after the absolute failure of his third major play, *Farque*, in Edinburgh in 1981, a second period of comparative obscurity ensued, during which *Hard Luck*, his first comic novel, was written, in Penury, in Bloomsbury and Northolt. Maw now lives in Manchester on the site of the Peterloo massacre.

JAMES MAW

Hard Luck

GRAFTON BOOKS

A Division of the Collins Publishing Group

LONDON GLASGOW
TORONTO SYDNEY AUCKLAND

Grafton Books
A Division of the Collins Publishing Group
8 Grafton Street, London W1X 3LA

Published by Grafton Books 1988

First published in Great Britain by
Quartet Books 1986

ISBN 0-586-07369-8

Printed and bound in Great Britain by
Collins, Glasgow

Set in Times

Preface

When certain avenues closed, and certain persons who had provided me with certain remunerations for work undertaken became reluctant to continue the practice, I found myself at liberty. So much liberty in fact that I was in the position of being able to cast myself upon the Parish. I was also at liberty to leave the house in which I lived, and to relieve myself of my possessions, and to learn how to live off soup. I moved then to a dull estate in Northolt, in the County of Middlesex, the rents being particularly convenient there.

This place was identical in every respect to the place where I had been born a little over twenty years before. Every corner I turned reminded me of things that I'd forgotten. One January day when my friend and former college mate, Julian Sefton-Green, was taking me to the chemist's with a bad ear, it became apparent to him that I should make a book of it – having so much liberty. So with his continued encouragement I have, and thanks to him, and to Mr Pickles and Mr Keegan, here it is, all boarded up in card and stitched at the edges, and ready to take its chance in the world.

Since no one, in the whole history of books, has ever read a preface, perhaps I could say a few words to my family, and save on the postage. You'll no doubt recognize certain things in here, and have certain things to say about it. The awful cooking especially will probably make Mum throw the book on to the electric fire, but if she doesn't know by now what a terrible liar I am then these pages will point it out. Dear Uncle Sid and Auntie Wyn,

I'm sorry that I used your old house in Wimbledon and put rather stuffy off-licensees, by the names of Peter and Cynthia, to live in it and be my uncle and aunt instead of yourselves. Dear Uncle Doug and Auntie Francis, I used yours in Basildon, and even broke the picture window and evicted you in favour of the awful Uncle Stanley. I'm sorry about this but you must understand that while you make marvellous uncles and aunts, you'd make lousy villains in a book, and I needed some. As for Uncle Bill and Auntie Gladys, well, I haven't used your house, I haven't even put you in at all, but you see, two villains are quite enough in chapter thirteen. And my dear Grandmother, I've used your bungalow down at Newhaven and I've made a terrible mess of the kitchen. I'm sorry that the grandmother in the story hogs the nuts at Christmas, but it really, really, really, isn't you. To my nephew Oliver, I'm sorry I used your brother Tom's name and not yours, but when you get to read Dickens you'll see why. As for all the other houses, schools, offices that I've wrecked, and the teachers, the doctors, the welfare people I've maligned, well, all I can say is that there are some exceptions here, and I hope you're furious.

For the historical detail I acknowledge the help of the ITN library, and, of course, *Hard Luck*'s copy editor Rosemary Graham.

I want to thank my brothers Michael and Derek for helping me out with some stories, and this book is inscribed, with love, to their children, in the faith that none of the adventures here will ever be theirs.

For

Jamie, Oliver, Tom & Juliet

Manchester 1986

Contents

I. *In which we are born, and then by a backward stroke of the clock we are merely expected. Our parents are cleared from the London slums to discover the new Garden Estate of Prospect, and its innovatory sewage system is explained* 13

II. *In which we are still expected and in which our parents fail to make a cup of tea. They explore Prospect and a surprising discovery is made which delights our father* 20

III. *In which we are born again, but in greater detail, and our story begins. The celebrations of our birth are described. We meet the young and idealistic Doctor Woodle, and the innovatory sewage system explodes* 27

IV. *In which we are to be sold to an advertising company and we have our photographs taken, which are thought by some to be successful but by others to be not so appealing* 34

V. *In which we are given every luxury that money can buy but our manhood is called into question over a Winceyette Sheet. Our grandparents are introduced, and our grandfather has a novel idea* 39

VI. *In which we are taken to the seaside for the first time on an original conveyance but we are not impressed with the*

*south coast of England, nor by the whelks, and in which
Uncle Stanley tells us about his wiggly tooth* 46

VII. *In which we eat our tea but do not enjoy it, and in
which we have a glimpse of the kind of conversation
common to our household, and touch on some of the
everyday problems facing Ellen* 57

VIII. *In which we get the television put on and our mother
has an adventure in the advertising world but on both
counts we are disappointed* 61

IX. *In which we hear about our father's job at Blake's Mill,
and Frank shows himself to be something of a poet, and
Ellen something of a chef. A recipe is included* 69

X. *In which we make friends with Charlie Rubbidge and
go tiddling at Five Arches, and Charlie tells us how his
mother fried his father's hand* 78

XI. *In which we have our sixth Christmas but there is
trouble with the tree and the turkey and Father Christmas
is not all that we had hoped* 85

XII. *In which we are beaten by our father and in which
we go to school and play the drums but our diaries say
more than we are at liberty to reveal, and in the longest
chapter of the novel we go on holiday to our grandparents
and a pig is killed* 99

XIII. *In which we go to pick peas with our mother but the
course of our lives changes. Uncle Peter and Aunt Cynthia
and Wimbledon are introduced and Ellen's childhood in
Kennington is described* 122

XIV. *In which Frank discovers that we have run off and we return to Prospect and witness a terrible and final event* 138

XV. *In which we are alone with our mother and the house is fortified against burglars but a surprising turn of events turns up to surprise us. The Pascoes are introduced* ... 146

XVI. *In which we are lied to by our mother on the draining-boards and we swap transfers with Kacky Fanakerpan and our mother is hoist with her own petard* 152

XVII. *In which we seek a new father and launch a campaign to marry our mother off to the rentman, and then the milk-man, but Ellen subscribes to a marriage bureau and Mr Norman Spanish comes into our lives* 162

XVIII. *In which we run away but come back again to find another turn of events which greatly affects the course of our lives for the remainder of the novel, and possibly beyond* 180

XIX. *In which we go to live with Mrs Bagbourne and we meet Mr Bagbourne who is most sympathetic to our plight but has possibly had a drink* 190

XX. *In which we go to school and struggle with our tables in the shortest chapter of the book* 204

XXI. *In which we are branded delinquents by the Bag-bournes and are betrayed into the hands of the state* ... 207

XXII. *In which we arrive at Crab Apple Road, a meal is eaten and a sausage is lost, and in which, as in other chapters, it rains* 220

XXIII. *In which our mother is disappointed with us and in which the reader sees a little of our lives at Crab Apple Road* 228

XXIV. *In which we ask to go to the cinema, and Mr Bumble makes a brief appearance to thwart us, and in which we are unhappy* 234

XXV. *In which we meet Hibedyhoy Harold and make plans to run away to join the fair and, also, in which a present is given to Miss Graterex and there is a shoot-out* 239

XXVI. *In which we go on holiday but we are found to be wanting at the table-tennis table, also in which several children are sick on a coach* 247

XXVII. *In which I get a bang on the head and I have tea with my mother* 252

XXVIII. *In which we sit our eleven-plus but the results change the course of our lives yet again and my fortunes in particular* 256

XXIX. *In which we get our new uniforms and I have a problem with a briefcase, and the headmaster of Broadfield is found to be a man of great investigative abilities and pomposity* 261

XXX. *In which we are split up and I begin to plot against my brother, and in which several boys in white polyester suits perform on the trampolene, and also in*

Contents

which I conduct a campaign against the Education Authority 271

XXXI. *In which Prospect is changing and the houses are improved and a most unexpected turn of events turns the events* 281

XXXII. *In which Mr Bannister is found to be a very great man and his influence changes the course of my life yet again, and in which a great scandal is uncovered by him and great steps are taken* 287

XXXIII. *In which we are reunited and arrive at a happy conclusion, and in which the sewage explodes, and in which Prospect is preserved in a very unusual way* .. 294

CHAPTER I

In which we are born, and then by a backward stroke of the clock we are merely expected. Our parents are cleared from the London slums to discover the new Garden Estate of Prospect, and its innovatory sewage system is explained

We were born at the end of the fifties. Our mother, Ellen, wanted to call us Pauline after a black doll she had as a child; our father, Frank, wanted to call us Heston after a cowboy. In the event we were born twins, with a single minute between us, which so confounded them that we had to be named by the nurse. Mercifully Agatha Ada Arbuthnot SRN sought no opportunity for revenge and named us Richard and Tom. The little tag tied to the toe of the first born worked itself loose on the way to the incubators. Which one of us is which, and who is the heir, and to what, is still hotly debated each Boxing Day over cold meats and pickles.

Ellen and Frank were moved to 127 Clover Gardens in the Great Slum Clearances of the nineteen-fifties just a few months before our birth. The new estate was called Prospect and it lay just outside London on the Orpington Road, a spot chosen for its valley, its clear view of Sidcup to the west, the North Downs to the south and the cheapness of the land. The London County Council had been through several policy changes since the *Housing of the Working Classes Act, 1890*, but this new period of building was the most important, instrumental as it was to be in rebuilding the shattered post-war economy, and the new garden estates were flagships of the newly created Welfare State. The queues outside the council offices in the poorer parts of London were so long that the LCC evolved a process of selection whereby sufferers from TB and diphtheria were given priority.

People collected their sickness certificates and ran through the streets to get their names down at the council offices for the new estate of Prospect. In Prospect clinics would be built, access for health visitors unimpeded, disease wouldn't be spread by shared bathroom and WC. Ellen's murmuring heart, coupled with pregnancy, was as good as TB so what had at first been deemed by Frank an accident was now hailed by him as 'the smartest move I ever made'.

Ellen still talks about the move down to Prospect as if it were any other great English migration: the sailing of the *Mayflower* to the New World or the shipping of the convicts to the Antipodes. They had been packed and waiting for a week. The council had provided them with tea-chests.

'We'll never fill all these tea-chests up,' said Ellen.

'Well we'll fill them up with newspaper, no one will know,' replied Frank.

In the bitter January weather, 1957, they moved to Prospect with a few dinner plates and a dozen copies of the *Daily Sketch*. For Ellen, after only two rooms, the house was a palace. The Authority had provided her with a coal-fuelled Burco in which to boil her washing, and which she quickly utilized for the making of plum jam from the fruit trees in her garden. There was a washboard hanging in the airing cupboard and a mop leaning inside, a bowl beneath the sink, a spade in the outside toilet, and a gas cooker, all provided. A card with fuse wire hung from the electric meter and lino had been laid throughout. She could obtain assistance with beds, curtains and carpets. Although Ellen and Frank didn't have two ha'pennies to rub together, and they were too proud to apply for everything, they lived in a dream house that they never imagined they would have. They were lucky to go straight in; the council had moved twenty-two thousand families all at once, all coughing and wheezing, in a fleet of vans and trucks, and many had to live in the little asbestos pre-fabs until their homes were ready.

Ellen walked round and round the house that first week, touching the walls and gazing out of the windows, continually changing her mind as to which view was the best. Every afternoon she set aside a little time to reflect on her good fortune and to sit halfway up the stairs to cry or to draw the blinds in the front room and dance with the mop to the wireless for the luxury of no one banging up from below.

Mr Edwin Bannister came to their front door on the first day and introduced himself. 'Well,' he said, 'I think you'll agree, Mrs Stone, that it's a pretty marvellous place isn't it?'

'Oh yes, it's wonderful, you don't know how grateful we are to you.'

Mr Bannister gazed around from his position on the front step with satisfaction and pride. He was an imposing figure in his pin-stripe suit, black spotted bow-tie, blue beret pulled dashingly to one side to cover an ear, as he rose on the balls of his feet to his full five foot two. He observed the way in which she was dressed and the tiredness already on her young face. 'Oh, I think I do,' he said.

From his brand-new leather money pouch, slung at his

side, he issued Ellen with her rentbook, the passport to her own home, and told her that he would be calling every Monday morning at eleven-thirty sharp for two pounds ten.

'Actually I had more than a bit of a hand, on several occasions, in the naming of some of the streets,' he said, with considerable pride.

'Oh yes?' said Ellen, impressed.

'Oh yeeeees!' said Mr Bannister. 'Well there's several hundred streets you know, probably more than a thousand, nearly.' Being a rentman he was always keen to be accurate with his figures.

'I bet there are,' said Ellen.

'It would be far too much for one man to name them all. Imagine the strain.'

Ellen shook her head slowly from side to side.

'I don't think an Einstein could do it.'

'No, I'm sure one couldn't,' said Ellen.

'Quite a few of us put our heads together. We had a "brainstorming session" and bingo! we came up with the names. It was touch and go for a moment though, the signs were made by a very good company in Swindon . . .'

'They're very good,' said Ellen, 'very clear.'

'Oh yes, they have to be clear. There's nothing more useless than a sign you can't read because it could lead a person to presume that it said something else.'

'Oh yes,' said Ellen, 'some of the signs in Kennington were so old that the places weren't there any more, they were somewhere else.'

'That is what happens without organization,' said Mr Bannister and then he returned to his original theme, '. . . but it was touch and go, because although they were made in Swindon they were painted in Slough. Makes you proud doesn't it . . .?'

'It does . . .'

'. . . to think that practically the whole country has taken part. I had many sleepless nights thinking that you would all arrive and the signs wouldn't be up in time. I could see you all not knowing where to move into, removal vans everywhere, up on the grass verges, even in the front gardens . . . but we all pulled together.'

'Well you have to, don't you? In a crisis,' said Ellen.

'The sewers,' he said, hopping a little with excitement, 'the sewers are something remarkable. There was, what? twenty cottages on this site before Prospect went up and you know what they had for a sewage system?'

'No?'

'Cess tanks.'

'Cess tanks?'

'Three between the lot of them. I can only presume they lived very regular lives.'

'They must have done.'

'Under our feet . . .' he said, stamping his foot so that the loose change in his pouch leapt up and down, '. . .is a tremendous operation involving many feet of piping not to mention valves. I had the honour of meeting the architect of our system,' he said, and here he bristled with pride, 'a brilliant man, who has formerly worked in Canada and places as far flung as Milan and Livorno. Dams, underground vaults, silage, there's nothing he hasn't had his finger in. He's entirely done away with the Stink Pole, you won't find one anywhere in Prospect. It's all controlled by valves under the ground. Under here, deep in the soil, is nothing but glistening aluminium. The detritus tanks themselves are situated two miles outside the Prospect boundary, two miles! The sludge which is produced in the houses is pumped out there, hydrauli-cally! Then it is entirely reprocessated and pumped back again. Marvellous.'

'It all sounds lovely,' said Ellen.

'When you think,' said Mr Bannister, 'about the state of this country after the last war, buildings flattened, food rationed . . .'

'You couldn't get nylons, you couldn't get bananas,' said Ellen, swaying him momentarily from higher things.

'. . . and building materials practically non-existent. All those brave men returning from the war, getting married, having kiddies, looking for work . . .'

Ellen began to wonder whether a list begun with such gusto could ever come to an end but pretty shortly, after he had said a few words about the aspirations of the young men who had fought he concluded: 'Who would ever think a place like this could be built?'

After a pause he began again: 'Not only massive slum clearances but new schools and a health service, and all at once! It makes you proud to be part of it.'

'I'm sure it does,' said Ellen.

'Fresh air, blue grass, green sky, it'll do wonders for your health, Mrs Stone, you won't believe the difference. You suffer from TB do you or is it your husband?'

'No, it's me,' she said, 'but it's not TB, it's a murmuring heart.'

'A murmuring heart?' he repeated with interest. 'I've another murmuring heart at 109. Very nice lady, such a shame.'

'Well it was a close run thing getting accepted really, it was touch and go until we found I was expecting.'

'Oh yes, well it would have been close run. I was present, myself, at many heart-rending scenes in the Authority offices where applications were close run. You can't entertain everybody to a thing like this. It's only the lucky few. It's one of the hard facts we had to face. Sometimes a thing would be so close run that they simply wouldn't know which way to turn so they'd turn to me and say, "Well, Mr Bannister, what do you think?" and I'd look at them and I'd say, "What do I think? . . . Well," I'd say, "I think we ought to give them the house – provisionally."' Mr Bannister smiled and gave a short laugh of pride and then looked up at the house. 'And what a place to bring a child into the world, could it have a better start?' he said.

'No,' said Ellen. 'When it was touch and go I just looked around our old place and I thought, "I can't bring it up here." Not that we were in what you would call squalor, but it was all flypapers everywhere and the people below fried a lot of onions.'

'Prospect!' said Mr Bannister, loudly, proposing it as a toast.

'Prospect!' said Ellen.

'Well, I suppose I'd better collect your rent!' he said at last.

Ellen took a quick tour around the house, ten shillings from her purse, eighteen shillings from a piggy in a cardboard box and twelve shillings from Frank, who was standing quietly behind the front room door. She handed it all to Bannister. He surveyed it in the palm of his hand with satisfaction and then he squeezed it in his fist saying, 'Well there it is, your first rent!'

'Yes,' said Ellen, 'and I'll be seeing you again next Monday?'

'Oh yes, I'll be here, don't you fear. I wish you many happy years in your new abode.'

'Thank you.' Ellen smiled with excitement.

Mr Bannister turned on the step, utilizing the new rubber soles to his shoes. Ellen stood at the door for a moment longer and then, as halfway down the path Edwin Bannister began to whistle 'On the Road to

Mandalay', she went indoors. She wondered how such a man, who had played such a vital pioneering part in the building of Prospect, a man so keen to extol its virtues, a man so keen to share his own enthusiasms, would ever get his rent round done by next Monday.

Frank sat down again by the window and expressed the opinion that the man was a bit of a twit. Ellen wouldn't hear this said.

'Yes,' she agreed, 'he was going on a bit, but he's obviously got a head on his shoulders or the council wouldn't have given him a position.'

Ellen sat down on the settee beside Frank and they both stared around the room.

'As soon as they've put those factories up they've promised us I'll be getting myself a good position,' said Frank.

'We haven't even got a Hoover yet,' said Ellen. They both stared out into the space before them.

CHAPTER II

In which we are still expected and in which our parents fail to make a cup of tea. They explore Prospect and a surprising discovery is made which delights our father

The builders' dust, the joiners' shavings, particles of plaster brought in by the plasterers, and fumes from the painters' drying gloss; the putty and the grease smells of the plumbers and glaziers; all these elements joined together to dry their throats and they were gasping, like mackerel at the end of the pier. They were gasping for a good strong cup of tea. The thought of it alone gave them pleasure and they began to feel at home. They had completed the labour of looking in all the cupboards and trying shillings in the new meter and turning the water on and off at the stop cock, and decided that they had earned themselves the cup of tea. It was to be a matter of great ceremony, but when Ellen turned the tap it spluttered and the first three feet of water was thick and brown. Shortly it cleared itself up with an astonishing burst of chlorine, and then Ellen filled the kettle while Frank looked in a tea-chest for some milk.

'Oh no,' said Frank, 'the bottle's bust – I said that driver didn't know what he was doing.'

'Oh well,' said Ellen, 'it'll give us the chance to find the shops.'

'What, both of us?' asked Frank, 'do you think we ought to go and find the shops and leave the house empty?'

'Well, we're going to have to some time,' said Ellen.

'The place is full of windows, anyone could get in and take our stuff.'

'We'll get insurance in the morning,' said Ellen.

Satisfied by this, Frank went into the kitchen to consult the map that the council had left in a drawer for them.

According to the map, the shopping parade was only a few streets away but when they got there it was just a set of hollow shells. The shopkeepers were loth to open up until enough custom had settled into the houses. Added to this there were great and furious debates over the terms of the franchises. The greengrocers believed that they should be allowed to sell tomatoes in tins, while the grocers believed that this would infringe their prerogative.

'Fancy sending people to a place with no shops,' shouted Frank as they marched along the streets in the vain hope of finding a corner shop. 'And the mud! Look at it!' he shouted, 'they've not even got any slabs down yet, it's a rotten shanty town. What have we come to? – we've come to the back-end of nowhere.'

'We'll get used to it, Frank. It'll be nice when it's all done.'

'But it's not London is it?' he said, plaintively.

Frank stopped dead in his tracks. 'Just a minute,' he said. 'We've been down this road once already, we're going in circles.'

'No we haven't.'

'We have. I've seen that house before, that one with the extra bit above the door.'

'No you haven't,' said Ellen. 'This is Marigold Road, you're thinking of the same house in Lily Road.'

'But the road curved just like this and then there were three trees with fences round them, look, there they are.'

'No,' said Ellen, 'those three trees were in Violet Road.'

'And I suppose all the roads are named after bloody flowers are they?'

Frank was right, all the streets were named after flowers. Ellen was charmed by the device but he didn't like it at all, he was used to proper street names: Newington Butts, Renfrew Road, Jubilee, Corporation . . . places with a bit of history like 'Elephant and Castle'. The notion that Prospect was a garden estate had gone to the planners' heads. They had started in good spirits and you could see which of them were named first because they extended from the Council Site Office outwards: Gloxinia Avenue, Saxifrage Street, Honeysuckle Close, Primrose Bank; but then, after a few rows of ordinary seed-packet names, they began to run out. You turned into a street named Leaf Hill or Branch Road, and then, as you proceeded towards the boundary you came across those named by Edwin Bannister: Dogwort Drive, Pigweed Way, Bladderwort Walk and Rubber Plant Place.

'Every road's the same,' continued Frank. 'I've never seen anything like it, all the houses are the same.' They were lost.

'They're not the same, Frank,' said Ellen, defending the brave new conurbation in which she intended to bloom, 'not when you look at them properly. They've all got different expressions . . .' By this Frank knew that she could only mean that some had curtains up and some did not. For every house was identical in all other respects.

'No picture palace,' shouted Frank, 'no pub, there's not even a church.'

'What do you want a church for?'

'I like to see them. You need a steeple here to find your way about.'

Ellen bumped into someone she knew. Frank shuffled about kicking the kerb as the two women engrossed themselves in conversation as if they were long-lost friends.

'Fancy seeing you,' said Ellen. 'Last time I saw you was in the laundry, Lambeth Road. I didn't know you were moving down.'

'Oh yes,' said the woman. 'We were among the first with our name down to get accepted through my Jack's polio and bronchitis which meant that we got separate bedrooms on medical grounds through his chesty cough which mustn't keep me up all night because of my kidneys.'

'Oh that was handy,' said Ellen. 'We were accepted straight away as well, they practically threw the house at us when they heard about my heart.'

'Really?' said the woman. 'I understood it was strictly polio or TB.'

'Oh no. Anyway, we're very happy with it.'

'Oh yes, so are we,' said the woman. 'It's by far one of the nicest houses on the estate, the wallpaper is beautiful and all the doors are flush. You've never seen anything like it.'

'Well, Frank's going to do ours in pink and green.'

'Oh you don't want to let him do it, get the council to do it, he's not fit is he?'

'Oh, yes,' said Ellen, 'Frank wants to do it. He's sound as a bell.'

'Are you sure?' asked the woman, 'he doesn't look fit.' She looked him up and down. 'He looks anaemic.'

Frank tired of this assault very quickly and turned away from the conversation humming 'Mademoiselle from Armenteers'. He thought about the men he'd be sharing the estate with: bronchitic, balding, divided from their wives by bedroom walls. He remembered the mates he'd left behind and wondered if there was a single man who could lift a snooker cue.

'We're up Geranium Walk,' said the woman. 'You and Frank will have to come round and have a look at it.'

'We will – and so must you, we're in Clover Road,' said Ellen, pausing to add rather grandly, 'it's a cul-de-sac.'

It was a good job no one had told Frank that this was French for 'bottom of a bag'.

'No more of those dirty, nasty streets,' said the woman, 'no more of that shouting and every other place a boozer.'

'Oh no,' said Ellen, 'and all these trees and verges.'

'There's every amenity, isn't there?' added the woman. 'Have you signed on with a doctor yet?'

'Give us a chance,' said Frank, 'we can't even find a bottle of milk.'

With this Ellen decided it was time for them to leave

the woman before he showed her up. They continued to trudge the streets, with Frank in a worse mood than ever.

'You could have asked her for a pint of milk,' he said.

Frank began to swear and curse the day. Ellen tried to soothe him by taking his hand but as each curse laid itself upon another so his grip increased and her wedding ring bit into her knuckle, but she did not let go.

As he scraped his heels around another turning, a movement in the air, a slight breeze, nothing more, brought a message to his nostrils. His eyes opened wider and a twinkle appeared, his nostrils enlarged, and, tentatively, he began to sniff, and then becoming more assured he filled his lungs with the invigorating aroma.

Forget the milk, he thought. He knew and loved each element of the smell: the dry, musty hop that formed its base; the rich, thick malt that fortified it; the grain that gave it body; and the yeast that crowned it with strength. His step quickened as his nose led him efficiently to its source.

'There it is!' he shouted as he saw the new-built and defiantly named Dog and Bucket. He paused for a moment to take it all in and then he threw away Ellen's hand and strode towards it, manfully. On either side of Ellen's wedding finger were the white indentations of the ring.

Casks of ale fresh from the brewery were being rolled up the open arms of the Dog and Bucket's forecourt by bronzed ostlers; leaded lights and dimpled glass adorned the Public and the Saloon; the landlord's wife was on the balcony above the painted awning planting out-of-season red geraniums, one after another, in a row of whitewashed tyres; the sign, with its cheeky-looking dog, a Jack Russell with a patch over one eye, drinking from a bucket, swung gently. The Great West Door of the Saloon Bar swung open as he approached it entirely without human aid. An orange light reflected on the copper plates and horse brasses and covered his face with an ethereal glow.

'Perhaps they could let us have a pint?' said Ellen.

'I wouldn't be at all surprised,' said Frank.

They went in, Ellen trailing nervously behind. Frank looked around with satisfaction. All the necessary accoutrements of drinking were there, brought from The Smoke to a new home in green pastures: the round board for the Arrows with its rubber mat before it; tall stools at the bar, short stools at the tables, a bottle for the blind, small square cardboard mats, ashtrays, and men, good, strong, healthy-looking men with their collars open and their ties in their pockets, their eyes sparkling and their noses red and gnarled. He satisfied himself that a pub is a place unchanged and unchangeable wherever it may be.

As he looked across the bar, between the upturned spirits, he saw his old drinking pal, Clancy, propped up against the pumps on the public side, and could barely believe it. 'Clancy, me old mate!' he shouted.

'Frank, me old mate,' returned Clancy.

'Where's your billet, Clancy?' Frank enquired.

'They've stuffed us up Clover Road,' said Clancy.

'Clover Road! I don't believe it!' he shouted and turned to Ellen saying, 'Here, Ellen, did you hear that? Clancy is in the same street as us!'

'I did hear,' said Ellen, 'he bawled it across the bar.' Ellen looked around the Dog and Bucket too but without appreciating the wealth of tradition as Frank had done.

'What bleeding number?' shouted Frank.

'One-two-five,' returned Clancy.

'One-two-five?' said Frank. 'Did you hear that, Ellen, he's our effing next door neighbour. All this way and he's our next door effing neighbour!'

'Bloody fantastic!' said Clancy.

'Bloody fantasticamagorical!' said Frank, and turned to Ellen. 'Look pleased, Ell,' he said, shaking her by the arm and turning back to yell across the bar, 'here, I hope you ain't going to be rowdy!'

'Rowdy?' said Clancy. 'I hope we bloody will be, we've just splashed out on a radiogram. We're going to have a right old laugh now I know you're down here – I knew you was moving down but I didn't reckon for a moment that we'd practically be in the same billet; we can knock a door through the bleeding wall.'

'Here, did you hear that, Ell? We're going to knock a door through the wall!'

'So this is Prospect then, eh?' said Clancy. 'What do you reckon on it?'

'It's all right,' said Frank, looking round the 'Bucket. 'It's all right!'

No higher recommendation for the new estate of Prospect could be made, and when he got home he made a sign, to hang on the garden gate, which said 'Timbuctoo'.

CHAPTER III

In which we are born again, but in greater detail, and our story begins. The celebrations of our birth are described. We meet the young and idealistic Doctor Woodle, and the innovatory sewage system explodes

On the night we were born Frank visited the hospital briefly before going on to the celebrations at the Dog and Bucket. There was a great deal of interest in our birth from other inhabitants of the cul-de-sac, from the woman in Geranium Walk and most especially from Mr Bannister, who had prefaced every little rent collecting homily for the last two months with,'Well, it'll be any day now, Mrs Stone.'

Frank felt it was his duty to run to the 'Bucket hotfoot from Maternity with the news that a great new brood had been born to Prospect.

'Well,' he said, standing on a stool because of the auspicious nature of the occasion, 'I was in the waiting-room with a man from the electric light company who'd lost the top of his finger, and he was just as flabbergasted as I was when they came out and said it was twins!'

'Well done, old son!' said Clancy, slapping his back and helping him down from the barstool and pulling up a chair for him to rest on after such an exhausting begetting.

'He's the father of twins,' said Clancy, 'two of them,' so that there should be no doubt in anyone's mind about the achievement of the man.

Ellen lay in a darkened ward, heavily sedated, wondering if she was still expecting.

'What is it?' asked the landlord, beaming over his pumps, 'a boy and a girl?'

'No,' said Clancy, 'it's two boys!'

'Good on you, my son,' said the landlord, leaning over the bar to shake Frank by the shoulders, 'let me give you a Scotch on the house!'

Frank was overjoyed and picked a Scotch up from the bar.

'A toast!' declared the master of the 'Bucket, raising his glass with all his regulars following suit. 'What are their names?'

'Heston,' said Frank, overwhelmed by his magnanimity.

'Heston?' said the landlord.

The bar repeated the name twice and swilled their drinks.

'They are indentical, are they?' asked Clancy.

'Oh yeah, totally identical, like peas in a pod.'

'Well then, if we're wetting the babies' heads,' said Clancy, 'I suppose we have to drink twice as much for twins, eh?'

'Certainly do,' said Frank, not one to be discouraged, and, by following the principle that Clancy had laid down, he managed to get himself twice as drunk as usual. By the middle part of the evening the Scotch had so confused him he announced that he had to be getting home because his wife was expecting and he wasn't having her lift the coal-scuttle. When Clancy reminded him that the great event had already happened he paused for a moment in disbelief, and then ordered another double round of drinks. From that night onwards our father's consumption of alcohol exactly doubled. By the end of that great evening the landlord found himself in the position of being forced to call the police to have Frank and Clancy removed. Frank kept a cutting from the local paper, reporting the incident, as a memento of our birth. Ellen, on the other hand, kept a column inch, run on another page, which was headed: BOUNCING TWINS FOR HEART MURMUR MOTHER.

After two weeks we were set free from our incubators, wrapped up and taken for a first ride on the bus to be settled into our parents' new house. When the doctor called, Frank asked if we would be getting free milk.

'Oh yes,' said Doctor Woodle, 'you'll be given everything at the family clinic.'

'Rosehip syrup?' inquired Frank.

'From the clinic,' replied the doctor.

'Oh good,' said Frank, 'I like that. What about free meat?'

'Not for babies,' said Doctor Woodle, frowning, 'they don't have teeth.'

'What about us, we have to keep our strength up,' said Frank.

Doctor Woodle smiled and preferred to pretend that this was a joke. Doctor Woodle was a young man and idealistic. He had moved to Prospect where he felt himself to be at the very heart of the National Health. Only a few short weeks after this meeting with Ellen and Frank he was to found the local communist party, and in a few, even shorter, years after that, at the time of a missile crisis in Cuba, his patients were scandalized by the knowledge of it and refused his medications. Frank had heard about 'sleepers' and was sure he was supplying the tablets. Frank improvised a crib for us from a kitchen drawer. When the doctor noticed it, at the conclusion of his talk with Ellen, while checking our lungs, he said, 'And I'll see about a crib, Mrs Stone, my mother still has mine somewhere, I think.'

'Oh no,' said Frank. 'We don't need charity.'

Ellen would have liked to have accepted the crib. It was an embarrassment to her that she had to show off her pride and joy to the world as if they were a new pair of serving spoons. She wanted everything in the house to be new and she got a passion for anything modern or brightly coloured. The few things that they did have in the house, at first, they had brought with them from Kennington or picked up cheaply from an open-air store on the way to Sidcup. In Kennington there had been no incentive, they had lived among a landlord's cast-offs and the rooms looked just as their parents' had in the thirties. In moving to Prospect they had suddenly jumped from the depression years to Macmillan's fifties. Here, anything old-fashioned was no good any more, it had no charm and no value. It took Ellen years to get rid of the last bits of evidence pertaining to the two rooms in Kennington, but she waged a furious war against them, and we were the inspiration for the combat.

They had a utility sideboard with wood so wafer-thin that if too much was put in it the floor fell out. Frank said of it that the only good thing in it were the hinges but when he dragged it out into the garden and made a hutch of it for the breeding of rabbits he was proved wrong. The buck rabbit kicked the doors off with his back feet and went to live in the woods.

In Ellen's attempt to jazz things up a bit she attacked her dressing-table with a hammer and knocked the standing mirror off the back.

'Well you've got no bloody mirror now,' said Frank when he got in.

They had a Victorian chiffonnier, inlaid with mother-of-pearl and standing, as if on points, on delicately carved rosewood legs. Ellen suddenly decided that it was a 'blooming eyesore' and made Frank smash it up in the garden. It was as if someone had walked on stage at the Royal Opera House and kicked a ballerina.

Ellen wanted a nest of tables, which were all the rage, so Frank stained the tea-chests left over from the move and made three little tables, none of which would quite fit into another.

As much as the house, Ellen loved the garden. There were some fruit trees left from when there was an orchard on the site and to these they added more. Frank loved to climb the trees to shake the fruit down for Ellen to make pies and jam. Most families had no more experience of gardening than they had gained from the annual LCC

Best Window-box Competition and so the cultivation of plants was a fussy affair: little pinks and pansies overcome by great expanses of mud. Their attempts to create gardens were not helped by the fact that Mother Nature made a bid, during the estate's first year, to reclaim the land on which it was built. Springs welled up in the gardens, forming little brooks and rivers which flowed around the houses and along the streets, meandering across the neat lines of the urban plan. Some families thought this to be the perfect atmosphere in which to rear ducks for the table but, on the whole, the ducks didn't like the uncertainty of it all, preferring their pond to remain in the same place two days running.

In the second year the gas began to build up in the innovatory sewage system and the explosions began. They terrified Ellen, and when they boomed in the night she would wake up and take us from our drawer as if she was living through the blitz again. The glass shook in the windows, the mirrors dropped from the walls, and the most awful smell filled the house. Mr Bannister assured her that these were just minor teething troubles and quite acceptable in a system so revolutionary. He began to be less assured in his tone, however, after arriving on our doorstep one Monday morning badly shaken, pale and in need of hot, sweet tea. He had narrowly missed being caught up in one of the explosions.

'Paving slabs flew twenty feet in the air,' he said, 'as the ground opened up beside me and gallons of sludge shot up.' But apart from a dreadful pong which hung about him, Mr Bannister had escaped a most ignominious fate. No one was actually killed by the innovatory sewage system. The engineers moved in very quickly and the whole thing was re-dug, but the purgatory of those living in the pre-fabs was prolonged.

All of the people were young with newborn families and, despite the chronic disablements of many of the tenants, there was a genuine pioneering spirit. The council had built brightly coloured schools which lay in wait for us under the cover of fences and shrubs. The roads were safe; no one had cars. Some, the totters, had brought horses which they let graze on the verges at the corners of the streets. Everyone got cats and dogs immediately because in two rooms they'd only been allowed canaries and fish. After only a couple of months the abandoned pets had formed themselves into wild packs, overturning dustbins in the night and, by day, marauding, ambushing the rentmen on their rounds and the sewermen as they sliced through the tarmac. Mr Bannister came in for another cuppa.

Both Ellen and Frank dedicated their lives, in these early years in Prospect, to our well being. They were intent on our having the best, Frank got a pram for us and pushed it all the way home from a lay-by on the Sidcup by-pass on only three wheels. It was a Silver Cross which he reminded Ellen was the Daimler of prams. He found another wheel and rejuvenated the chassis with green gloss. The hood was re-covered with orange curtaining and a second hood was made for the other end out of a meat-safe. We spent many hours in this grand contraption because although Ellen was a little ashamed of it, we were lucky to have it and it afforded us one of the greatest opportunities: that of soaking up the sunshine. Ellen believed in sunshine with a naturist's zeal.

'It doesn't matter,' she said, 'whether a baby's rich or whether a baby's poor – it soaks up the sun just the same.'

As well as a belief in the beneficial effects of low-level radiation on babies, Ellen also became an ardent admirer and advocate of the carrot. The Germans were beginning to do terribly well after the war, something which upset Frank and the boys at the 'Bucket greatly, but gladdened Ellen. She disliked cup finals because she felt that after getting so far it was a shame that one of the teams had to loose. Part of the basis of the German rejuvenation, she was sure, came from the carrots they were given as babies. Ellen had got friendly with a German woman who had married a member of the Rhine Occupation Army and had moved with him into one of the pre-fabs where they were re-digging the drains. No doubt it reminded her of home. It was Eva Tinkle who gave her the recipe for infants' carrots.

3 lge carrots
2 nice size lemons
2oz gran. sugar

Grate carrots into bowl. Put away. Crush the lemons careful to exterminate the pipins. Smother the carrots with juice. Leave to stand up for 3-4 hrs. Bury in sugar, leave standing for 30 mins. Serve to kinder.

CHAPTER IV

In which we are sold to an advertising company and we have our photographs taken, which are thought by some to be successful but by others to be not so appealing

It was one afternoon when we were enjoying our German carrots that Frank, who didn't approve of them, looked at Ellen and said, 'I've had an idea.' Whenever he had an idea the last thing he would do was to supply the details of it to Ellen in the early stages lest he should be discouraged while it was still forming in his mind. He guarded it closely like a patent pending and disappeared from the house under a great cloak of secrecy, to gather all the elements he would need. On this occasion he returned with a little paper bag containing his *fait accompli*: a small pot of apricot and honey pudding.

'Go and get my Halina Prefect,' he said to Ellen. 'It's still got some film left in it from Christmas.' When Ellen had taken the camera from the chest of drawers upstairs she returned to find Frank spooning the food out of the pot and trying to get us to eat it.

'What are you doing?' she asked. 'You've not even put it on the heat to warm it up for them.'

'That don't matter,' said Frank, 'I'm taking photographs.'

Ellen handed him the camera.

'Right,' he said to her, 'you make them look as if they're enjoying it, do your jigging about and get some smiles on their faces, and make sure you've got the label on the pot turned towards the camera.'

'What's all this in aid of?' asked Ellen.

'Our future,' said Frank. 'We won't want for anything once I've taken this snap. They'll be falling over themselves.'

Ellen said nothing but waited for him to continue. He took the photographs while she complied with his instructions. Finally he gripped the camera in his hand saying, 'I'm going to send the photo in. It'll be a great advertisement for them.' Frank had heard of a man in the pub whose brother had twins and all the babyfood companies queued up in his front garden offering him money.

'They wanted to buy them everything, clothes, food,

even a bungalow and all they had to do was to eat their stuff and nobody else's.'

'But what if they don't like it?' said Ellen.

'Well, I don't know,' he said. 'You could sneak them something else, on the sly, when no one's watching.'

'They wouldn't send someone round to make sure?'

'I don't know,' said Frank. 'Not at breakfast, they wouldn't send someone over just for breakfast would they? But for other meals I expect he'll be there.'

'But it'd just be dinner and tea?'

'If that,' said Frank. Ellen was unsure about his project. It was a well-known fact that companies would do anything for advertising. Rationing was newly ended and modern mass advertising was a novelty in this country. As soon as the snaps were printed up Frank sent them off to the company.

Ellen read him the letter which came back:

Dear Mr Stone,
We were so pleased to get your lovely photograph of your babies. You must be proud of two such fine little girls, and we are thrilled that they enjoy our very fine products. You say in your letter that they 'live on' our apricot and honey pudding 'morning, noon, and night' and 'won't touch nothing else'. We are very pleased that the product is proving satisfactory but I have included a list of our full range of babyfoods in the hope that they may also enjoy a varied Berber Diet.

Thank you for your interest in our public image, we really do try our best! I'm sorry if it's not up to your own very high standards.

Yours,
T.L. Timberlake (Public Relations)

'Is that all?' said Frank. 'Don't she say nothing about free food and a bungalow?'

Frank was undaunted by this. He was determined that

his sons should have the best, that he was going to do his complete duty by them as a father. He began working on a plan to sell us to an advertising company.

'But won't they take them away?' asked Ellen.

'I don't know,' said Frank. 'I mean, they'll be required for photo sessions and the like and as soon as their faces have been on every billboard in the country, well they'll be famous won't they? They might have to stay in a hotel, but, I mean, they'll have the best of everything.'

'Oh no,' said Ellen, 'I don't like the sound of it.'

'Well, we'd go with them, naturally. I mean as their mother you'd have to open shops.'

'Oh no, I wouldn't want to do that, anyway I haven't got a hat.'

'Well you'd get a hat. The advertising company would provide you with one.'

Frank speculated over the problem for many hours in the Dog and Bucket. Sometimes, it's true, he would despair, but Clancy would encourage him, assuring him that if anything in the world were true it was that twins, and pretty twins, were worth money, no one could say they were not.

By the time we were two, Frank was getting a little bit desperate. He began to think that unless he had one final push at getting someone to put up a contract we would not fulfil our early promise.

One day we were playing with a cardboard box in the garden when Frank suddenly yelled, 'Quick Ellen, get my Halina Prefect!' Ellen came out with the camera. Frank sat us both inside the cardboard box.

'What are you doing,' said Ellen, 'putting them in a filthy dirty box that's had veg in it and everything?'

'Ah!' said Frank, 'but it hasn't had veg in it. Look, it's

Leyland Motors, see, it says "Leyland" on the side of it –
it's had parts in it.'

'I want to know what you're doing of?'

'Look, we put this little bucket on the back and it
looks like a car, see? And Tom's driving it and Richard's
having a nice little ride in it.'

We watched our dad with bemused faces and Tom
began trying to eat the box while I dribbled over my end.

'You're off your rocker,' said Ellen.

'Get them to smile and I'll take the snap, quick before
they've ruined the box. Who's having a nice ride in the
little mote-mote, then eh?'

Frank showed the photograph to Clancy and Clancy
said it was brilliant.

'Yeah, I know,' said Frank. 'And Ellen said I was mad
when I took it.'

'You'll get a packet for that! Get it off to Leyland first
thing.'

'I've already sent the copy. You look out for it, Clancy,
it'll be on every billboard in the country. They'll be the
Leyland Babies. They'll give us a free car and everything.'

'They will, Frank,' said Clancy, 'for a picture like that
they definitely will. What do you say we go down and
have a celebratory lemonade at the 'Bucket?'

Ellen wasn't so sure about the picture, and she certainly
hoped that nothing would ever come of Frank's schemes,
but she said, 'Yes, the picture's nice, they look like
they're driving a car and everything but they won't give
you anything for it will they?'

'Of course they will, it's advertising!'

'They won't think it makes their cars look like a lot of
cardboard boxes, will they?'

Frank paused for a moment and looked at Clancy.
'Naw,' he said.

'Naw,' said Clancy, and they got off to the 'Bucket sharpish.

Leyland never wrote back, they never even returned Frank's snap. In response to this Frank refused ever to accept a lift in one of their cars. We remained the property of our parents.

CHAPTER V

In which we are given every luxury that money can buy but our manhood is called into question over a Winceyette Sheet. Our grandparents are introduced and our grandfather has a novel idea

The notion that we should have the best of everything swept through our family like fever.

'Winceyette!' said Frank's father when his wife and Ellen returned from the Peckham Rye sales. 'Nothing but the best, eh?'

'Oh yes,' said Nan, 'and feel the quality of it.'

Frank picked up the call in the kitchen and came through to the front room saying, 'Winceyette! Luxury! No more of those old linen things of your mother's.'

'There's nothing wrong with those linens of my mother's,' said Ellen.

'No, I know,' said Frank, 'except that they've gone yellow. How long did she have them before she gave them to you?' Frank's parents laughed.

'He's a card, our Frank,' said his mother proudly. Ellen didn't consider it right that one mother should laugh at the expense of another and so she rounded on Frank, and defended the old linen sheets. 'They're good quality,'

she said, 'better than anything we could afford; they
came from Eaton Square.'

'What, when she was in service?' said Frank.

'Yes,' said Ellen, 'admittedly. But she didn't take them,
the lady gave them to her when she got married.'

'But that was in the First War,' said Frank, smiling at
his parents. 'No wonder they caught my toes, they must
be forty years old.'

Frank's father computed the distance, in years, between
the Great War and the present day and said, 'Yes, they
must be forty years old – or more!'

'Well if you didn't toss and turn you wouldn't have
ripped them,' said Ellen.

'Ripped them?' said Frank, defending himself to his
parents. 'They went threadbare, you can see through
them, they just gave way.' It was an indisputable fact that
they had given way. Frank woke us up at night when his
leg went through the sheet and he got all caught up in it.
We always knew when he'd gone to bed because we
heard the rip.

'Anyway,' said Ellen, 'the Winceyette is not going on
our bed, so I don't know what all the argument is about,
the Winceyette is going on the twins' bed.'

'The twins' bed!' shouted Frank. 'But I can feel the
buttons in my back!'

'All they've got is a bit of old curtain,' said Ellen.

Frank shook his head, his father shook his head. 'A
man's got to get a good night's rest,' said Grandad, 'he
can't sleep with buttons in his back.'

'The Winceyette,' said Mum, finally, 'is going on their
bed until you give me the money to buy some for our
own.'

With this the subject of the linen was dropped, but not
before it had established itself in Frank's mind, and in

the mind of his father, as a bone of contention. We were very happy with our new sheet and because it had come into the household so heralded and so much disputed it came to be known as 'The New Blue Cuddly Sheet', and we felt ourselves to be much pampered possessing it.

After only a few weeks of sleeping each night in the luxury of it we developed the habit of pulling it off our bed in the morning and carrying it about with us all day. I would tuck one corner around my thumb and Tom would tuck the other around his so that we could each suck a corner. It travelled with us everywhere, flapping between us like the sail of a catamaran.

'What are those blinkin' kids doing with that sheet?' our father would inquire of our mother.

'It's their comforter.'

'Comforter,' said Frank. 'what do they want with a comforter?'

Sometimes Tom would want to go one way and I the other, which provided us with one of our first great dilemmas. The difficulty was solved by Mum, who would lay the sheet at a point equidistant from the two of us. As long as we could see it, and return to it whenever we felt it necessary, then we were happy.

Frank's parents were frequent visitors to our house in those days. Nan declared that she didn't want to miss any part of her grandchildren's growing up, and didn't want to deprive our mother of the advice and instruction that she could offer. Our grandfather too enjoyed the spectacle of our infancy, but more than this he enjoyed the long discussions with our father about what we should become, and what signs we were manifesting towards that direction.

'They've got a comforter now,' Frank informed him.

'A comforter,' said his father, 'what do they want that for?'

They settled down with a couple of bottles of stout to discuss it.

'When I was a baby,' said our grandfather, 'a child didn't have such things, and when you was a baby,' he said poking our father in the ribs, 'you didn't have such things. You were happy with a bit of stick to chew, and by their age you was kicking a ball in the street and fighting.'

'Yes I was,' said Frank, remembering every detail of his second year.

'Children,' continued his father, 'have to be watched. You can't pamper them. Some families revolve entirely around the kids, every stupid little thing they do people think is marvellous. Well do you call wandering the house slobbering over a bit of sheet marvellous?'

'No,' said Frank. 'I don't.'

'Do you call going "gar gar gar " and "da da da" marvellous?'

'Nope,' said Frank, 'and I don't think people should.'

'Do you call standing up, tottering a few steps and falling over marvellous?'

'Definitely not,' said Frank.

'We brought you up to be a man,' said his father. 'I wouldn't allow none of this namby-pambying around. If I strapped you, I strapped you and that was that, wasn't it? You let them get away with this sort of nonsense and you know what they'll turn out?'

'I do,' said Frank, 'I do.'

They resolved that this dreadful situation couldn't go on a minute longer, the women had been soft, it was time for a father's influence to be fully felt. It's up to a father to point the way for his son, they decided. No one else can do it.

'Here,' said Grandad, calling us over by slapping his hands on his thighs like people summon dogs. 'Watch this, Frank,' and he turned to us. 'Why don't you let Grandad have that horrible old sheet? You don't want it do you?' We didn't have the greater part of the language at our disposal at this time but we intimated by signs (rolling the sheet up and sitting on it) that we preferred to remain with it. 'I'll give you half a crown for it,' said Grandad. Money meant nothing to us; we'd been brought up to believe it was simply something which must not, under any circumstances, go into the mouth, which valued it far below a cuddly sheet.

Grandad's offer had no effect so, having tried reason and having tried bribery, he resorted to the thing to which they are always the prelude: brute force. He tugged at the sheet, pulling us over, and gained possession of it. There was a moment's perfect silence while we filled our lungs. Then we bawled. Tom's bawl was just a little higher in pitch than mine and the effect of our bawling in tandem was shattering to all who heard it. It had, to Grandad's ears, all the dissonance of Indian music coupled with a klaxon-like quality which reminded him of the blitz.

The great noise summoned our mother and our grandmother from the kitchen, from which they ran wiping their hands on their aprons.

'Whatever's happened?' called Mum, above the bawling.

'Is the house caving in?' said Nan.

'Dad's set them off,' said Frank (as if we were some kind of alarm).

'What have you done?' asked Nan.

'What have you done to my babies?' said Mum.

Grandad sat, cowering in his chair, a broken man.

'All I did,' he pleaded, 'was to try getting that blinkin' sheet off them, that's all I did. I offered them money.'

'Well they won't be parted from it, they love it, you know they love it.'

Mum assured us that the New Blue Cuddly Sheet wouldn't be taken away. As suddenly as our bawling began, so it stopped, leaving a ringing in the air and Frank and Grandad plugging their fingers in and out of their ears.

After we had all recovered Grandad took the opportunity to say a few more words on the subject of our upbringing.

'If you let a child go round with something like that he's going to grow up soft. A comforter, what do they want a comforter for? It's not natural.'

'Yes,' said our dad, 'when I was their age I was kicking a ball in the street and boxing. What are we bringing up, a bunch of ninnies?'

'And pansies,' added Grandad for good measure.

'And nancy boys,' added Dad to fill it up to the brim.

There was a pause and then our grandmother took off her apron and looked at our father.

'When you were their age you were kicking a ball in the street and boxing?' she asked. Frank nodded his head. 'Well as far as I can remember, and I remember pretty well,' she continued, 'you had no such thing as a ball.' Shock ran around the room. 'You had one once, yes, but before you could use it your father and his mates had lost it under a tram.' It was not often that Nan had the opportunity of addressing the family on such a great subject so she made the most of it. She affected a stern face and spoke slowly and regally and commanded the attention of all. When Frank made to interrupt she would simply raise her hand and continue. 'And as far as boxing goes, well I remember you coming in crying because you'd been scratched by a tabby but I'd hardly say it was done by the Marquess of Queensberry rules. What I do remember, on the other hand, is you playing with the little girl across the landing, and you taking one of her dolls, in a frilly white dress, and you refusing to give it back, and you bawling the house down for a week.'

Frank sat white-faced; his father's mouth was open and his left hand rubbed slowly up and down on his chin. A second silence descended and then the two men erupted at once with shouts of 'Did I? my foot I did!' and 'a son of mine?' and 'frilly white dress?'

Mum and Nan marched back into the kitchen.

Dad refused to believe such stories, and his dad refused to believe them about him. Dad had an image of his childhood in his mind: the tenements, the hard life, the street fighting, the raggy clothes and dirty faces, which he would never, ever, erase.

Later that evening when all but the two men were in bed, and they were downstairs drinking, Grandad said to our father: 'Look, I'll tell you what, Frank, I've had an idea.'

'What's that, Dad?'

'You've got a pair of scissors haven't you?'

'Yes.'

'Now we're here for a week. I'll tell you what I'm going to do. Starting tonight, each night when they're asleep I'll go up there and cut a couple of inches off the sheet and chuck it away bit by bit.'

Frank shook his head from side to side astounded at the simple brilliance of the plan, and then he nodded it up and down to give assent.

We didn't notice, of course, even when the couple of

inches of the first night grew to great chunks being sliced off as the nights went by. By the end of the week we were walking around the house clutching a New Blue Cuddly Sheet that was no more than twelve inches square, and not a word said. We couldn't understand the mystery at all.

As Nan and Grandad were leaving to go home we were standing at the front step to wave them goodbye.

Grandad sneezed. 'Oh coo blimey,' he said. 'I'm getting a cold. I'd better blow my nose, lend us your handkerchief, kids.' Saying this he grabbed the little square sheet that we held between us, blew his nose on it and chucked it in the dustbin by the door as if it were a paper tissue.

We looked towards the dustbin, we didn't cry. Mum led us back into the house.

CHAPTER VI

In which we are taken to the seaside for the first time on an original conveyance but we are not impressed with the south coast of England, nor by the whelks, and in which Uncle Stanley tells us about his wiggly tooth

Frank took a great deal of interest in the world. As a boy in the nineteen-thirties he collected his father's cigarette cards celebrating the land speed trials. He loved the smooth futuristic shapes of the speed cylinders: Malcolm Campbell's *Bluebird* as it tore across Daytona Beach at 276 mph and John Cobb's Railton on the Bonneville Salt Flats, burning up at 394.19 mph. As soon as Frank earned his first wages he wasted no time in joining a roller skating club.

Ellen, on the other hand, took her pastimes more sedately, as befitted a girl with a dubious heart. Her brother, Peter, was secretary of the Kennington Clerical Cycle Club and he persuaded her and Frank to join in the great forays, with hundreds of cycles, into Surrey of a Sunday. When Ellen and Frank became engaged they bought themselves a tandem which they brought down to Prospect with them.

The great cycle trips had ceased by the fifties, the roads were not as free as they had once been, but the annual Bank Holiday beano to the south coast still remained and Frank wouldn't miss it for the world. As a child he had gone with his parents to Southend on the *SS Imperial Star*, a packet steamer, embarking at Tower Pier and disembarking at 'the longest pier in the world'. It invariably arrived with its passengers so drunk that none could manage the mile and a half walk to the mud flats.

Frank contrived to fix a kiddy seat to the back of the tandem. He was very proud of his work but it still only made it possible for one of us to go.

'We'll have to go by train,' said Ellen. Frank knew that this would cut down on the beer money substantially.

'No,' he said. 'We like our biking, it's exercise. Put one of them in with next door.'

'No,' said Ellen. 'We can't take one and not the other.'

Frank thought about this for a moment. He knew the necessity of keeping everything equal between us. If he did not, we would hold our breath until we suffocated. 'All right then,' he said. 'Put both in with next door.'

Ellen wouldn't entertain the idea so Frank came up with a plan. He went in to see Clancy and a few moments later Ellen heard a great banging in the back garden. Ellen went to the kitchen door to see what was going on.

'Oh, Frank, what on earth's that?' she said.

'It's Clancy's sidecar from his Harley Davidson, he's let me borrow it.'

The sidecar was painted in black gloss and had RAF insignia on the side. It was known by all in the Dog and Bucket as the 'Dresden Bomber' because everytime Clancy drove it into the forecourt bits dropped off.

'I'm going to fix it to the tandem, see, and we'll have one kiddy in here and one in the kiddy seat.'

'Oh no, Frank,' said Ellen. 'You can't put a kiddy in that, it'll scream all the way.'

'Well, I thought we'd give it a tot of brandy before we set off.'

Ellen tried to save as much as she could so that she'd be able to afford the train fare for us all but when the Bank Holiday came around there was not enough in her purse. It was the Dresden Bomber or no Brighton at all. Ellen gave in and Frank slipped Tom a tot of brandy and tied him into the sidecar with a fluffy duck. I was on the back. It was quite a contraption, people cheered us as we passed them. Ellen was very embarrassed but Frank was spurred on by it. He cheered back at the people and pedalled faster and faster, trying to beat the cars. It was clear from the start that the project was doomed, there was too much machinery and human frailty involved. The disaster didn't strike until Poll Hill, one of the steepest hills in Kent, on the edge of the North Downs. It was Dunton Green, a mile on, before it was discovered and Ellen screamed.

'Frank, Frank, stop!' she shouted.

'What's the matter, love, ain't you enjoying it?'

'The sidecar's dropped off,' she said. Frank looked down to his side.

'The bolt must have sheered off at the top of the hill, I thought I heard something go.' Frank took off his goggles.

'My baby's dead,' muttered Ellen. Frank looked momentarily worried.

'I reckon we'll have to go back,' he said.

'Of course we'll bloody have to go back,' said Ellen, dismounting and beginning to run back up the hill. Frank told her to get back on.

'It'll be quicker with the two of us pedalling,' he said.

'Stuff the pedalling,' said Ellen. 'Forget the rotten pedalling, my baby's been killed.'

Ellen ran up the hill erratically, dashing from one side of the road to another, narrowly missing the cars. Every time she saw something flattened on the road she fell on it thinking it was a part of the Dresden Bomber, and then ran on, expecting to find a little group standing around her smashed child.

'I'm going to kill that Clancy if anything's happened,' panted Frank, as he cycled up behind her. 'I'm going to bloody kill him. I told him he gave me the wrong bolts.'

When they found the sidecar Tom was sleeping peacefully inside. It had veered off the road, mounted the kerb and come to rest among the trees. Frank pulled Tom out and Ellen woke him up with her hysterical sobbing. Tom began to cry and I was pale and shaking from being thrown about on the kiddy seat. Frank began to inspect the 'Bomber's damage. He shook his head. 'I don't know what Clancy's going to say when he sees this,' he said.

After we had sat by the roadside for a while, and broken open the thermos of tea, Ellen forced Frank to dip into his beer money so that we could put the 'Bomber and ourselves on the train at Dunton Green. Frank sat with the 'Bomber, as if it were a sick horse, in the mail wagon, while we stood in the corridor.

We walked, in the bright sunshine, down the hill to the George where we were to meet up with the rest of our

relations. On the way our father bought us a spade and a
bucket. We were three years old and, although a little
nervous of the pebbles on the beach, we were very
excited about being at the sea amid all the noise and
colour. Frank put his head around the door of the
George. The pub was packed and so Tom, Ellen and I
waited on the step while he pushed his way through to
the family. They came out, briefly, to see us. Our paternal
grandparents had a passion for shell fish. They'd already
been to the stall by the pier to stock up with punnets of
whelks. Grandad loved his whelks with lashings of pepper
and vinegar, and he was particularly fond of the largest
and most gristly. He insisted that the first thing we should
do was to sample one of these unearthly specimens for
the benefit of the hairs that it would put on our chests.
Unfortunately our mouths were not quite big enough for
them, but Grandad managed, by using his two thumbs,
to plug them into our mouths. This created an expression
on our faces that delighted all. Everyone agreed that they
were very good for us and that we were thoroughly
enjoying them.

Ellen's two brothers, Peter and Stanley, with their
wives, Cynthia and Dot, were there too. Uncle Stanley
was not at all like Peter, he was broader and tougher and
could easily have been taken for Frank's brother rather
than hers. We knew Uncle Stanley well, much better
than the rather aloof Uncle Peter, and if it had not been
for the whelks we should have shouted and leapt all over
him in our usual fashion.

Every second Saturday Stanley and his second wife,
Dot, travelled through the Blackwall Tunnel from their
home in Basildon to visit Stanley's former snooker part-
ner, Bill, who also lived on Prospect. Afterwards they
dropped in on us. Tom and I looked forward to these

fortnightly visits. Uncle Stanley always gave us half a crown when they left and Aunt Dot brought Mum her cast-offs.

Uncle Stanley was a great storyteller. He would settle himself in the winged armchair, put his tobacco tin on the arm and wait while Dot told us all about the traffic in the Blackwall Tunnel, how the motorbike had performed, and how Mum could alter the cast-offs. All this time Uncle Stanley would not say a word, not until he judged that the conversation was beginning to wane. Then he'd pick his moment.

'When was it, Dot? Last Tuesday?' He didn't need to say any more, we knew that his story was about to begin and rushed to sit on the pouffe in front of him. Aunt Dot would go quiet and light up a cigarette. If Ellen still had something to say to her she would whisper it very quickly as you would if a film were starting.

His stories were most often to do with complaints: his dealings with the local council, the catalogue companies, the managers of caravan parks, and the purveyors of faulty merchandise who were forever at Aunt Dotty's elbow. We understood very little of what he spoke about, it all being so ridiculously complicated, but we loved the deep resonance of his voice.

Sometimes the brevity of his complaint would be breathtaking. His letter to a stretch cover manufacturer, for example, which ran:

Dear Sir,
    My wife bought one of your stretch covers. It's stretched.

Then he'd go on to describe the battle for reimbursement. Tom and I pondered the mysteries of reimbursement and decided that when we were grown up this is what we should like to pursue. His stories could sometimes last several hours, during which Frank would retreat to the garden to shake the fruit trees. Uncle Stanley always felt the need to give us the full historical background to his stories. They always involved his first job after school and the outbreak of war. This historical detail naturally led to a certain amount of embellishment of the facts and once he had found that this was acceptable it would inevitably lead to a little free licence with the imagery and, of course, little flights of imagination would suggest a much more satisfactory conclusion to the tale. All that he required from us was that we believed every word. One time he was telling us about his shoelaces, which kept breaking, and his correspondence with the Cherry Blossom Boot Polish Company, when he noticed that Tom was wiggling one of his teeth. He broke off and began a new story. 'Well, when was it, Dot? Last Tuesday?'

Aunt Dot answered in the affirmative and lit up a cigarette. Mum quietened down. We scampered over to the pouffe.

'Let me fill you in,' he said.

'When I was at Kennington Elementary there was a boy called Jimmy Pearson who knocked me against the railings. When I got up my tooth was loose. "If that tooth falls out," said your grandmother, "I'm going to go round to see Mrs Pearson," but of course it didn't fall out, it just kept wiggling for the next five years. It drove me mad. I used to wake up with my tongue aching from wiggling it in my sleep. I lost my first job because of it. I was working at the butcher's in the Walworth Road and the boss came in and caught me poking it with a stick. Anyway, war broke out, and I was on leave. I only had two days but I said to your grandmother, "I'm going to have this blinkin' tooth pulled." So I booked an appointment with a dentist in East Lane. I was sitting in the waiting-room and I was the next in line to go in when a buzz bomb came over. We all had to go down the shelter. When I came up after the all clear the surgery had been flattened, there was just the drill left sticking up out of the rubble.

'Anyway, come the fifties I was getting well fed up with it wiggling all the time so in 1955 I made another appointment at the dentist.' We were all terribly impressed by his perseverance. 'And I was all set up to go but the night before we'd had a works do, so I missed the appointment by five minutes. "I don't think I'm ever going to get this tooth pulled," I said to Dot, "it isn't meant." But one night in 1960 we'd just got back from the WMC and I says, "Right, where's my hammer – I haven't been able to enjoy a beer for twenty years." I goes out into the kitchen and I smashes it out. Of course it bled a bit but I was relieved. It fell on the kitchen floor, didn't it, Dot? And I says to it. "There you are you bugger, you won't give me any more trouble," and I stamps on the thing. But of course, I'm only in my stocking feet aren't I? The tooth cuts my heel. I couldn't walk for weeks, I thought, "Oh no, I'm going to have a blinkin' foot now." We couldn't find the tooth. Dot said to me, "I bet it's gone under the fridge," but it hadn't, it was imbedded in my foot. Now, you've heard about these blokes in the war who get bits of shrapnel in them what travel all over their body. Well, I didn't hear nothing from that tooth for seven years until last Tuesday. I was having a drink and all of a sudden the glass hits something. I put my hand in my mouth and there it was, it had found its way back to its gap . . .'

Tom and I sat open-mouthed. Uncle Stanley opened

his mouth too, and sure enough he was right. I put my finger on it, it was still wiggling.

When Dot and Stanley got one of the new houses in Basildon they were well pleased. Stanley told Mum and Dad how much better their estate was than ours, because it wasn't just an estate, it was a new town, with more amenities. Aunt Dot told Mum about her pride and joy, a picture window, something else which Prospect did not have. They were so pleased with the new house that we were all invited to a House Warming – not something we'd ever been to, nor was it something usual on a council estate. We got very excited about going to such a high society event.

Uncle Stanley, naturally, got quite drunk and sat in the corner with his toreador's hat on, telling his stories. He was in the middle of describing how one goes about finding the latrines when one is in an international army camp of twenty-two thousand tents, when Frank, with no garden to escape to, hit on a plan.

Frank and Clancy announced to him that they were going to play a game, the centre of which would be himself. Uncle Stanley was most enthusiastic and helped them take down his bookshelf to use as a plank, and gave himself over to them to be blindfolded. Uncle Stanley stood on the plank and was told that Frank and Clancy were going to lift him up until his head touched the ceiling. Everyone gathered around to watch. Frank and Clancy lifted the plank only six inches off the ground and then someone put a drinks tray on his head to make him think that he had been lifted right up to the ceiling. Then they pulled the plank away. The idea was that he should yell, thinking he had a long drop to the floor, and then laugh when he found it was only six inches. Instead of this he dived head first through the picture window, an event cataclysmic enough without the added attraction of the living-room's being situated on the second floor. The noise was tremendous and the sudden departure of our host left all the women screaming and the men reeling back in shock and shouting blasphemies.

Frank and Clancy crossed over to the broken window and looked down, everyone's eyes on them. Without saying anything they dashed out of the house and ran down to the verge where Uncle Stanley was lying on the grass, still with his blindfold on, his toreador's hat firmly on his head and a pewter mug in his hand, saying: 'Was that it? Did I do it right?' Fortunately a drunk man never feels his fall until the morning. The party continued until the early hours, minus the window and minus Aunt Dot who sat with Frank and Clancy in the local outpatients, suffering from shock. All the way home on the train Frank hotly denied that he had deliberately defenestrated Uncle Stanley.

But this tremendous event was still several years ahead. Tom and I were still standing outside the George on Brighton front. After our grandfather had plugged our mouths with whelks, and Uncle Stanley and Uncle Peter had patted us on the head so hard that they could have made flagstones of us, and their wives had kissed us and tickled us, smothering us with lipstick and perfume, our father had promised us a lemonade. We waited on the steps for an hour. Mum had made us promise to be good little boys before she had disappeared with the rest of the family into the darkness of the bar. After a length of time Tom got up and tottered to the public bar door.

'Oh coo blimey, one of them's on the rampage, Frank!' said our grandfather. He came out to us. 'Now what's all this then?' he said 'I thought you were going to be good boys. Aren't you happy at the seaside?' Tom said nothing but simply looked so downcast that Grandad was forced to flick him around the ear.

'Dad said we could have lemonade and crisps,' I said.

'Did he?' said Grandad. 'I'll tell you what, you sit down on the step like good little boys and I'll see what I can do.'

We sat down, looking as much like good little boys as we could, watching the other kids heading toward the beach, and tapping our spade and bucket against the pub step. We felt that we had been forgotten. As other people came into the bar they smiled at us and shook their heads and some of them gave us money 'to get ourselves a lemonade'.

Finally Grandad came out to us with some crisps. He had stripped down to his vest and had a tattoo-like impression of a barmaid's lipstick on his neck. He swayed a great deal, almost as if he were dancing. 'Here you are, kids,' he said. 'A packet of crisps each.' We took the bags. They were already opened. He'd bought one bag and tipped half the contents into another he'd found in the ashtray. This was a special treat – not having to share. We looked for the lemonade, but this he'd forgotten. The crisps served to make us more thirsty. After, perhaps, another hour, Frank appeared with two pints of lemonade, and doing the same dance as his father. After he had spilled the lemonade over our heads our mother came out to wipe us with the corner of her handkerchief.

'When are we going down to the beach, Mum?' I asked.

'Soon, soon,' she said.

A little later, when our relatives had got to the morose stage of drunkenness, we received a constant stream of visitors to the steps. Stanley appeared, plying us with more crisps and declaring us to be 'poor bloody little mites – sitting here while we're in there'. Grandad insisted that we try our first taste of Guinness. They all agreed we had been very good, but we never got to the beach.

When we arrived home that night it was discovered that Tom still had his whelk in his mouth. It had been there since eleven in the morning, Tom being unable to chew it. I'd put mine in the bucket.

'I thought he was quiet,' said Mum, 'poor little mite.'

'Oh, I knew it was there,' said Frank. 'I thought he was enjoying it.'

We dreaded being taken to the seaside.

CHAPTER VII

In which we eat our tea but do not enjoy it, and in which we have a glimpse of the kind of conversation common to our household, and touch on some of the everyday problems facing Ellen

At half past six each evening, on an ordinary day, we'd all be sitting around the tea table enjoying our evening meal.

1lb yesterday's greens
1lb yesterday's mash
2 tabl. spoon Brown Sauce
Leave greens standing overnight to stink out house. Scrape remaining mash from plates and pans. Fry in lard and sauce until solid. Serving suggestion: throw.

This was the recipe for 'Bubble and Squweak' which Ellen was especially fond of. It was the meal that we and Frank most feared. All the supplies that came into the house were the most basic. Ellen used no seasoning other

than salt and white pepper and we had never even seen a
hamburger or a pizza. Packet meals and frozen foods
were in their popular infancy and we lived in ignorance
of them, suffering the over-boiled blandness of the standard six dishes:

> Mince *boiled until grey and swollen*
> Stew *simmered with the knuckles of the ox tail*
> Steak and kidney *steamed in china and muslin*
> Bangers *stuck into mash*
> Hearts *braised in brine*
> Liver *murdered in onions*.

Dad would sit silently at the table, never looking up
from his plate. In turn, Ellen sat nervously staring at
him, always hoping that he would say 'Oh this is nice,
love, thanks', but he never could. She would never risk
taking her apron off. She used it as a shield between
herself and the table and it meant that as soon as Frank
said anything adverse she could dash back to the sink and
crash the pans around. After half the meal had been
eaten in silence she could bear it no longer.

'Are the spuds all right?'

'Yeah, they're fine,' he'd say.

'Only you're a bit quiet, so say if they're not.'

Frank would lean back on his chair impatiently and
sigh. He was letting her know that if she 'started' he
would become awkward. Ellen fought to stay silent, and
tried as hard as she could not to fish for compliments for
her awful food, but something in her drove her to ask,
'What about the carrots?'

'Don't start.'

'But what *about* the carrots?'

'They're fine, they're nice.' But Ellen couldn't leave it

there, the mad impulse drove her on. 'You don't think they're salty?'

Frank swallowed his food and glared. 'No!' he shouted.

Ellen still would not be satisfied. 'Then why have you pushed that carrot to the side of your plate?'

'I haven't pushed it there.'

'It walked I suppose? It's salty, that's why.'

'It's not.'

'I put the salt in and I went to peg some bits out and when I came back I thought "did I put the salt in? – no" so I put more in and then I remembered I had so it's got two salts in. Does it notice?'

'No,' says Frank, exasperated. 'For the last time, no. They taste fine.' He'd turn to us, 'You like them, don't you kids?'

'Yes,' we said, as we tried to stick them under the table. 'We like them, Mum.'

Ellen would leave it for a moment and then casually get up and go over to the tap where she would pour two glasses of water. She put one down in front of Frank.

'Thanks,' he'd say and drink some. She had caught him.

'There! I knew it, you were gasping. I said they were salty.' Now the floodgates were open: 'And the beans are stringy, those parsnips yesterday were woody, that turnip was earthy . . . I just don't seem to be able to do anything do I?'

All this was a desperate plea for Frank to say, 'It doesn't matter, I know you try your best, what more can I ask?' The tea table was the means by which Ellen tested her worth and the affection of her husband and sons. We dreaded the ordeal of it; sometimes it would be absolute misery from the very first mouthful. Frank only had to

make the simple observation 'The meat's chewy', and all
hell would break loose. Ellen would grip her fork.

'What do you mean, the meat's chewy?'

'It's tough.'

'Tough? I suppose you want it bloody?'

'I'm just saying it's a bit chewy, it could have done
with another five minutes.'

'Five minutes? You don't know what you're talking
about, it's had another five minutes already. Don't eat it
then if it's uneatable.'

'I'm not saying it's uneatable.'

'It doesn't sound like it.'

'I'll eat it, I'll eat it.'

'Push it to the side of your plate, leave it if it's so
horrible. Spit it out, spit it out,' and Ellen would cup her
hand beneath Frank's mouth for him to spit it into.

'Don't force it down,' she'd say. 'I can see you are
heaving against it. What do I ever do right?'

Right at this point we were longing for one sound only:
that of the bells at the bottom of the cul-de-sac which
signalled the arrival of Mr Tonybell, the ice-cream man.
He alone could save our teatime from disaster; the
soothing taste of the ice-cream, beloved as much by
Frank as by ourselves, brought the first peace to the
evening, although it must be said that this peace began in
total panic when the cart was first heard.

Something that the carts did then, which I don't suppose they do much now, was to serve ice-cream in your
own bowl. Mum had our afters ready on the draining-
board – tinned peaches or mandarins – for us to carry out
to the cart for a threepenny squirt on each. It was a good
way to buy ice-cream because you didn't waste money on
the wafer. We watched from the window, steaming up
the pane, getting into trouble for crumpling Mum's nets

and breaking the settee, as Mum tore around the house looking for her purse. The tension was terrible.

'Quick, quick, Mum, or the cart'll go, THE CART'LL GO!'

The next obstacle between ourselves and the ice-cream would be our runny noses. These would have to be wiped before they were seen by the neighbours. 'Quick, quick, Mum, the cart'll go.'

Finally we'd be released from the front door to tear down to the cart. We would get there just as it was pulling away and have to chase it to the next turning, both of us with a bowl of mandarins in each hand. If we caught the cart we'd invariably dropped all the mandarins along the road, if we missed it, we threw the bowls down in temper and returned home, inconsolable, for a smack.

CHAPTER VIII

In which we get the television put on and our mother has an adventure in the advertising world but on both counts we are disappointed

Everyone was getting the television put on, Mum maintained, and she wanted to see an aerial go up on our roof by the end of the week. Frank wasn't so keen. He was loth to spend out on something which breaks up family life, stultifies conversation and turns children violent, when that money could better be spent preserving the age-old oral traditions at the Dog and Bucket – where they already had a set.

Mum decided to get a job and pay for it herself. A great many of the women on the estate were working as leaflet distributors, posting door to door. Suddenly there

was more money around, new supermarkets were opening, TV rental companies setting up, mail order cata-
logues establishing themselves and all these endeavours
were advertised through the leaflet. All over Prospect
letter-boxes were stuffed full with them and the women
swapped product coupons amongst themselves. It was the
golden age of the free gift. Great excitement was caused
in a street when the Camay Queen was spotted alighting
from her pink van and coming to knock on the doors. If
you could produce a bar of Camay soap and answer three
simple questions then the most fantastic prizes would be
yours. Several of the washing powders and margarine
companies followed suit with lavishly decorated trucks
and glamorous soap queens sitting atop. It gave the estate
a carnival atmosphere. One never knew at what time one
of them would come and so Mum kept a table by the
front door stocked with all the products that might have
to be produced, should she be lucky.

Tom and I were playing on the verge when we saw the
Camay Queen's Float approach. We stood open-mouthed
for a few moments and then raced as fast as we could
back to our house, our hearts beating as we kicked the
front door, unable to reach the knocker. 'Quick! Quick!
Mum, she's here, she's here!'

Ellen flew into a fluster. 'Oh no,' she said. 'I'm not
ready, I'm not prepared, what if she asks me something I
don't know?'

By the time she knocked on the door all the other
women were on their front steps. We stood behind Mum,
staring up in awe at the Camay Queen. She had a tiara
and a silk sash and we were starstruck.

Mum was terribly nervous, we could sense it, and when
asked to produce the product she bungled it and picked
up the packet of Lux. This drew the interview swiftly to a

close. Mum was furious afterwards and she took the table away from the front door saying, 'I can't live with this kind of strain, it's making me a nervous wreck.' Frank agreed with her when he got in from work.

Still in her quest for a television set, and with her confidence not too shaken by her encounter with the Camay Queen, Mum joined the other women who gathered at 8.00 each morning in a builders' hut on the industrial estate. It was here that the promoters met to hand out the wodges of leaflets to the women and to brief them about distribution. We had started school so this left Mum with all the hours she wanted to trudge the streets, pushing the leaflets in our old pram.

Frank said she was mad but she was determined to get the set. Ellen did very well delivering leaflets and was popular with the promoters. One evening she announced to Frank that the company had made her an offer. 'They want me to be a Toothpaste Queen.'

Frank's mouth fell open and we jumped up and down as Ellen described how she'd have her own float and a sash and have to go on a training course to learn how to ask the questions. We thought it was wonderful, we couldn't believe that it could happen to our own mum.

'I don't know what the blokes are going to say,' said Frank. Ellen made him a cup of tea. Half of him hated the idea and the other half enjoyed the thought of having such a glamorous wife. He hoped it wouldn't change her. He'd always had an interest in advertising, as we know, but he hadn't dreamed for a moment that he would achieve success in this field through Ellen.

'Well, I've said I'll think about it until the end of the week, I mean, I don't know if I shall be able to ask all those questions.'

As the week went on Mum began to sing like a bird

and there was a dance in her step. It was as if she were being transformed, by a strange power, before our eyes, into something magic and glamorous. She even wrapped a scarf around herself to see what the sash would be like and Frank, as a joke, put a foil cake tin on her head as a tiara. 'How smashing it will be,' we thought, 'to have our own mum driving around Prospect on a float with a tiara on her head and all a-glittering.'

Ellen never told us what her decision was but, if she had decided to become a Toothpaste Queen, it was on the Tuesday of that week that she was disappointed. She sprained her ankle falling over a low hedge nipping between gardens when she was delivering free coupons. She knew that the promoters wouldn't want a queen who hobbled from her float. It was surprising, really, that a woman of such a nervous disposition had been tempted at all. I can only presume that she had been overwhelmed by the ad men whose business it was to sell glamour to women such as Ellen.

Frank felt sorry for her as she sat weeping over her foot. He put his arm around her and said, 'I'll tell you what, doll, I'm going out tomorrow to get that telly set you wanted.'

'Don't bother,' said Mum. 'I'll get myself another job, one that doesn't involve my feet.'

Frank went down to the Dog'. When we got in from school the next day, however, the set was there, in the space she had cleared for it. She was very excited. It had a screen that was much rounder than they are today and it was set in a heavy synthetic wood cabinet looking more like an old-style oven. Mum couldn't stop talking about it.

'I've done nothing all afternoon,' she said, 'but watch

it. I've seen everything. I watched *Criss Cross Quiz* and *Space Patrol*. I haven't even made a cup of tea.'

When Frank got in we all sat squeezed up on the sofa, to simulate being in the cinema. We didn't bother with a meal and we took it in turns to run out during the adverts to put the kettle on. I remember it was the first occasion Tom and I made a cup of tea by ourselves. It was a cold November night and when the coal ran out in the scuttle we huddled up closer to keep warm as Frank refused point blank to go to the coalshed.

We watched *People in London, True Adventure* and *Out of Town* and thoroughly enjoyed them all. At seven o'clock *Double Your Money* came on. We thought the host, Hughie Green, was wonderful; the last time Ellen had seen him was in *Midshipman Easy* when he was a child star.

'It's just like he's in the room with us,' said Frank.

'Yes I know,' said Mum. 'I watched this programme this afternoon with a donkey in it. It came up so close you could smell its droppings.'

At half past seven the *Dickie Henderson Show* came on. Ellen and Frank found it strange at first because of the laughter from an invisible audience but by part two they were laughing along out loud themselves – new members of the invisible audience. We all agreed that it was the funniest thing we'd ever seen.

Frank sat in the middle of the settee with one arm around Ellen and the other around us. We didn't bother to switch the light on when it got dark but sat in the dull glow of the dying fire and the blue flickering of the screen. It was the cosiest thing we had ever known. Eventually when Frank did go to the coalshed, during a break in *My Favourite Martian* (examining the sky closely as he did so), he brought back a great scuttleful and heaped the fire right up. Because of this we all fell asleep in front of it and woke, confused, to the ear-piercing scream of closedown. Mum and Dad were furious with each other. 'Why did you let me drop off?' asked Frank. 'Why didn't you stop me? I've been at work all day.'

'I didn't hear you snore,' said Ellen, 'so I must have gone off before you did. You should have poked me – now look what I've missed,' she said, reading from the newspaper, 'I've missed *Tools for Science* and I've missed The Queen, she was coming on tonight.'

'And we've missed *Closedown*,' said Frank. 'I wanted to see that.'

'It'll be on again tomorrow night,' said Ellen.

Nevertheless we all went off to bed happy that night, Frank promising to get home early from work the next day and not go on for his big Friday-night drink-up, and Ellen planning to get all the food for the weekend cooked in the morning.

Friday evening we settled down, once again, to watch our moving wallpaper. Fishpaste sandwiches, always present at an 'occasion', were lined up on the best plates on the sideboard. Frank had built the fire up. After the children's programmes, which Frank particularly enjoyed, Ellen looked through the evening paper and chose a selection of light comedy and hospital drama. Everything was set for a fine cosy evening, there was nothing to indicate that it should be otherwise. At seven o'clock on that evening *Take Your Pick* came on to the screen. An inoffensive little show, where nervous representatives of the public were taunted into vying for gaudy prizes. Gameshows were much as they are now except that they were not so heavily draped in models. We enjoyed the show enormously. We liked the part when the contestants were asked questions by the avuncular host, Michael

Miles, while a little man hovered behind them with a gong which would be struck should they answer directly with the words 'yes' or 'no'. The tension was unbearable, and when the first contestant slipped and answered 'yes' Ellen shrieked with the excitement of it all. The drama was so basic it was irresistible.

At 19.17 hours we were getting ready to enjoy the commercial break, to sing along and to play our game of guessing the product before they stated the brand name. It was at this point that our screen went blank.

'Oh no!' screamed Ellen. 'What's happened? What have you done, Frank?'

'Nothing, I haven't touched it,' he said.

'You did, you were fiddling with the back. What have you done, you've bought a duff set.'

As Ellen was saying this a caption came up on the screen in white letters which read NEWSFLASH. It was our first encounter with such a thing, all of a sudden the world of real events was upon us. Against the blank screen the voice of a newscaster announced that the American president was critically ill, having been shot while on a visit to Dallas. (The newsflash should have come during *Take Your Pick* but the Network didn't consider it an important enough event to interrupt the show.) Ellen and Frank were deeply shocked. At 19.30 hours *Emergency Ward Ten* began. The localized, banal drama of the hospital, ideal for television, appealed to Ellen. Frank didn't think much of the lead actor. At 19.40 hours a second newsflash blacked out the screen. Kennedy was dead. The bulletin lasted for three minutes at the end of which a piano recital began, given by Joan Burns. The music was a bit highbrow in Frank's opinion and he got the fidgets but Ellen said, 'What do you expect, Nat King Cole?'

At 19.56 a third newsflash confirmed that the president was dead. The Halle Orchestra followed with more sombre music.

20.40 Announcement of programme changes for the rest of the evening. Frank considers going down to the 'Bucket. Ellen says 'How can you?'
20.42 Piano recital, Robin Wood.
20.55 Obituary.
21.15 The News. The effect of what has happened is beginning to sink in.
22.10 *Roving Report* (special edition).
22.40 News Headlines.
22.42 *This Week* (special edition).
23.01 Tribute to President Kennedy.
23.25 Closedown.

Over the next three days our little family watched the events in America on our little screen. On the Saturday we watched the body brought to the White House and in the evening we saw the assassin, Oswald, arrested. By this stage Tom and I had realized that a real man and not an actor had been shot. It was a little confusing. We had imagined that the TV was simply like having a cinema in the living-room; we had been under the impression that the whole thing was created by some kind of direct line to the Commodore in Orpington and that whatever was shown there was seen also in our home. It was inconceivable to us that as things happened in the world so we should be a party to them also. On Sunday we watched Oswald himself being shot, and on the 25th the funeral procession in which someone was killed by the president's train. On the 26th we watched him laid to rest at Arlington and came out of the whole thing with an entirely different, and more cautious, attitude toward the machine that we had taken lovingly into our home.

The things that she heard on it worried Ellen. Our Christmas was spoilt that year by news of African students rioting, unlikely though it may sound, in Red Square; of clashes in Cyprus between Greeks and Turks; and of a state of emergency in Somalia. When the British Foreign Minister, Duncan Sandys, flew out to Cyprus, Ellen was convinced that another war was about to start. Because of the urgency of the news presentation she was deeply and immediately affected by it and found it difficult not to presume a relationship between one story and another. When Ellen heard of riots in Salisbury she was deeply disturbed. 'I knew a girl,' she said,'who was evacuated to Surrey in the war and she had an aunt who lived in Salisbury, near the cathedral. I do hope she's all right, I'll have to write to her.' Perhaps if our set had had a better picture she would have realized that the riots were in Salisbury, Rhodesia. But she didn't, and wrote the letter.

CHAPTER IX

In which we hear about our father's job at Blake's Mill, and Frank shows himself to be something of a poet, and Ellen something of a chef. A recipe is included

At the very edge of Prospect, just beyond its boundary to the south, was Blake's Mill, where our father worked. The mill was owned by old Colonel Blake and had stood there, in one form or another, since the Napoleonic Wars. Before that other mills, all powered by the water of the River Kray, had been on the site since the Romans had first forded it. The mill stood in stark contrast to the industrial estate which was rising around it. Frank was proud of his job there. The other industries had no place for traditional labour or craftsmanship; on the whole they employed the women to watch conveyor belts and the men to sit in stockrooms. They produced soft drinks, plastic saucepan handles, kiddies' penny novelties, and rubber bands – nothing of quality, nothing to inspire a romantic, like Frank, as the great white sheets of vellum did.

The mill employed local craftsmen. As well as master papermakers, who came from generations of Blakemen, there were carpenters, boilermakers and bricklayers – all manner of skills could be harnessed to the mill. There were even gamekeepers employed to look after the wildlife of the grounds. Unlike the other factories which polluted and covered with tarmac all that was around them, the Blake family had turned their environs into a nature reserve. There were two lakes, salvaged from gravel pits, which were well stocked with fish for the Blake's Mill's Fishing Society, and the trees were well arboured for the Blake's Mill's Ornithology Club. The members of this latter society could themselves be spotted, as they walked to work each morning, with their sandwich boxes and binoculars.

When Prospect was built old Blake put up a new mill called 'X Machine' which made a lower quality paper – kitchen rolls and computer printout – and employed the unskilled people from the estate. This was indicative of the attitude of the locals toward the new estate dwellers: a great army of riff-raff who must be organized into machine fodder. Nevertheless the Prospectors respected the mill and showed willing which mellowed the attitude of the paternalistic Colonel Blake. He enjoyed the challenge of new recruits. Even jobs at 'X Machine', then, were greatly prized because the managers were keen to teach the newcomers and they could graduate to the Old Mill. By rising up the ranks in Blake's a man could be somebody when he walked into the Dog and Bucket.

It was a man's world at the mill and Frank enjoyed telling us the story of his day as a member of the Heavy Gang Lifting Team, which was about the lowest employment that could be gained at the mill. One night he came home and told us a story which made a great impression on Tom and myself. The story was about his foreman, Harry, whom he hated. He told us how they had been moving a roll, one of the great steel rollers that pressed the pulp.

'Harry was shouting at us,' he said, 'calling us all a bunch of apes. He doesn't think we can do anything right. In the end he says, "All right, stand back, I'll shove it in myself," and he pushes the roll and it comes back on him. It bloody crushed his legs, completely shattered them. You could hear the bone go, it didn'aff make a bang.'

'Oh no,' said Ellen. 'Were you all right?'

'Oh yeah. I had more sense than to stand near. There was a lot of blood though.'

'I bet there was.'

'It was like that time when, what was his name, used to live over the road?'

'Ernie Wilson, you mean?'

'Yes. It was like the time he slipped when he was guillotining that paper and had his head sliced off in my first week.'

Our eyes were wide open as we pictured the scene.

'Oh yes, that was terrible,' said Ellen.

'Terrible?' said Frank. 'I was nearly sick.'

'So what happened to Harry, what happened to Harry?' we asked.

'Well, we were so shocked, we had to laugh. And then we kind of stood there until this new lad says, "Shall I go and get an ambulance?" So I says, "Yeah, you might as well," but of course he passed out on the way to the phone so poor old Harry was under the roll half an hour. You should have heard his language.'

'Annoyed was he?' asked Ellen.

'I should say so.'

Tom and I weren't sure whether we were looking forward to working at the mill when we grew up or not.

'I made the lads laugh, though, before I came home tonight,' continued Frank.

'Did you?' asked Ellen. She liked it when he was popular with his mates because if all was well between Frank and his mates then all was well with Frank.

'Yeah, I wrote a poem, didn't I?'

'You did what?' asked Ellen, astonished.

'I wrote a poem,' he repeated proudly. We were all very impressed, we had no idea that Frank had such things in him.

'I got a bit of chalk and wrote it on the roller after they'd taken him away. The blokes thought it was fantastic, so I copied it down for you.'

'You copied it down for me?' said Ellen.

'Yeah.'

Ellen ran her hand through her hair with nervous excitement.

'You've never written a poem for me before, oh dear, I hope I like it.'

'Well I won't read it to you if you don't want me to,' said Frank.

'Oh no, I want to hear it,' she said and looked at us,

excited. Frank moved a little nearer to her and reached into his overall pocket for a screwed-up piece of paper. He held it in his big, metal-stained hands. Ellen's lip twitched in anticipation of the honour that was being paid to her. Frank began to read.

> 'Poor old Harry tried to shift me.
> He huffed and puffed but couldn't lift me.
> Our foreman's got a great big gob
> and humping ain't his ******* job.
> So I rolled on him and had 'is leg –
> now he'll have to have a peg.'
> And we can swing the lead.

We all applauded.

'You've written it very well,' said Ellen, taking the piece of paper from him to read it again to herself.

'It rhymes and everything,' she said.

'That's what Clancy said,' said Frank.

'Did he?'

'Yeah, he said, "I don't know how you made it rhyme like that, it's really professional." He said it should be in a book, he reckons I should take it up.'

'Well you should,' said Ellen.

'Yeah,' we said, 'you should!' We were very keen on the idea of our father becoming a poet. Even though we tried to pretend that the stories he told us, of the mill, didn't worry us, they did. We were frightened that Frank would get hurt. We were also worried, I think, by the lightness with which grown-ups seemed to treat these awful accidents. When I told Tom that his wish would come true if he threw the horseshoe that he had found up in the air, and he wished for some sweets, and it came down and split his head open, I was upset for hours.

Ellen had tried several jobs since her sprained ankle. Her favourite was as an orderly at the hospital. The hospital had been put up as a temporary measure for Canadian soldiers during the Great War. Although only a collection of asbestos huts, they were built in mock Elizabethan style. The corridors were all in the open air and wound among a maze of lagged pipes which pumped out great clouds of steam. The hospital was infested with wild cats who enjoyed the rich pickings of its bins. Ellen felt very grand in her green uniform and linen hat. She would dress up in it for us, before she went to work, and impersonate the matron. It made up for the fact that she never became a Toothpaste Queen. She taught us all how to tell the difference between a Sister, a Student Nurse and a State Registered Nurse, by the different colours of their belts. At the drop of a hat she would speak up on behalf of the medical profession and advise everyone on their pills and treatments, something which made her very popular at the shops. She came home every evening full of fascinating accounts of incurable diseases and motorbike accidents.

The biggest bonus for her was that she could bring home the food that the patients didn't eat, which was mainly boiled fish and scotch eggs. At first Frank was pleased that she'd got a job at a place 'where you can bring something home'. Since he had resolved to be a poet he found the perks in his own job particularly useful.

But after a few weeks Frank tired of the scotch eggs. 'Oh no, not another blinkin' scotch egg,' he'd yell as he sat down at the table.

'What's wrong with them?' said Ellen. 'There's a lot of goodness in them. They wouldn't have them at the hospital if they weren't full of goodness.'

Frank disputed this. 'Look at this egg in here,' he said, poking it out of the sausagemeat casing with his thumbs. 'It's blue. It's grey and blue.'

Ellen looked at it and shook her head.

Frank took it off his plate and banged it on the table where it bounced like a rubber ball. 'It wasn't in that hospital as food, Ellen,' he said. 'It was there as a patient.' We all laughed.

Ellen tightened her apron and marched over to the sink. 'I don't have time to cook for you when I've been out at work. You should learn to cook for yourself . . .'

Frank looked so astonished by this that we began to giggle.

'And you two can wipe the smiles off your faces as well,' she said. We went quiet, knowing that the evening's hostilities were about to begin.

'You can't even boil an egg!' she said to us. We shook our heads from side to side, admitting that we couldn't.

'And you,' she said, poking Frank, 'you couldn't even boil the water!'

The three of us giggled at this as Ellen got more cross. Sometimes it appealed to us to side with our father.

The Scotch Egg, then, became a token for their conflict, an emblem, just as the New Blue Cuddly Sheet had been when we were a little younger. Frank threw down the challenge: 'I'm not having another one of those scotch eggs in this house or I'll walk out. Choose what you want, the eggs or me.'

Ellen replied to this with only a tight pursing of her lips. When we got home from school the next evening we were quite worried. Tom and I had told our teacher at milktime that if our mum didn't make a nice tea our dad was leaving home. Our teacher often had cause to puzzle over the little reports we gave of our home life. We went into the kitchen and there on the table was a brown paper bag with bulges inside. Tom and I looked at each other and went into the front room. When Frank got in from work we begged him not to leave us, but he was in a bad mood and ignored everything we said.

Ellen called us to the tea table and we went through. There were four empty plates on the table; Ellen was stirring something on the stove when we sat down.

She served Frank first, putting something on to his plate with a ladle. It was something we'd never seen before. Frank smelled it, suspiciously. 'What's this?' he asked.

'Risotto,' said Ellen.

'It looks good,' said Frank. 'What is it, a new thing?'

'Yes,' said Ellen. 'Everyone's making them.'

We all tucked in and thoroughly enjoyed it. Ellen smiled for the first time in weeks. After the meal Frank sat with her on the settee.

'We've got some vacancies for women at Blake's,' he said. 'How would you fancy working at the same place as your old man and not having that long walk over the hospital but coming with me instead?'

Ellen smiled and thought seriously for a moment. 'What would the work involve?' she asked.

'It's a good job, working in the Old Mill.'

Ellen was very happy that Frank wanted her to work for the same company as himself. She could picture them having their sandwiches together, both sitting in the locker-rooms in their overalls. It was quite usual for whole families to go into Blake's. Ellen took the job, which was in the rag shed. The fine papers were made from rags instead of wood pulp and the shed was the place where the rag-and-bone men brought their stock to be prepared for pulping. It was set high above the rolls, in the roof, and the rags were winched up through a mill door. Here the women sat at long benches tearing the rags to shreds; the air was thick with fibre and their clothes took on a fleece-like quality.

You could easily spot the women who worked in the rag shed as they walked home. They were all of a uniform colour and texture. Sometimes their colours would change. One time there was a big shipment of purple cloth, from a theatre that had closed, and all the women had purple-rinsed hair and deep purple bands around their wrists where their gloves stopped. Mum scrubbed and scrubbed when she got in each evening.

Another time she had been ripping industrial towels which whitened her hair and face. All the women of the rag shed looked as if they'd aged twenty years in a single afternoon. We thought that it must be tremendous fun and thought Mum to be very lucky to be paid for tearing things up all day. Ellen wasn't so keen on the job, it exhausted her and affected her chest, but she wouldn't give it up because she liked walking to work with Frank in the morning, and also because she thought it would be bad for him because he'd recommended her. She was very loyal to him and the harder the work was for her the more she felt as if she was doing it for him.

Here is the recipe for Ellen's risotto (should you like to gain similar success).

Smash up scotch egg, fry with peas and chips and left-over rice pudding. Serve: quickly.

CHAPTER X

In which we make friends with Charlie Rubbidge and go tiddling at Five Arches, and Charlie tells us how his mother fried his father's hand

Tom and I made a great friend of Charlie Rubbidge, a boy of our own age who lived on the other side of the verge. Charlie was something of a legend in the neighbourhood; he was the boy who, in the great winter of '63, got lost in the snow because he was so short, and the police came with dogs to find him. He was also the first boy in our class to contract the measles, and produced a fantastic display of spots. He followed this success by introducing the whole year to chicken-pox and whooping-cough. He was a little like a barometer for any infection which was around. Even though he missed a great deal of school the speed with which he recited his times tables amazed all. It was universally acknowledged that he would grow up to be a great scientist. He knew everything about the demise of the dinosaurs and the bouncing bomb. He was a great fount of knowledge to us.

It was Charlie Rubbidge who came knocking on our door every time the chip-shop was on fire – one of the great sights on Prospect. We would go tearing up the Parade on our bikes to watch. The chip-shop had a particularly incompetent manager who let the fat catch fire every couple of months. They could barely get the Formica stuck down on the counter and the shop opened again in time for the next fire. We could stand for hours amid the blue flashing lights on the engines and the water

which flowed in great torrents down the street, and talk
for weeks about how the flames melted the plate-glass
windows, and how the vinegar in the big pickle-jars
boiled, and how the jars exploded and shot boiling pickled
onions at the firemen, and how the firemen had to sit on
the pavement, with their heads in their hands, overcome
by the thick smoke of the burning fat and the acrid stench
of the vaporizing vinegar.

Charlie Rubbidge it was who introduced us to 'chippings'. When the shop was in business we'd go in with
him and ask for the little bits of batter that collected at
the bottom of the stainless steel fryers. The chippings
were often black, they'd been fried so many times, and
they were always ninety per cent grease, but we loved
them because they were free and the manager wrapped
them up in newspaper for us so that we could walk along
the street making out to the other kids that we were rich
enough to buy chips.

In the summer holidays Charlie took Tom and me up
to Five Arches – so named because of the bridge which
spanned the Kray at this point. Charlie described it as a
'beauty spot'. It lay between our estate and the next and
was too wet to build on. The council cut the meadow
grass and cemented little bins along their gravel paths for
us. Nevertheless it was still a place of great mystery to us.
There was the marsh, blowing with yellow water iris
which grew out of a black mud thick with tubers. Many
men had been sucked into the mud and had died horribly
there.

Upstream from the bridge the river widened. This place
had once been the ornamental lake of the manor house,
but the whole estate was now open to the public since the
manor had been burned down by Teddy Boys. The
summer sun would dry the banks and the quicksand

would appear. A whole troop of Boy Scouts had been
lost there and never seen again. Charlie showed us the
cap lying in the sand. Charlie was very useful for this
kind of information.

The tiddlers harboured in deep pools made by the fall
of the water from the arches. This was the best place to
fish, said Charlie, but it was dangerous: many men had
been pummelled to death by the waters.

Tom and I were a little afraid of the place. Water
always meant death; we'd seen the posters at school
from the National Swimming Campaign, but here, at the
Arches, mere swimming couldn't help you, you could be
sucked in, or pummelled under. It was the kind of risk
that we, as fishermen, simply had to take, he told us.
Charlie was a much bolder fisherman than either of us,
but then he was a month older, and, coupled with this,
he had a proper net. We had made our nets from canes
with a wire hanger looped inside one of Mum's unwanted
laddered stockings. They weren't too effective because
the mud didn't pass through the toes so when we did
catch something we were unlikely to see it until we
washed out the silt, then it would escape. If this wasn't
the case then they would, of course, escape by using the
ladder.

Charlie also told us about the rapids. Even though the
water was only six inches deep in our river, the speed of
it could break your ankles and carry you off down to
Sidcup. Charlie was the only one brave enough to fish the
middle stream because of it.

Our dream was to catch minnows (although Charlie
fancied sharks). On the whole we ended up with half a
dozen sticklebacks, normally the five-spined variety but
sometimes the seven. The five had three spines on the
back and one either side by the front fins (which meant

that you could stand them up when they were dead).
They would stick these spines out when we lifted them
from the net. It was mainly the prick of these spines that
made us want to catch minnows instead, because they are
soft, green, mild-mannered little fish. The sight of a dead
stickleback, with its spines sticking out and its eyes
whitened, like a trout on the table, and its body bloated
with tapeworm, still makes me feel slightly sick.

We also caught newts although not in the river. We'd
go over to Hobblingwell Wood for these, where there
was a pond that had been created by bad drainage. The
newts thrived here, especially the Great Crested, of which
Charlie caught several. They were spectacular things.
The females, smooth and buff-coloured, the males, dark
green with a stegosaurus crest and an orange and black
spotted belly. We fed them on ants' eggs. Unfortunately
most of our captives very quickly hung up their harps and
we were required to conduct frequent funeral services,
sometimes several dozen a day, with Charlie reading the
service. The plot of garden that Mum had given us to
cultivate began to look like a toy cemetery. Charlie
showed us how to make coffins and crosses and we tended
their graves with flowers which we stole. We enjoyed
these funerals enormously and would stand solemnly by
their gravesides, and, after an hour or so, dig them up to
see if they'd gone to heaven, or better still started to rot
so that Charlie could cut them up and put the bits into
jam-jars. Sometimes we'd have no pets left alive and so
we'd have to make do with killing a worm and burying
that instead. Worms, on the whole, are not very good for
burying, they are not very well behaved at their funerals.
No matter how many pieces they've been chopped into
they all tend to wriggle, independently, throughout the
ceremony, and then escape from their coffins and start up

again on their own as a whole lot more worms. It is a most remarkably difficult thing, we found, to bury something in its own element.

The newts were the hardiest of all our creatures. Charlie would insist that they were lizards, however, because lizard sounded so much more dangerous than newt. But there were real lizards on Prospect. They lived on the dump, a waste piece of ground that had been created when the builders put a street up in the wrong place and cut off access to a plot of land at the centre. It had grown over with grasses and crab-apple trees. The lizards moved in, like rabbits into the heart of a cornfield at harvest. This was the only place they liked and they would bask in the sunshine, right up by the iron railings, defying us to catch them. The railings were bent and shiny at this point. We'd lie in wait for hours but it was as if they could dissolve into the ground as soon as we blinked. They darted into the nettles as if they knew it was their great weapon against us. We were always mottled white with stings and Charlie would go off looking for dock leaves.

Everywhere the kids made openings and gaps. It was regarded as vandalism by our parents, but it wasn't by us. We were just making an alternative route around Prospect, Charlie said, just as a cat marks out its territory and will always go a particular way around a table leg. We left the pavements to grown-ups and travelled by a much older way, tracks, gullies, cuts and slips, made from the sweat of our own plimsolls. Each path had a meaning. A track curved in a particular way because there was an especially good blackberry bush almost on the route. Some railings would be more polished at the top of the gap in the bars because the secondary school kids used it to get home or to have a smoke. We'd know not to use this way unless we wanted to run into trouble, and although Charlie was always ready, we were not. Another fence might be broken down low and you would know that the younger kids used it to get to their back-gardens and so it probably wasn't worth visiting.

Places developed new names. The Sandy Mound was where the lizards sunned themselves. It was no more than a foot high and two foot long and had begun its life as a split cement bag but because the lizards had chosen it for a castle so had we. There was also the Old Haig Stump, an old witch-like remnant of a tree. Eventually the whole wood became named after it, changing from Hobblingwell Wood (as the planners would have it) to 'The Stump'.

'I'm going over the Stump.'

'Is Charlie coming out to play?'

'He's already out, Richard, he's over the Stump.'

The parents began using our names. When there was a public meeting about the future of the wood (there had been some attacks) everyone who spoke referred to it as the Stump.

It was we, not our parents, who broke in the new estate of Prospect and smoothed its rough edges by bending a few railings and doing a bit of carving. We knew the place much better than they. Barry Foster was the first person, in living memory, ever to climb the Gnarl Tree by the Drain Pond. Charlie Rubbidge was the first ever to fall in. These were true pioneers. We discovered together the magic places: a certain combination of mud, water and shrubbery which suggested something romantic to our imaginations and around which we could build our folklore. What had been a building site only a few years before had now been colonized by a secret life. A life of lizards, water boatmen, salamanders (rumour only),

invisible snakes (only Charlie saw them with the magic
glasses he'd invented), climbing trees, camps and wild
children who had run away from their parents to form
tribes until teatime.

When teatime did come a very special ritual was always
observed. The women, our mums, would appear at the
doorways to yell into the air as if they were summoning
the dead. 'Barry!' 'Billy!' 'Malcolm!' 'Dirk!' 'Richard,
Tom!' 'GET IN HERE THIS MINUTE. TEA'S ON THE TABLE.'

Then the women would stand on the steps and wait,
chatting to each other across the gardens, every now and
then letting out another ear-splitting yell, 'RICHARD, TOM,
GET IN HERE. I'M NOT CALLING YOU AGAIN.'

'We've got to go,' we'd say at last to Charlie, 'Mum's
calling us in.'

It didn't matter even if we were a long way over the
Stump, we could still hear the call. It might not be our
mum we heard, but as soon as the calling started we
knew that our mum must be among them. Even if Mum
wasn't watching the time, when she heard the others
calling she'd think, 'Oh, I must get their tea on or the
neighbours'll think I don't feed them.' So she would come
out whether there was food on the table or not.

As we got nearer our own cul-de-sac we'd start to
recognize the voice of our own mother among the rest.
The dogs and the cats would be running along with us
too, leaving whatever they were doing to dash across the
gardens and under the hedges in the hope that their
mums would think to feed them at the same time. It was
inconvenient sometimes if a good game had just got
going, and annoying if there was no food available at the
end of it all, but on the whole we approved of the system.
We would have been ashamed and upset if our mum
hadn't been among the callers. Charlie's mum never

called him in. We'd run off and he'd just stand there, in the middle of the Stump, kicking his heels with his head down.

We feared Charlie's mum greatly. He told us how she would get a wire, plug it into the mains, and try to electrocute him while he was asleep to punish him, and how she chopped off his dad's hand and fried it. We were quite nervous when we went to knock for him – but knock for him we did because Charlie knew all the places and all the games and was our best friend.

Charlie went through a particularly bad patch with his body at the end of the holidays and going to knock for him was a terrible ordeal. He was rarely available.

'Is Charlie coming out to play?' I would ask, from halfway down the path where I had retreated when his mother opened the door.

'No,' I'd be told, 'he's having his adenoids out.'

Poor old Charlie. By the time we went back to school Charlie had lost his appendix, his tonsils, his foreskin and three new teeth. When Mrs Rubbidge told us he was at the doctor's having his ears drained, Tom said, 'Will there be anything left of him to play with?'

We were convinced that Mrs Rubbidge was murdering him bit by bit – or at least that's what Charlie told us.

CHAPTER XI

In which we have our sixth Christmas but there is trouble with the tree and the turkey and Father Christmas is not all that we had hoped

'We've had six Christmases here,' announced our mother, 'and we've never had a tree.'

'And you know why, don't you?' replied Frank. 'It's because you say they drop bits on the carpet.'

It was true. Ellen always began the Christmas festivities with a list of dampening observations on the yuletide season: the fairy lights would only fuse and then they'd burn the house down; setting fire to the pudding was a waste of brandy and blackened the ceiling; Christmas cake was too rich and Tom and I would get constipated all through New Year; wrapping paper must not be torn but used again next year; and she would never, never allow decorations to go up because she said, 'When they come down again it depresses me.'

This year, however, her mood had changed because we were growing up.

'I wanted a tree last year,' said Frank, 'but you said no.'

'You were drunk.'

'What difference does that make?'

'You want everything when you're drunk. I just thought it'd be nice to have a proper Christmas for the twins before they get too old to enjoy it.'

'Well all right then, I'll get a tree, but it'll mean having a smaller bird.'

'We can't have a smaller bird, not with your father and mother coming over. I need a bird that's going to last me three days.'

And so the great discussion went on all through Easter, and most of the summer until the falling leaves and the first frost made it a matter of even greater urgency.

When Christmas did approach Ellen was still of the same mind and Frank agreed to provide both bird and tree in plenty.

The run up to Christmas Eve was made fraught by Mum's nagging until it all came to a head on the Eve itself. 'I don't know what you're thinking of,' she said, 'leaving the bird to the last moment like this. What am I going to do without a bird? And the tree, I even went out and bought a star for it. The twins have been looking forward to it. What do you mean to do? – you'll let us all down again. When I'm dead and cold in my grave you'll be sorry we didn't have any decent times.'

This parting shot deeply disturbed Tom and me and made the issue of the tree and the bird even more urgent. Frank could not let this go unchallenged. He put his coat on with a great flourish, like a man about to face the wild elements in search of bear, and thrust open the door as he buttoned up his gaberdine. 'Right,' he said. 'I'll get them now.'

'Before you go,' said Ellen, 'let me get the twins into their duffles so you can take them with you.' Frank growled with frustration. 'I want to wrap up their you-know-whats,' whispered Ellen.

We were very glad to hear this and eager to give her the opportunity to do so. Frank shuffled on the step and waited. 'You'll have to give me some money out of your purse,' he said. Ellen gave him her money.

By the time we had pulled on our wellingtons, got our hands into the mittens that were secured to our coat sleeves by elastic and had our balaclavas pulled down over our heads so that we looked like little human cannon balls, Frank was in a mad, blustery mood and was already striding down the path. We scampered after him, like hunting hounds around the horse.

We had been walking, at this infantry pace, for three or four minutes when he suddenly stopped, causing us to walk into the back of him, and said, 'I've had an idea.' He about-turned and went straight to the Dog and Bucket.

'He'll be sorry when Mum's dead,' said Tom.

'And cold in her grave,' I added. It was bitterly cold, also, outside the Dog and Bucket, sitting in the porch waiting for him, and we got some idea of exactly how cold Mum would be when Dad was sorry. Holding the lemonade was agony.

'What will Mum say when he ain't got a bird?' said Tom.

'And no tree, neither,' I added.

We could hear his voice soaring above the rest as they passionately sang 'Once in Royal'. This being the Christmas season, no one rolled out of the pub until four. When, at last, we strode, although in a less forthright manner, up to the Parade, most of the shops were already shut and in the half-light the others were closing. There was a ghostly feel to the place as woozy shop assistants with little bits of tinsel in their hair meandered from one shop to another offering around the sherry. Frank took us into Matthews'. The butcher's boy was hosing down the slab. We were fascinated by the blood as it streaked across the white marble. 'Christmas colours,' we observed. All the meat had been cleared to the cold store.

'Got a turkey then, mate?' said our father. The butcher stepped back slowly from his counter as if he hadn't heard correctly and then looked at our father with such puzzlement on his face that he was forced to repeat the one obviously offensive word. 'Turkey?'

'Turkey?' said the butcher, 'you've left it a bit late for a turkey.'

'Oh come on, it's Christmas, you must have a turkey.'

'I've had turkeys in the shop the last fortnight. All the meat's been put out the back now, it's all in store.'

'And there's a turkey is there?'

The butcher raised his eyebrows and reluctantly admitted, 'I think I've got one left, yes.'

Tom and I cheered, jumped up and down a little and kicked the sawdust around that lay on the floor.

'And those two young 'uns of yours can stop that as well,' said the butcher. We stopped dead in our tracks not wanting to jeopardize the turkey.

He came out of the coldstore with the bird, weighed it, named its price and handed it to Frank, who, in turn, handed it to us. We bowed under its weight but made for the door with it nevertheless.

'I can owe you for it can I?' said Frank, beginning to follow us.

'You can do no such thing!'

'Oh, come on,' said Frank. 'It's Christmas.'

The butcher was obviously keen to get shut up and to go home. He agreed: 'But only until New Year.' This meant that ever after Ellen had to walk to the butcher's in Orpington.

Frank took us home by a new route, one which passed the electricity transformer. There were several of these little chapel-like buildings on the estate and they intrigued us. They had art-deco flourishes composed of chopped-up bits of housebrick cemented at bizarre angles. The effect of the whole was entirely out of character with the rest of the estate. It was as if a private battle over urban taste was being waged by the Electricity Board. We couldn't imagine who lived in them and why they needed to be protected by so much electricity. There was strictly no admittance if the sign on the fence was to be believed but Frank managed to make an opening in the fence. He commanded us to follow him in but we were frightened to go through the gap. 'You can't stand out there, someone'll see you,' he growled. We were aware that our father was up to no good and it made us uneasy.

Growing beside the transformer was a fir tree about seven foot high, and this was the object of Frank's interest. He began pulling at its trunk and rocking it backwards and forwards in an attempt to work it free of its roots and liberate it from the prison in which the Electricity Board had placed it. The tree would not come away but hung on tight to the ground beneath it. Frank attempted to reason with it, and then tried to take it by surprise with one big pull. This resulted in Frank sprawling on the gravel while the fir tree swayed over him like another drunk puzzling out the condition of his companion in the gutter.

He stood up again and, as soon as he had composed himself, kicked the tree, not without considerable injury to his foot. He put both his arms around it and hugged it like a bear, endeavouring to transfer the whole of his own weight on to its roots. After kicking at the gravel around the base of the tree for some time he sat down on his haunches, took out his key ring and began to saw with his Yale at the trunk. Frank had beads of sweat on his forehead but the snow had formed solid skull caps on the tops of our balaclavas.

'Ain't you pulled it up yet, Dad?' said Tom.

'No, ain't you pulled it up yet?' I added.

'No, I B'haven't,' he said, 'have you got any suggestions then, eh?' and he took a swipe at Tom.

'No, we haven't,' I said, boldly.

'You two go back through the fence and keep watch for the police,' said Frank. 'You'll be more use out there.'

We quickly clambered back through the gap. Tom

looked one way and I looked the other, like two little sentries, with ice packs for busbies.

When the tree finally did come crashing down it slumped over the electrical apparatus, on to which Frank climbed to free it. If we had been more sensible of the danger we should probably have come dashing back through the fence but we remained on watch. To get the tree out of its enclosure Frank had to remove several more planks from the fence. He pulled it into the street and began dragging it along behind him by its stubborn roots. When we got back to the house he remembered that he'd left the turkey behind at the transformer, and he made us hide in the alleyway beside our house until he returned with it.

'Whatever's kept you?' said Ellen. 'I've been worried silly. Whatever possessed you to keep the twins out so long in this cold?' Our balaclavas were irremovable and we had to sit in front of the fire until the ice had melted.

'Where's my bird and my tree?' asked Ellen.

Frank dragged the tree into the front room.

'Oh no! Look at the size of it,' exclaimed our mother.

'I know,' said Frank. 'It's a real good 'un isn't it, I've had my eye on it for weeks.'

'But it's far too big, Frank, my tinsel will look silly on it. Bring it over here, I've got a bucket of dirt ready.'

Frank attempted to stand the tree up to its full glorious height, but the glorious height combined with the depth of the bucket of dirt made the total span larger than that of the floor to the ceiling.

'Mind!' said Ellen. 'It's too big, you stupid fool, you've bought one that's too big.'

'No I haven't,' said Frank. 'It's you. You've put too much dirt in the bucket. What do you expect it to do, start growing again? Take some dirt out.'

Eventually, after much toing and froing with trowels of dirt, Frank had to concede and he sawed off the topmost twelve inches of the tree. This action made it look rather strange – it appeared to be extending itself through the ceiling.

'It looks like a great big lavatory brush,' observed Ellen. 'Whatever was you thinking of, buying such a big one? It's the sort of thing you would have in a hotel at a function, not a private house, and look at it, where am I going to put my star?' Saying this Ellen took a closer look at the tree. 'How much did you give for it?' she asked.

'Ten and six,' said Frank.

'Ten and six?' repeated Ellen, shocked. 'You've been done. This isn't a Christmas tree, it's not got needles, it's something else, like what you have in graveyards.'

'And electricity trans – ' said Tom.

'No, I know it's not got needles,' said Frank, jumping in quickly, 'that's why I got it. Nothing to drop, see?'

Ellen couldn't bear to look at it any more and went out into the kitchen to inspect the bird. We were still by the fire warming up when we heard her shout to Frank. 'Oh my gawd, Frank, get in here.'

'What's he done now?' said Tom.

'Less of your lip, kid,' he said and clipped Tom around the ear. He went out into the kitchen.

'It's forty-five pounds!' said Ellen.

'Well you wanted a big bird, you've got a big bird.'

'I suppose you left it right until the butcher's was closing and this was all he had because no one else wanted it.'

'No, no!'

'And you know why no one else wanted it?'

'No?' said Frank.

'Because it's too bloody big to get in the oven.'

Frank got angry. 'Well I'll saw its sodding legs off then,' he said.

'I'm not serving a legless bird to your mother and father. There'll be enough leglessness around this Christmas without the bloody bird as well. I'm just going to drink the gin and show you up for a change and see how you like that for once. You can cook the bird, if you can, I'm not serving up a monster. I've done my best. I've been putting aside nuts, mandarins, fancies, what for? I've tried my best for your rotten parents, I've been wasting my time.'

As usual during one of these speeches Frank stood on one foot first and then the other, first looked at the floor and then at the ceiling, and then he ended his shuffling by hurting his hand on the table, and making everything jump off it on to the floor. This was our favourite part of the performance.

'I've been going short myself,' continued Ellen, 'just to stock up and try to make this a nice Christmas for us all, and now look! You've tried, I know you've tried, but as usual you've tried too hard. I'm not cooking that bird and that's final.'

As Mum pronounced the last part of her speech we looked at the monster as it sat on the draining-board. In life it must have been something like an ostrich, and its death, we imagined, must have been quite a drama.

'You can tell your mother that Christmas is off this year,' said Ellen at last.

'Come on, don't be silly,' said Frank. 'I'll cook the bird.'

'You will cook the bird?' said Mum. We all looked at Frank. 'And how do you propose to do it, dig a ditch in the garden and barbecue it?'

Frank stormed out of the house. Mum sat on the settee and had a cry.

'If we don't have a bird,' asked Tom, 'we will still get presents from Father Christmas won't we?'

'If you're good,' said Ellen.

When Frank came back in two hours later he said he'd worked it out. He'd met a mate of Clancy's at the 'Bucket, called Arnold. Arnold worked at the crematorium.

'I saw a mate of Clancy's in the 'Bucket,' began Frank, 'and he said he'd got a big oven we could use.'

'What?' said Ellen. 'You mean you'll cook it in someone else's oven and then walk the streets with it when it's done?'

'Yeah,' said Frank. The idea obviously quite appealed to him. It would be another story told at the 'Bucket with great relish.

'What about them, aren't they going to be using the oven?'

'No,' said Frank, and then he paused, 'they always go down to her mother's at three o'clock and have their dinner there.'

'Well it's a forty-five pound turkey, that's twenty minutes per pound plus twenty minutes. It'll have to be in for over fifteen hours, do you realize that?'

'It'll be all right, Arnold says it's a very hot oven.'

'It had better be a hot oven,' said Ellen. 'Are you sure it's going to fit in this oven of this Arnold's then?'

'Oh yeah, it'll fit in easy.'

'Are you sure? Why's he got such a big oven, then, what's he had in it?'

'Well . . .' said Frank, 'he does a lot of catering . . . for parties . . .'

'Oh, I see,' said Ellen. 'So it's not a household oven then, it's professional.'

'Oh yeah,' said Frank. 'It's a professional oven all right.'

'Well,' said Ellen, 'if you want to look a proper fool parading the streets on Christmas morning with that monster, looking like someone from the Welfare, it's your business.'

'I shall use a wheelbarrow,' said Frank.

'Yes, you do that,' said Ellen, 'and put some fancy chains around it and carry a wand.'

Ellen was at her wits' end with the whole subject of Christmas. She made one more stipulation and that was that Frank should inform his parents of the true history of the whole saga so that she could be exempt from any blame as a mother and wife.

Our grandparents arrived shortly before we were due to go to bed. Nan helped us to leave a bottle of beer and two carrots for the reindeer, on the back step, and we checked the chimney to see that it was clear. The adults seemed much more taken with the whole palaver than we did. We were keen to get to bed and to get to sleep so that St Nicholas would come quickly. We sent a quick reminder up the chimney and went to bed.

Downstairs the 'dults, as we called them, quickly got to the philosophical stage, brought on in the men by stout and in the women by advocaat snowballs. Every year Grandad brought his bust of Sir Winston Churchill which he set up on the mantelpiece. He had little firework cigars, which, when lit and placed in Churchill's mouth, intermittently puffed out little white rings of smoke. With the bust of the great man looking down on them they were inspired to great thoughts about the nation and the state of the world since the war. They reflected upon the great days of the war and bemoaned the economic recovery of Japan and Germany. Then came the greatest discussion of all, which fired them all to a passion: The National Debt. They laid curses on the profiteering Americans, and Grandad would vow that if every working man took a pound from his pocket then we would finally be rid of the great shame of the nation. Why on earth did we give in to India and sail the Empire down the Swanee? The Queen should put her foot down. Why hadn't Harold put up a better fight at Hastings? That was when the rot set in. It was us who had to bail them out last time, and the time before . . . Tom and I grew up with the great weight of The National Debt upon our shoulders and the profound impression that the Queen always had one leg in the air. 'If only she would put her foot down . . .'

After the philosophy came the remembrance of times past, of the great Christmases of the blitz when they had nothing but swede and a candle between twelve of them, no nylons, no bananas, but a true spirit of Christmas. It was at this point that the maudlin songs would begin:

'Oooh-oooh what a rotten song,
what a rotten singer too-oo-oo.'

Tom and I would lie in our beds listening, frightened and disturbed by the drone. 'My baby has gone down the plug-hole' was a particular favourite with our grandmother. We felt so sad that such an event had befallen her and wondered if we would have had another uncle even though he would obviously have been very thin.

'I had a little drink about an hour ago
and it's gone right to my head.'

There was something in the songs which frightened us, especially when they got to the line in 'Knees up Mother Brown' which went: 'Under the table she must go.'

'Why must she go under the table?' asked Tom.

'I don't know,' I said. 'Who's got to go under the table, not Mum?'

'No, I think it's Nan,' said Tom. 'I can hear her screaming.' We pictured in our minds what must be going on downstairs: our grandmother on her hands and knees, while everyone else pushed her under the table. When they really got going they'd sing a whole medley, confusing bits of one song with another. They'd be:

> 'Underneath the Arches
> I'll dream my dreams away'

which made us cry, and then:

> 'Where did you get that hat?'

which we liked better, and then they would all cry as they sang:

> 'Maybe it's because I'm a Londoner
> that I love London Town.'

'I'm not singing those songs when I'm a 'dult,' said Tom.

'No, neither am I,' I said.

We had also noticed that our father kept coming up the stairs and going down again, apparently for no reason. We wished he would stop it because he might come up just as St Nicholas was leaving our presents and disturb him.

'The little bleeders are still awake,' said Frank when he got downstairs. 'How am I supposed to go in there?'

'What's he want to come in for?' asked Tom.

'I don't know,' I said.

'We'll have to wait, Frank,' we heard Mum say. 'If they know it's you it'll be terrible for them.'

'Oh yes,' we heard our nan saying. 'You don't want to spoil it for them, we've had enough setbacks this year already, what with Ellen not getting the bird properly organized. Christmas is what Children are all about.'

'Yes, Frank,' said Mum, 'don't drink any more.'

'But Dad's just opened a party-seven! It'll go flat if it's not drunk straight away.'

We dropped off to sleep for the hour or so that it took Frank and his father to drink the party-seven, then we woke up again and Tom said to me, 'Has he been yet, Rich?'

'No, Tom, he ain't.'

'Have a look, see if the stockings are full. He might have been and we didn't know.'

'He's not been, Tom, go to sleep or he won't come.'

'Perhaps we haven't been good and he's not coming.'

This was worrying and we went to sleep thinking that we had been bad children and that we didn't deserve a visit.

At about three in the morning there was an almighty crash. We woke to discover that it was our father. He was wearing his black dufflecoat with the hood up and he appeared to have fallen over the rug. I heard Tom's stocking rip as he tried to get something into it. 'Sod it,' he said.

Then he got off his hands and knees and swayed around for a while. He walked across the room. 'Done it,' he muttered and walked straight into the cupboard where

Ellen kept her clothes-horse. 'Where's the effing light?' we heard him say. Then we heard him being sick in the cupboard and finally saw him crawling out, on his hands and knees, towards the landing light, and then we heard him tumble down the stairs in a succession of bumps.

There was silence for a moment and then I felt Tom tugging the sleeve of my pyjamas.

'He's been,' said Tom, ecstatically, 'I saw him!'

'So did I,' I said.

'He had a big red coat and a long white beard and I could hear the reindeer on the roof!'

'So could I,' I whispered.

CHAPTER XII

In which we are beaten by our father and in which we go to school and play the drums but our diaries say more than we are at liberty to reveal, and in the longest chapter of the novel we go on holiday to our grandparents and a pig is killed

Every street on the estate had what our mother termed a 'rowdy lot'. 'Please God,' prayed Ellen, 'please God don't let it be us.'

Up until our father's not entirely successful impersonation of St Nicholas; and up until the Great Boxing Night Row in which our grandmother was accused by our mother of sitting on the nutcrackers in order that she might hog the brazils, the rowdy lot had generally been supposed to be the Hardys at 109. On Boxing Night we had outstripped their reputation to such a degree that, breaking with tradition, it was the Hardys themselves who sent for the police to quieten us. Ellen was crushed by the visit; as the constable stood in our hallway she demanded to be thrown in the back of the Black Maria and taken away – 'anything to get out of this madhouse.'

Ellen's mother had once played 'In a Monastery Garden' loudly on the piano to cover the sound of her husband's accusations of infidelity. Ellen had a mortal fear, now, of disturbance. 'My heart can't take it,' she said, 'nor my brain neither.' Living in a cul-de-sac, as we did, meant that the plan of the houses formed an amphitheatre. The sound of disturbance could leave by our windows (particularly by one pane through which a turkey leg had already successfully passed) and swirl around the amphitheatre, gaining in volume, so that all the stands lit up and the spectators could hear every word and follow the course of the argument. One particularly painful moment for Ellen, during the Boxing Night Row, was when she shouted, 'You'll be sorry when I'm dead', and the woman over the road called out, 'I won't, we might get some quiet', and the whole cul-de-sac cheered. The next day our grandmother refused to stay in Ellen's house a single minute longer and as soon as she'd eaten a large lunch of cold turkey and piccalilli and packed herself up some sandwiches for the trip, they left.

The strongest remaining impression I have of that day is of our mother, in a fit of anxiety, throwing the toy piano at me that I had been given by my grandparents. It hit the wall, where it shattered, and the little white keys fell behind the sideboard. I remember that the keys had black rubber dongers on them that so much resembled crotchets that I believed it was the music itself which had flown out and dropped behind our sideboard. I still can't look at musical notation without hearing the sound of pianos being smashed.

Frank seemed quite cheery throughout the whole episode. He took these arguments in his stride, perhaps even enjoying them. He sat for the next few days surrounded by his cans and bottles. Because of the hostilities Ellen had lost all desire to cook the rest of the food that she had in stock. For the rest of the holiday we lived off the fancies that remained – the chocolate log and the marzipans – which we were perfectly happy to do. We did, however, stay as quiet as we could, knowing that both Mum's and Dad's nerves were very easy to get on to. We were glad when the Christmas holiday was over and we could go back to school.

Frank was rarely in from the pub before we were in bed. One night we heard him remonstrating with our mother in the hallway. He was insisting that he should come up and kiss us goodnight.

'If you'd wanted to do that,' said Ellen, 'you should have got in from the 'Bucket in time.'

'But I've written a poem,' said Frank. 'I've got to tell them.'

'They don't want to hear your poetry,' said Ellen.

'Yes they do. I've wrote it on the way home, I've got to tell it to them before it goes out of my head.'

'I'm not having you waking them up and ruining them for school in the morning.'

'But it's poetry, it's educational.'

'Don't talk such rot,' said Ellen. Frank went and sat at the kitchen table where he sucked the end of his pencil and tried to commit his verse to paper. When he'd completed it we heard him insisting again that he should come up and sing it to us, since it was in the form of a lullaby.

'They're fast asleep,' bellowed Ellen

'No we're not,' Tom called back. Because of this Frank could not be held downstairs any longer. As he leaned over us we could smell the drink on him, which disturbed us as much as the poor state of his overcoat, which bore the marks of his having fallen in the mud. He still had a bruised eye from the difference of opinion he'd entered into outside the 'Bucket two nights before. He got out his piece of paper and began to sing.

> 'The sun has gone to Australia
> to see a kangaroo
> so little boys must go to bed . . .'

and here he coughed, spat into his handkerchief and bristled with pride as he approached the rhyme,

> '. . . and that applies to you.'

His voice was sometimes deep and sometimes high and sometimes the tune matched the line and sometimes it didn't, but it was all rendered in an eerie, old music-hall kind of way.

> 'So climb the wooden hill and go to sleep,
> and if I hear you make a peep
> I'll hit you with a shoe.
> The flowers have closed and so have the bars,
> your mother's boiling socks;
> your dad's been out for a couple of jars
> but it's bedtime on the clocks . . .'

'What do you think?' he asked when he'd finished the performance.

'It's really good,' said Tom, through his yawns.

'I thought you'd like it, and you know what, your

bloody mother downstairs didn't want me to come up with it.' At this point he belched.

'Do you want to hear it again?' he asked.

'Dad,' I said, 'I want to go to sleep or I'll be no good at school . . .'

Frank looked at me with anger and disappointment mixed in his eyes. 'Sod school,' he said.

'I can't sod school tomorrow,' I said. 'I've got to say my six times table.' Frank seemed entirely unaware of the pressures we were under. I was very worried about my six times table, the whole subject of tables worried me. It was not that I was lazy in my lessons, I had worked hard to learn the tune to all the tables, it was merely the words I was lacking. I didn't mind it when we all chanted them together, but when we were called upon to recite individually I always ended up having to stand on my chair. Having to stand on my chair was the worst punishment I knew, at this age, and the thought of it terrified me. The feeling of instability as the little chair rocked on its uneven legs compounded my feelings of vulnerability and shame as I stood there, above my peers. The hostilities at home didn't help me to concentrate any better on those tables. Tom wasn't much better but he didn't mind standing on his chair, with his hands behind his head, as much as I did. I think he rather enjoyed it, just as, I'm sure, Frank would have done.

We were very fond of our teacher, Miss Graterex. When a dispute broke out over who was to have the sidedrums during music and movement she generally decided in our favour because we were so gentle with them and looked, she said, like two little drummer boys. Barry Foster hated us for this, he liked to bash the drum in the manner of Bill Haley and the Comets. Poor Charlie Rubbidge got himself banned on the triangle because, although he was a delicate player, lifting it to his drained ear to enjoy the enduring tone, he always managed to get his finger stuck in the ring.

It was during one of these sessions in the school hall, where the girls were in their blue knickers transformed into fairies, and we were in our white, bashing out the music for them to dance to, that Miss Graterex called me to one side. While the fairies were asleep beneath their toadstools she had noticed an ominous blue mark on my shoulder. I told her that I'd fallen down the stairs running away from the toilet. (Charlie had told me that if you didn't get out quick the turds would come back up and get you.) Miss Graterex was surprised by this news, and laughed, but then she turned more serious again and called Tom over to join us. 'And do you keep falling down the stairs too, Tom?' she asked.

'No,' he said.

'So how did you get that mark on your arm?'

'I dunno,' he said.

'Do you know how he got it?' Miss Graterex asked me.

I stared at the blue bloody wound beneath his skin. 'I dunno neither,' I said.

'And this one here,' she said to Tom, laying her hand gently on the tip of his shoulder blade.

'I dunno,' he said sullenly. All the class stared at us and we shivered, wanting to put our clothes back on, or to play the drums again, or even dance around the room with the girls, anything to stop the inquiry. We were so fond of Miss Graterex that we often cried at the pain of being told off by her. I wanted to say that I didn't mean to have these marks and that I was sorry if I shouldn't have them. Every morning before we had our milk she supervised us as we washed our hands and scrubbed our nails at rows of little sinks in the boys' latrines. We were not allowed back into the classroom until our hands were as clean and white as the sinks themselves. I presumed that she regarded the big blue marks I possessed in the same way she regarded dirt. Miss Graterex could see that we were upset, and she sent us back to the band.

Ellen worried about the marks too, and on the night before we had a music and movement lesson she'd sit us on the draining-boards, either side of the sink, and lay little pieces of beef or bacon, whatever was to hand, on our arms and back. In the morning she'd lightly rub our bruises with her sweet-smelling talcum powder. She constantly talked to Mr Bannister about the problem she was having with cold sores, which got so bad sometimes that, as he could see, they flared up into a Fat Lip.

The first task of every school week was to write up a diary of the things we had done over the weekend. We had barely learnt to read, of course, but Prospect provided an ideal opportunity for experiments into innovatory teaching systems. Miss Graterex supplied us with sample cards, of things we might have done, with an accompanying picture to identify the words. The idea was that we could copy the cards. *On Saturday we went to the shops* was a great favourite. *On Saturday I watched the television and I saw . . .* was the most popular, although we were unable to fill in what we had seen, of course. For this part we had another set of picture cards: *dog, cat, elephant, egg, rhubarb*, so that we could put, 'On Saturday I watched the television and I saw some rhubarb.' Miss Graterex had amended my card and Tom's card to read '*On Saturday we . . .* instead of '*I*'. We were very proud of the doctoring.

Miss Graterex began to look at our diaries closely, for sometimes little tell-tale things would appear in them to worry her. She called us both up to her desk one Monday afternoon to query our entries. Tom's had run:

'On Saturday we went to the shops. We went to the shops with Mum. We bought some bakon and a eg. Mum made a cake.'

I was very keen on my diary and liked to use as many of the cards as possible, cramming a trip to the coast, a birthday party, the pictures in Orpington, and going to church (we didn't) all into the same weekend. I was more ambitious with my juggling of the cards than Tom was and always attempted too much with them. My entry for this particular weekend ran:

'On Saturday Mum made a cake. The cake is v. bad. Dad give Mum a blak I. I went to the seaside. I went to a birthday party. I went to church and sang.'

Miss Graterex decided to walk home with us from school and talk to Ellen. Our emotions were mixed as we walked along the street with her because although she was being very nice to us, we felt ourselves to be in the most serious trouble we had ever been in. This time we had really been bad, we felt, worse than the time Tom spat at Grandad and he was unable to identify which one of us did it, worse than the time I took the goldfish out of the bowl that the rag-and-bone man had given us, and let it dry up in the cutlery drawer.

As she was telling Ellen how worried she was about us, Frank got in for his tea. As soon as he saw Miss Graterex he walked through the front room, without stopping and left by the back door. He hung around in Clancy's until he heard her leave. Ellen found our teacher's visit very hard to bear, the shame showed on her face and while she spoke she pulled at the threads of her cardigan.

When Frank came back he was furious, and he accused Ellen of inviting the visit, and of collaborating with the Welfare. 'I suppose you want a whole stream of them calling at all hours to see what our business is?'

'No,' said Ellen. 'I didn't get her round here, she saw the marks on the boys.'

'I suggest we make up a bed in the hallway for the School Board, and the Department of Health can sleep in the bath, will that make you happy?'

'I told her that they fight a lot, that's how they got them . . .' Ellen began to cry.

'You make me want to weep!' shouted Frank. He began marching round the house, throwing things. He went into their bedroom and smashed the crystal vanity set that was Ellen's mother's, and threw our jigsaws out of the window in a great shower.

We were wearing corduroy dungarees on this occasion and Frank utilized the straps to pick us both up and hurl us out of his way as he left for the Dog and Bucket.

News of the activities in our house had reached Mr Bannister and he could barely believe it. He had been sitting in the council offices, resting with his pouch, when conversations taking place in the rooms off the corridor he used as his office drifted to his ears. The Education and Welfare were the first to become alarmed, and they had spoken to their fieldworker, Miss Barnes, an elderly spinster of Roehampton, rather out of her depths in Prospect, who had opened a file on us and placed it with great care in a green cabinet. In turn the Works and Fabric Officer had come to hear of it, and it was he who approached Mr Bannister to ask him to keep a close watch on us, and if possible gain admittance to the house. 'Report directly to me,' he had been instructed, 'any doors off their hinges, any gross abuse of the paintwork, wainscoting dislodged, attempts at arson, damage to the plumbing, violence against the fitted cupboards.'

Mr Bannister agreed enthusiastically. 'You can put complete trust,' he said, 'in the boys at the front line.'

After Frank had cast us aside by our straps, and knocked Ellen to the floor, Ellen began a front line of her own. She bolted the doors and set furniture up in a barricade against his return. We spent the evening huddled together in front of the television for comfort. We stayed up until half past eleven when Ellen decided to take us to our beds, declaring, 'He won't come back now, he's gone off to kip with one of his cronies.' By cronies Ellen meant Clancy, who was no good, and had led Frank astray from the start.

At two in the morning we woke in our beds to the sound of a great crashing and banging at the front door. We gathered up our eiderdown and, wrapped up in it, like two little bugs in their cocoon, we wriggled our way to the top of the stairs. Ellen was holding on to a dining chair secured against the front door and shouting, 'It won't do you no good banging!'

Frank was calling for admittance in furious language. We heard him beating on the door with the milk bottles from the step and, as one of them shattered, watched the little bits of glass come in through the letter-box.

'Why don't you go and sleep with one of your cronies!' called Ellen.

Frank called again for admittance. Ellen looked up at us. 'Go back to bed you two,' she said, 'there's nothing to see.'

We remained where we were; if he got in it wouldn't matter where we were, our fate would be the same, and besides, there was plenty to see. Suddenly, and ominously, the furore at the front door ceased. Ellen listened for a while, and finally released her grip on the dining chair. She looked up at us and said, 'He's gone off to sleep with one of his cronies.'

By this stage we had a very strong picture in our minds of what a crony might be: a hobgoblin-type creature who drank, broke things up and lived somewhere beneath the ground; it was they who inhabited the sewers and produced those deep shudders and groaning noises which still plagued the innovatory system. We pictured our father descending into the earth to join them and perhaps choosing to remain there, living like a smuggler in tunnels full of barrels beneath Prospect, only returning to the surface to steal bread and margarine.

In actual fact this was not the case. Frank had not gone off to join the cronies, but had instead gone to rummage around in the garden shed. In the shed he had found Ellen's old ironing-board, which the council had supplied, and he'd carried it out into the middle of the verge and set it up at the centre of the cul-de-sac. Going back to the shed he found a piece of cardboard and some red paint. He made a placard which read:

> JUST TO LET YOU ALL KNOW
> THE BITCH HAS KICKED ME OUT AGAIN

The placard he set up against the ironing-board and then he clambered up on to it and settled down to sleep for the night. The board was too short for the comfort of his calves, and several times in the night the whole memorial toppled over but Frank felt it to be such a worthwhile project that he stuck with it until morning.

In the morning the milkman knocked for his money. Ellen noticed that he had the most peculiar grin on his face and that he treated her with definite disdain. The

milkman had already vowed to buy Frank a pint the next
time he saw him in the 'Bucket.

When Mr Bannister called for the rent a few moments
later Ellen detected a note of deep concern in his voice.

'Is everything, as it were, all right in your household,
Mrs Stone?' he asked.

'Yes, yes, fine, and yourself, Mr Bannister, and Mrs
Bannister?' said Ellen.

'Fine,' said Mr Bannister. 'It's just that, I can't help
noticing that you're looking a little drawn of late. I
wondered if everything was all right between yourself
and Mr Stone?'

Ellen feigned surprise at his uncustomary forwardness.
'Certainly,' she said, 'but I must get on and make his
breakfast or he'll be late for work, and then where will
we be?' she said.

It was at this point, probably through embarrassment
at the confrontation with Bannister, that she looked over
his shoulder, in order to avoid his eyes, and saw the sign,
and the ironing-board with Frank upon it, sleeping. She
whimpered a little, thrust the money into Mr Bannister's
hand, and shut the door on him. Bannister stood on the
step perplexed for a few moments, unable to think what
to do. He could hear Ellen sobbing with shame inside the
house. He looked back to Frank, aware that his weight
was putting a great strain on council property. He debated
with himself whether he should make Frank aware of the
fact. He decided against it. He continued on his way to
the next door, deeply worried about Ellen and us and
deciding that whatever he could do, both in his capacity
as an officer of the council, and as a man, he would do.
He did not knock for the rent at the next door until he
had placed himself in such a way that he would block the
sight of Frank upon his ironing-board, and thus save

Ellen any further embarrassment. It was a noble act, he felt, befitting an officer.

Very shortly, and much to Bannister's relief, Frank climbed down from the position he had stuck to so resolutely. In her upset Ellen had neglected to replace the dining chair in front of the door and Frank let himself in with his key. Bannister braced himself at the bottom of the cul-de-sac, to rush in manfully, as soon as the fracas began, not simply to save the fabric, but to save the poor young woman and her children. His heart beat, and he secured his money pouch firmly to his side, but no sound came from the house. Sober, Frank was gentle again and he was more concerned with towelling the dew from his hair and changing his damp clothes. He and Ellen agreed on a silence and we ate our breakfast. Ellen walked us both to school, because we wouldn't go without her. We vowed that we would bash him if he did anything to her. For this suggestion we were rewarded with a sharp telling off. We were not to dare to strike our own father.

'Not even bite him in the knee?' inquired Tom. No, not even this.

During the course of that day, while we sat at our desks dazed and confused, Ellen and Frank decided that we should all go on a holiday. Ellen was desperate to do anything to save the situation, motivated not so much by love for Frank as by the fact that the house was in his name, and if he left, she felt, she would lose it. She saw herself returning to the slums and was determined to avoid that. Nothing would part her from her dreamhouse, not even the nightmare of living in it with Frank.

When we got in from school the atmosphere was so relaxed, Frank having taken the day off work to mend the things in the house that he had broken, that we

cried with relief. Frank had telephoned his parents and
arranged for us all to go and stay with them for a
fortnight. They had retired and moved from the Guinness
Trust Tenements in Kennington to the Guinness Trust
Bungalows in Newhaven. We were very excited about
the prospect of two weeks off school, and of going to the
sea, and we liked the sound of living in a bungalow,
which we imagined was something like a caravan. We
saw ourselves pushing it from one happy glade to another.

On the next Saturday, after five days of truce already,
we all boarded the train and travelled down to Newhaven.

As it turned out the bungalows were not on wheels but
nevertheless we liked them, they were very quaint: a line
of thirty little homes in the design of almshouses or a
parish hospital. At the centre of the terrace there was a
two-storey clubhouse, with a room below provided with
board games and easy chairs and a room above for
community singing which was led by the local charities. It
was like a little holiday camp and was set high up on the
brow of a hill, looking down across thick meadow grass,
matted with poppies and speedwell, towards the goods-
yards of Seaford and then the coastal defences and the
sea, which shone like silver foil.

From the moment we arrived a great pretence was
afoot. There was laughter as soon as we stepped into the
house, laughter and smiles, and our grandmother ran
around unable to do enough for Ellen. There was no
mention of her having sat on the nutcrackers to hog the
brazils. We were all the best of friends. Grandad gave us
both half-crowns with the proviso that we waste them on
whatever we wanted and then come back for another
one. The best china was used for every meal and every
cup of tea.

Our grandfather even suspended his thoughts on the

National Debt and changed to a new theme of hope. 'When you look,' he said, 'at the green grass, and the beautiful sky, and all the tarmacking and new lamp posts the council have put up, well it can't help but make you happy, can it?' We agreed that it couldn't. 'All those poor bloody Japs slaving over soldering irons. Who'd want that?' We agreed that nobody would.

In return for all this effort our parents put across the image of being ridiculously happy, as if they were in the first flush of love. In turn our grandparents attempted the same, and made out that they were deliriously happy with each other even though we all knew they had been trying to kill each other for years. They put on a show of domestic bliss by way of an example to Ellen and Frank. Nothing must go wrong, there must be no unhappiness, everything was to be nice. It was going to be a terrible strain.

Grandad had attempted to adapt to retirement, but found it difficult, never having really adapted to work in the first place; it was for him a second-hand affair, he'd watch the other old men and copy. He built some cloches from little panes of glass in which to grow strawberries, and set them outside his front door. He fearlessly defended these cloches against the slugs – it was the only part of growing the strawberries that I think he enjoyed. The plants themselves withered and died, scorched by the sun under the glass, but the slugs kept coming and he amused himself by pouring salt over them. We sat outside the bungalow most of the day watching the slugs die and playing with Grandad's outdoor fridge. It was made from chalk with a dip in the top of it into which he poured water. As long as it was kept in the sun where the water could evaporate then it kept cool inside. We heaped water on to it all day long in an attempt to freeze

grasshoppers to death. (Charlie Rubbidge's mum had an
electric fridge and he had frozen a grasshopper in it for
two days and later revived it in the bath.) We never did
achieve our goal, and cursed Charlie once more for
having the proper equipment; instead we got sharp slaps
around the ears from our grandmother when she discovered the grasshoppers wriggling in the butter. Ellen
and Frank were out at the time, walking along the front.
When they came back Tom and I were crying. We saw
them holding hands and so we stopped crying immediately
and our grandmother spoke nicely to us again so that
they wouldn't know anything unhappy had happened.

Nan and Grandad suggested these walks for Ellen and
Frank, especially if an argument between either couple
was brewing. As soon as Ellen and Frank were off on the
walk our grandparents would explode into screaming,
each blaming the other for the sorry state of their son's
marriage. Tom and I would begin fighting over the few
toys we had brought with us, or the fridge, but as soon as
Ellen and Frank returned silence and happiness would
descend. A sentence beginning 'You miserable old sod
. . .' would mysteriously end '. . . shall I help you peel
the spuds, my dear?' In our case, 'It's mine, it's mine, I
got it first, I'll bash you . . .' would become 'Do you
want to play with this for a while, Tom?' It may be, of
course, that as soon as Ellen and Frank turned the corner
in their approach to the bungalow a similar truce broke
out between them, and they held hands so as not to
disappoint us because we were all making such an effort.

Tom picked Ellen bunches of flowers, because flowers
made her happy. He practically cleared the meadow, and
had a few as well out of the post office garden.

One day he came in with some may blossom from a

hawthorn tree. 'Take that horrible stuff out of the house right now,' said Nan. 'It's bad luck.'

At that moment Ellen and Frank appeared at the doorway. 'Oh they're nice,' Ellen said to Tom as he went to rush past her with them. 'Are they for me?'

'Yes they are,' said our nan. 'Isn't he a thoughtful little boy! Shall I get you a vase for them, Tom?' Our grandmother got the vase and arranged the may blossom, but she didn't put any water in.

Grandad showed Frank his next door neighbour's cabbages and tried to get him interested in the soil. He told him how much he enjoyed growing his strawberries and said that he liked to do things about the house and in the garden. It was better than just sloping off down to the pub every five minutes. He hoped this would be a good example to his son, and undo all the years of bad example he had set him – he even went so far as to hang a picture of the royal family in the room where they were sleeping.

'You seem happy down here,' said Frank to his father.

'Well,' he replied, 'I've a lovely bungalow and a wonderful wife, what more does a man require?' As he said this he squeezed our grandmother around the waist which so surprised her that she dropped a jug of sennapods she had been soaking on the sill.

'Oh, silly me,' she said.

We were enjoying our holiday enormously, conscious of the fact that we were getting away with blue murder. We hoped that Mum and Dad would put off making up completely, and just hover on the edge of it, so that everything would carry on like this in a state of holiday limbo. Every evening we'd all take a walk along the seafront together. Grandad would stand for half an hour or more in one spot on the sea wall, mesmerized by the movements of the Channel. He loved it when the water was high and the spray hit him in the face. Tom and I shrieked every time a high wave drenched him, frightened that he'd be washed over and drowned. It was the possibility of this, he told us, that made the drenching fun. The sea spray frightened Ellen too, but our grandmother was unworried by the possibility of his being washed over. He loved standing there. He said that the noise of the sea reminded him of Lambeth Laundry. On the way back we would all sit outside the Flying Fish and have a drink. It was a real treat to have the 'dults sitting outside with us for once, all lined up as a happy little family. We listened to the midges and the frogs and the wagons rattling down to the Seaford docks.

'I can listen to those trains all day,' said Grandad. 'It's not like city noise, well it's the same noise, I know, but it's in the fresh air.'

Whenever Grandad made one of those pronouncements we all leaned forward to listen and then sat back at its conclusion with satisfaction. There was something very calming about the pronouncements of a retired man performing his role as the head of the family.

'When I was younger,' he said, 'I could go for years without even a look at the sea. Now I can look at it every day.'

This was something which our mother gave great assent to. Whenever we had been on a trip to the sea she would say, 'Well this is my first look of the sea this year.' If we didn't have a holiday, or a trip, Ellen would bemoan the fact by saying, 'I didn't get a look of the sea last year, and now I won't get one this,' as if there was something medicinal in the fact of having looked at it.

Ellen found it very soothing to be sitting outside the Flying Fish because, in her book, beer drunk in the open air was less alcoholic. She could find no direct scientific reason for this but, nevertheless, she felt it to be true. She found the setting of a country pub much removed from the dark, beery, male world of the pubs she had known in Kennington and their replicas on Prospect. Grandad said 'good evening' to everyone who passed by and attempted to engage them in conversation about the quality of the evening, while the rest of us craned forward to hear him. He was trying to show us that he was just as well known and respected here as he was in Kennington. It was lucky for him that when people are on holiday, as those were who passed by, it is a fact that they are disposed to be more friendly and talkative than they would normally be, and that they get an inordinate pleasure out of talking to the locals. He couldn't have pulled the same stunt inland.

At the end of the first week the strain of all this began to show on our grandparents. Nan developed a nervous tic beneath her left eye, Grandad began tapping things: his fork on the dinner table, his tobacco tin on the arm of his chair, his foot on the floor. They had need to get at each other's throats. Frank rattled the change in his pockets as soon as it got to opening time at the 'Bucket, knowing that he couldn't spring up, suddenly animated for the first time since they'd shut after lunch, and say, 'Right, I'm off down the boozer.' He would have to wait for his father casually to suggest it at around about eight o'clock when it would be mooted as a family outing after that interminable walk along the seafront. Frank would have been much happier getting drunk with his father in the corner of the snug. Ordering two sweet sherries and two lemonades was an ordeal for him.

At the beginning of the next week Nan and Grandad were twitching and tapping at an incredible rate. Ellen and Frank went out and a great row blew up between them. It concluded with Nan throwing a shaving mug at him; she missed and it smashed against the kitchen wall.

'Oh no, you've broken your lovely mug,' said Ellen to our grandfather when she came in and found them both in the kitchen and Grandad saying, rather nervously, 'Shall I help you peel some spuds, my dear?'

'It slipped while I was shaving,' said Grandad.

'It slipped a long way,' said Ellen.

Our grandparents seemed to have derived great relief from the smashing of the mug; it had been in the family a long time and celebrated the ending of the Boer War. They sat a lot more peacefully in their chairs and the percussion abated.

By lunch the next day, however, Grandad began rapping his finger nails on the window pane and Nan was clinking the pearls of her necklace together, like an abacus. 'I think I'll go down to Stan's farm and see how his pig is,' said Grandad at last, and he sloped off to the Flying Fish and went into the snug. He did indeed have an interest in Stan's pig. He'd been a butcher for a short while and had learned to make black puddings.

1 gall. fresh pigs' blood
2 lbs pork fat, chopped into cubes
1 oz black pepper
tabl. spoon salt
  Simmer blood and fat over low heat for three hours until congealed. Hang in muslin bag for twenty-four hours. Serve in skins (to the strong-willed).

Grandad began talking about his pudding and telling us about the exact state and health of the pig. He was waiting for the moment when the pig should be killed and he could go down to Stan's farm at the bottom of the hill and catch the blood in his bucket. He was very excited about the prospect of such a large pudding, one which, he believed, would cause quite an impact in the neighbourhood: he'd promised parts of it to all the locals, the landlord of the Flying Fish, the postmaster, the chairman of the community singing room, and the vicar. Every time he met anyone he would promise them a lump and those to whom it had already been promised would have it promised again. I think he felt that his pudding gave him the air of a great provider for both his family and the locality. He was like a man preparing himself for religious orders, every day saying, 'I'll just pop down to see the pig,' and returning two hours later smelling of beer. When this was commented upon, Frank eyeing him jealously, he would simply reply, 'Well, I had to take Stan in for a quick half, after all he is letting me have his blood.' Frank racked his brains for a similar ploy and hoped against hope that his father would invite him on the pig visits; but he never did.

A few days before we were due to leave for home Grandad sat in the front room tapping his fingers on the white enamelled bucket into which the blood was to be put. Nan's tic was ticking. When it got to eleven o'clock he got up and wandered down the hill to the farm. We sat out front, playing with the fridge and watching for him to go into the Flying Fish with Stan as he usually did. An hour or more went by without any sign of them, then we heard a great squealing. Stan was slaughtering the pig. We asked Nan if we could go down to the farm and watch it die but she said, 'No, it'll muck up your new shoes.'

We waited to see the blood. We were hoping that Grandad would give us some of it to play with. Finally we saw him come out of the farm with the bucket, full, by his side, and then we watched in disappointment as he

went into the Flying Fish to show off to the landlord and
reaffirm his promise. Another hour later he staggered
out, worse for celebratory drink, with his bucket of blood
swinging by his side, like a bell, splashing drops over his
brown serge trousers. He started up the hill, walking
through the long grass and the poppies, and tried to get
over the flint wall, gripping the bucket precariously in his
arms. He slopped a little and then disappeared into the
post office to reinforce his promise and to share a tot of
brandy from his hip with the postmaster. Tom and I were
reminded of the Christmas when Dad had dropped the
turkey; the smell of disaster hung over the hill. Our
grandmother came out on to the step to watch his
progress. Ellen and Frank, fortunately, were walking
along the front.

'Sod him,' said our grandmother, 'he's going to drop
that bucket, and we've got the whole neighbourhood
waiting on us because of the way he's been going on
about it.'

He staggered up the last part of the hill, puffing and
blowing, with a silly grin on his face. He arrived at the
bungalow in triumph. We were sitting by the cloches. He
put his finger in the bucket and dabbed a thick red line
on to my nose. Then he dabbed some on Tom. We
chuckled but we didn't really like it. We followed him as
he carried it proudly into the kitchen where Nan was
rubbing out on her washboard, banging her soapy smalls
against its ridges. He was amused by our red noses and
being in a triumphant mood he dabbed his own as well.
This didn't get the expected jubilant reaction from our
grandmother so he flicked some blood on to her nose as
well.

'Oooh, get away from me,' she yelled, her tic ticking
and her knuckles turning white where she gripped her

washboard, restraining herself from smashing it down on his head.

'It's only pudding,' he said, and repeated the gesture. She threw her washboard into the bath.

'You make me sick,' she said. 'You're nothing but a kid. Oh yes, your son takes after you. Look at what he's doing to these poor bloody kids! What chance do they stand in life, dragged here, dragged there. She'd be better off shot of him now, while she's still got some life to lead, just as I'd be better shot of you. But will you go, you buggers, when you're told to?'

Grandad stood there smiling, shifting from one foot to the other. He was all excited about making his pudding; it was the only thing he'd attempted to do all year, and he expected her to be excited too.

'What sort of life have we had?' she continued. 'What sort of life have you given me? Two rooms, lousy jobs, rotten neighbours. You make me want to spit. Watching you staggering back from the pub every day, and you just stand there and grin, don't you? With that stupid smile on your face because you're thinking, "Oh yes, just let her go on. I'll be all right, Jack," and you can go down there to the Flying Fish and tell them all how I make your life a misery. I know you do it, you old sod.'

Something in this speech touched a nerve in Grandad. Our grandmother was standing there defiantly in a flimsy white cotton summer dress. He swung the bucket under his arm and threw the whole gallon of blood at her. We watched it cross the kitchen like a thick, dark, lump. It hit her quite hard, knocking her back; it saturated her dress, her hair, and it cascaded down the yellow-tiled wall and flooded across the floor and over our shoes. She fell on him screaming. We began screaming. It was a

sight of sheer horror and it was the nearest they'd yet got
to murder.

Right at this point we heard Dad yell, 'Surprise, surprise,' from the doorway, and he and Ellen came bouncing into the kitchen bearing toffee-apples for us and
holding a glass mug for them, engraved with the words
'Mum and Dad'. Our grandparents ignored them and
continued their screaming and we continued ours while
Ellen and Frank looked on, flabbergasted.

We left for home that evening, as soon as Ellen had
helped clean up the kitchen, even though she heaved as
she mopped up the blood. Nan wanted to leave Grandad
for good and to come back with us, but Frank was on his
father's side and so she came with us as far as the station
and then went to stay with her sister in Eastbourne. Ellen
didn't speak all the way home on the train. Tom got a
soot in his eye from leaning out of the window and cried
all the way home. Frank stood in the corridor, he seemed
to be shocked by his father's action.

CHAPTER XIII

In which we go to pick peas with our mother but the
course of our lives changes. Uncle Peter and Aunt Cynthia
and Wimbledon are introduced and Ellen's childhood in
Kennington is described

When we got back home Frank was still very quiet and
deeply disturbed by what he had seen at Newhaven. He
brooded around the house. It worried Ellen, she found
his quietness disturbing, a harbinger of a greater storm.
He wasn't returning to work until the Monday and Ellen

found it a strain to be in the same house with him and she wanted to get out. She had given up her job at the mill because it had worsened the murmuring of her heart. To get herself some extra pocket money she would take us peapicking. Whenever she suggested it we'd get excited and tear around the cul-de-sac looking for Charlie to tell him where we were going and he'd go back to his mum and demand to go. He was designing a machine for the shucking of peas. While Ellen packed up sandwiches and headscarves, to protect the backs of our necks from the sunshine, we would jump up and down in the middle of the front room singing the signature tunes from television programmes at the tops of our voices, occasionally breaking off to poke our heads out of the window to shout to passers-by, 'We're going peapicking.'

'Don't let everyone know our business,' Ellen would say, but how could we help it when our business was peapicking? We would sing all the way but as soon as we reached the peafield and saw all the people bent double, with great sacks in tow, we remembered what hard work it was. When Mum suggested going peapicking again the following day we ran around the house shouting, 'Oh no, not peapicking AGAIN!'

It was a peapicking trip, then, that Ellen suggested to get us out of the house the day after we returned from Newhaven. There were only small farms in our locality and they had all turned themselves over to market gardening: cabbages, greens and fruit – just a hint of the Garden of England on the hills around Prospect. Ellen always knew when it was pea time, she could smell it in the air. The men waited at the corner of the street in the early morning, if they wanted work, and the farmers drove round in their open-backed trucks and picked them up. The women and the children had to walk, trudging up the lanes that wound around the foothills of the North Downs, and hope to find a farm that needed labour. The peafields were never in the same place two years running, because of a policy of rotation, and so sometimes we'd think that we'd never find peas among the acres of cabbage and burning yellow rape, and we'd curse the unfairness of the men in their trucks. The farmers would take on as many pickers as would come. They were, on the whole, the poorer families and those of gypsy stock. There was no formal arrangement with the farmer, you would simply pick up one of the large mesh sacks and start filling it. The peas grew on bunches of dry birch twigs. Tom and I would do one sack between us, dragging it as we went. When a sack was full you took it up to be weighed at the back of a lorry. If it was a hundredweight they gave you seven and six. If you put too many leaves in it'd be called a spoiled bag and you would have it tipped out in front of you to be refilled. We would be continually dragging our sack up to the lorry to be reweighed, but it never seemed to reach a hundredweight. We ate a great many of the peas.

When we got older we tried putting lumps of flint, conveniently abundant on the Downs, in the sack to make it weigh more. Tom once made only half a sack weigh the hundred. We dragged it up to the farmer. He seemed a very big man, in his elevated position on the back of the truck, flanked on each side by two teenage ruffians who lifted the sack to the scales.

'What is this?' said the farmer as his gaze fell on our sack. 'Only half a sack? Weigh it and give them three and six.'

The ruffians weighed it. 'It's an hundredweight and more,' said the boys.

The farmer halted momentarily from his overseeing

and looked down at us. 'My goodness, these little lads put the rest of you to shame, they must have noses for extraordinarily healthy peas. In which part of the field did you uncover these monsters?' he said.

We smiled with pride. 'Just over there,' said Tom. All the other pickers looked in the direction to which Tom's finger pointed.

'I must have double fertilized that section of the field,' said the farmer and he extended his hand to us with the seven and six, composed of three large half-crowns, lying in his palm. Tom stepped forward to take them and as his fingers lighted on the silver the farmer snatched them back again. He grabbed the sack from the ruffians and hurled it into Tom's belly, knocking him to the ground and the air from his lungs. 'Go,' he bellowed, 'and scatter the flints along the lane.' The assembled pickers laughed, and the gypsies, and a few more besides, left the group to remove their own flints.

On the second day after we had returned from Newhaven we had all had a silent breakfast together and, a little later, after elevenses of orange squash and biscuits, again in silence, Frank announced his intention of going to the Dog and Bucket.

'Right,' said Ellen, 'then I'm going out as well. If you're going out then so are we. It's not only you who can go out. I can go out if I want to. Come on, we're going out.'

'Where are you going then?' asked Frank.

'Out,' said Ellen. 'Come on, kids, get your coats on.' We rushed to get duffled. Frank quietly removed himself from the house.

'Where are we going, Mum? Where are we going?' we called.

'We'll show him,' she said.

'Where are we going, Mum?' we asked again, jumping up and down. Ellen looked at us resolutely and said, 'Peapicking.'

We followed her out of the house, downhearted.

When we got to the field it was in a terrible state. There had been rain the night before and the peas were sodden, the shucks had yellowed and the crop could not be picked. All the plants had been beaten down to the ground and in the sun they were rotting. The fresh pea-green of the day before had given way to a mottled yellow draped over the black of the birch twigs. Ellen sat down in the mud on her haunches and began to cry. We watched our mother as she shuddered and heaved as if her ribs would break. We didn't know what to do and looked around the deserted field for help. Tom moved a little nearer to her and said, 'All the peas have got wet.' She didn't look up but began to lose her balance and she put her hand down so that her fingers sank deep into the mud. We felt as if she would never get up, but squat there until the plants grew up over her, or the truck came and ran her over. After quite a while she looked up at us and stretched out her hands for us to help her. Tom took her left hand and I took her wrist and together we pulled her to her feet.

'So we can't pick any peas then,' said Tom, and shrugged his shoulders.

Ellen began to walk us out of the field and back down the lane toward our home.

When we got back she told us to leave our dufflecoats on and she went down to the telephone-box to speak to her brother, Peter. Ellen came back and began to pack things into a suitcase.

'Are we going away, are we going back to the sea?' asked Tom.

'We're going to stay at Uncle Peter's,' she said, 'but we've got to get out of the house before he gets back, so I want you to be good boys and go upstairs and get your toothbrushes and a toy each that you want to take with you.'

'Are we running away?' I asked.

'Yes,' said Ellen, 'we can't take any more of it.'

Tom and I went upstairs and got our toothbrushes out of their pot and got our large cardboard toybox out of the cupboard. We began dragging it across the landing, determined to take all our possessions, unsure as we were about the future. The box was very heavy and the task of moving it was made more complicated by the fact that we had our Noddy toothbrushes gripped in our fingers. We got the box to the top of the stairs and down the first step but at that point we lost our grip. It tumbled, scattered its contents of toy cars, farm animals, broken parts of clockwork and diamonds from Ellen's brooches, all down the stairs and into the hallway. Ellen dashed from the front room.

'What on earth's happened?' she shouted. 'I said a few toys. How am I supposed to get all this cleared up before we leave? Do you want me to leave the place like a pigsty? Come down here.'

We were frightened to go down the stairs and so we waited until she shouted at us a second time before descending. She slapped us both hard and then began to cry herself.

Ellen watched the clock for the next hour, every five minutes saying, 'They won't close until three, he won't be back till half past.' She was very nervous and everytime she heard a car at the bottom of the 'sac she sent us out to see if it was Uncle Peter's Wolsely. She decided that Uncle Peter would take the cases out, and our toys, and then he would sit in the car, in the next turning, and keeping the engine running. As soon as the coast was clear, with no neighbours watching from their nets, then we were to dash to the car, with her following a few minutes later. Under no circumstances should the neighbours realize what she was up to. No one was to see us leave. The whole thing was organized. We were not 'doing a bunk like some fly-by-nights', Ellen maintained. She posted us permanently at the garden gate, both to watch for Peter and to keep a lookout in case Frank should return early.

We were swinging on the gate, excited, when one of the neighbours, Mrs Pascoe, came past and spoke to us. 'You'll break that gate if you swing on it,' she said.

'Don't matter,' said Tom.

'No,' I said, 'we're running off,' and I waved my toothbrush. I think it was the toothbrush which made Mrs Pascoe realize the seriousness of the situation because her face changed considerably, and she looked towards our house where she could see Ellen taking things out of her wardrobe upstairs.

'We can't take any more of it,' Tom informed her.

Uncle Peter arrived and I introduced him to Mrs Pascoe. 'This is Uncle Peter and he's got his car round the corner,' I said.

Peter hurried into the house while Mrs Pascoe gazed after him, looking him up and down and presuming that the 'uncle' was an honorary title which we'd been encouraged to bestow. He brought out the suitcase, Mrs Pascoe stepped out of his way, and Charlie's mother, whom she'd beckoned over, made way for Uncle Peter too. A few other people were at their windows. Peter hurried off to his Wolsely and sat in it revving the engine. We continued to swing on the gate.

When Ellen came out, her cheeks flushed, carrying a little china pot, Mrs Pascoe said to her, 'Good Luck, love, I think you're doing the best thing,' and Mrs Rubbidge added, 'Yes, good luck, love,' and they both crossed their arms sympathetically.

'I'm only popping down to the shops,' said Ellen, and we dashed off down the road. When we got into the car Ellen asked Peter if he would drive past Clover Gardens. 'I have to have one last look at the house,' she said. As we passed it she wiped her nose and said, 'And I've just put those climbers in for round the door.'

We didn't like cars very much. We were not used to them and we felt that whereas with a bus you could get the next one back, a car gave no guarantee of return. They can run out of petrol.

'If only it hadn't rained,' said Tom.

Uncle Peter drove us to Wimbledon. We had never been there before, or anywhere like it.

'Are we in London or in the country?' asked Tom.

'London,' said Ellen.

This seemed to upset Peter, who had a very high opinion of his environs. He turned to us and said, very proudly, 'We are in the suburbs.' We were very impressed by this. Wimbledon, where the ribbon development is tied in tight knots, impressed us because of the number and the opulence of its shops, with their Elizabethan facings. Peter was manager of an off-licence in the High Street and he and his wife Cynthia lived above it in great splendour in a three-roomed flat. The opportunity of living above a shop made Wimbledon even more exciting and exotic to us, and we began to relax at having left the familiarity of Prospect for the first time. Peter pointed out shops that stayed open until seven or eight in the

evening, selling weird foreign luxuries: aubergines and
tinned walnuts. So we knew we would not starve.

Uncle Peter's front room, which Aunt Cynthia termed
the lounge, was a tremendous place with two settees and
lamps with blobs of wax that floated up and down. In the
corner of the room was a bar, which he'd made himself
from fluted hardboard and surrounded with fairy lights
and bottles in baskets. If the rest of the lounge had not
been overwhelming enough then this most certainly was.
It was more the sort of thing we would have expected to
see in a stately home or Buckingham Palace. Tom and I
longed to stand behind it. Peter had even gone so far as
to add the finishing touch of two collection boxes on the
bar, one for the blind and one for sick donkeys – he was
a man of great social conscience. Cynthia made Ellen a
cup of tea and Peter poured us each a lemonade, to
which he added ice from a pineapple with a lid. As soon
as we were settled Peter went down to get our suitcase
from the car. Cynthia told Ellen that we could stay as
long as we wanted to.

'I suppose it's too early to think about the future?' she
asked.

'Yes,' said Ellen. 'I'm at my wits' end corner this
afternoon.'

'Well, you are sometimes,' said Cynthia, sympathetically. 'I know what it's like. When I was choosing this
carpet I went from one to another until I just couldn't
think any more. My brain was like a thick brown sauce,
like yours is.'

Ellen looked down at the carpet. She was trying to
keep her mind on ordinary things. 'It's new, is it?' she
asked, trying to show some interest. Ellen and Cynthia
barely knew each other. Cynthia had been a committee
member of the Kennington Clerical Cycles.

'My Ewbank's stuffed with fluff,' said Cynthia.

'It looks like it'll wear well,' said Ellen.

'If it's not walked on,' said Cynthia. We wondered how this could be avoided. Harnesses, suspended from the ceiling?

'Do you mind me asking, Ellen, I realize you've come away in a rush, but did you bring your slippers with you?'

'I think so,' said Ellen.

'Well, when Peter brings your cases up, perhaps you and your boys will put them on. You've got to stay on the safe side of Pile.'

Ellen looked a little distraught again and so Cynthia touched her on the knee and said, 'Can I offer you a whisky liqueur?' and reached for a big round box of chocolates from which she'd already eliminated the other choices.

'No thanks,' said Ellen, 'they stick to the roof of my mouth.'

In turn Cynthia seemed to be made distraught by this observation and so the conversation died, and we all sat in silence, the three of us in a row on one of their settees and Tom and I lusting after the whisky liqueurs.

Uncle Peter returned empty-handed and stood in the doorway looking perplexed. 'I'm very sorry, Ellen,' he said, 'I don't know how to tell you this but someone's forced the boot of my car and your case has gone. I knew I should have garaged the car.'

'It never rains but it pours,' said Cynthia.

'So I've lost everything?' asked Ellen. 'My clothes, the kiddies' things, my prayer book was in there.'

'Your prayer book?' said Peter.

'It had the family tree in the front and a pound between each page.'

'Was it insured?' asked Cynthia.

Ellen had also lost the little card that the barber had given her with the locks of hair from our first cuts, and a snap of the house on Prospect.

'Perhaps you'd like that liqueur now,' said Cynthia, 'it might buck you up.'

Ellen pushed her tea aside and began to weep. It was a wonder to us that she could still do it but seeing that she could we joined in as well, which threw Peter and Cynthia into a state of anxiety. They hopped about offering chocolates. Ellen wanted nothing. Tom and I didn't know whether we should continue drinking our lemonade under the circumstances. We stared at it longingly on the black glass coffee table as we sobbed and watched every bubble leave.

'I've got nothing left,' said Ellen, 'not even a change of clothes for myself or the kids.'

'Oh, it's not as bad as all that. I'll see if I can hunt out some of our old slippers,' said Cynthia, kindly, and tiptoed lightly across the room and out of the door.

'We'll have some fish fingers in a minute,' said Uncle Peter. 'You've got to keep your strength up.'

Ellen wiped her eyes and smiled at him. Cynthia fitted her out with a pair of her old fluffy slippers and she provided us each with a pair of Peter's. To cross the room we had to slide in them, like skis, the slippers having, as they did, the capacity to contain much larger feet than we, at this stage, possessed.

We settled down to the table in their dinerette. Peter touched Ellen's hand and said, 'It's just like old times, when we were kids.' This simple statement set them both off on a great recollection of their lives in the Guinness Trust Buildings. Ellen had never spoken very much about her family to us, Frank's parents had dominated our lives so completely, and the little things we had picked up were too confusing for our young minds.

There had been great excitement in their family when they had moved into the Trust's Tenements, comparable to Ellen's delight in moving to Prospect. While Cynthia frowned, and withdrew her food from her mouth and let it hover, in protest, on her fork, they recalled their first encounter with an inside lavatory.

'Mum was worried by it,' said Peter. 'She didn't think it was hygienic, she worried about it overflowing, and she didn't like the idea that everything went down a pipe and passed through the flat below. She liked it even less that what happened in the flat above passed through ours!' Peter roared with laughter at this recollection but Cynthia placed her fork heavily on her plate. The past brought out a rare, and tasteless, excess in her husband, she felt, and she became less and less keen on the intrusion we had made into her household. We heard how William, our maternal grandfather, had sat for hours together, like a king upon his throne, on the lavatory; and how each Friday night the family sat around a table, playing beetle drive and tearing newspapers into four-inch squares and hanging them on a string.

In many ways the Guinness Trust was even more paternalistic than the Prospect council: they insisted that their tenants should be working people with preference being given to labourers and the lower paid. They gave them free venetian blinds, a peculiar gesture designed to combat the expense of curtaining and following the principle that privacy breeds dignity. They were good thrifty philanthropists and they bought up coal at summer prices and sold it at cost to their tenants in the winter months.

At the far end of the court around which the tenements

were built there was a water porter's hut where they could get free hot water. To Tom and me hot water seemed a funny thing to want to give away, especially after the glamorous prizes of the Camay Queen. 'It saved you boiling a whole kettle if you only wanted one cup of tea,' said Ellen.

The gap between her and Cynthia was steadily widening. Cynthia earnestly believed in her airs and graces, they were not affectation alone, they were marks of the fact that she had struggled to develop and cultivate herself. She had barely nothing in common with Ellen who, after all, had been brought up on the sixth floor of a charity tenement while she had been brought up on the first.

Uncle Peter conjured up 'Alf the porter' for us, by huffing and puffing and making his face go red, and then, as Alf, he showed us how each evening, at seven in the summer and five in the winter, he'd call 'all-ee-in'. After Alf had called it no child was to be seen in the streets or in the court, and he'd tour around, huffing and puffing, and sending every child back to their homes. Tom and I were delighted by Alf, forever having to chase up alleyways and leap railings, in his quest to banish the children from the streets. I dare say that had the Prospect council decided to retain this feature from its charitable models, Alf would have been the most feared figure in our lives.

Ellen would do anything she could for the pleasure of being out of the flat after all-ee-in had been called. She would get the two tin buckets from beneath the sink and take them to be filled with the free hot water. To carry the buckets invariably meant that she would have to tip the greater part away before she could drag them up the stairs. The sound of little Ellen's buckets scraping up the stairwell echoed all around the buildings and people would say, 'Ellen's got out again, I see. You'd never think she had a dodgy heart.'

'I'd do anything to be out when I was supposed to be in,' said Ellen.

Peter and Ellen talked so much about the old days that Tom and I could only understand so much of it; there were so many people, and so many names, and so many strange events that we began to get a very mixed-up picture of it all. Our maternal grandparents were dead, we knew; we learnt that our grandfather had dropped dead in a sewing factory from hard work, and that our grandmother had been killed while varnishing the inside of a beer vat – but it may, of course, have been the other way around.

As far as I can recall, and here I may still be a little confused, the subject being far too delicate ever to be brought up again, our mother's grandmother had been coshed on the head in the General Strike and had gone completely out of her mind. She walked the streets all day, thereafter, picking up pieces of paper and putting them into a bag. It was her, I think they said, who was known in the locality as 'Silly Lilly the paper queen'. At first she was a harmless entertainment in the neighbourhood, and Peter, Stanley and Ellen would often walk along with her, picking up paper as well, too young to realize that it was anything other than a reasonable activity. Just before the last war, or just after, she began to get a little violent with her bags of litter. It started gradually with stamping and shouting in the street. Then she began waiting at bus-stops and pelting the passengers with the contents of her bag as they got off, shouting, 'You filthy rotters, I have to pick all this up.' She took exception to the fact that some of them failed to place their used tickets in the box provided. If she saw anyone throw so much as a matchstick on the ground she would fly into a rage with them. She attacked a high court judge for littering the coastline when she saw him drop a cigar butt into a drain.

The greater part of her day was spent in hunting down new places to dispose of her own litter. She stuffed it into people's letter-boxes and filled up the pillar-boxes with it. She set upon newspaper sellers, and vandalized cigarette machines; she fought against anything or anyone responsible for providing the public with what became litter. She said, 'the only good paper is toilet paper', presumably because it was flushed away, she knew not where, and she was deeply in awe of the modern lavatory, continually recommending it to her daughter, who was not convinced.

As the state of her mind worsened, however, her confidence even in the toilet paper waned. She was found one day by a neighbour, in a state of nervous collapse on the floor of the shared lavatory on the landing, presumably attempting to retrieve a previous occupant's paper. Silly Lilly the paper queen was admitted to Bethlehem Hospital in Kennington. Bethlehem was the place known as Bedlam in the eighteenth century, where, on a Sunday, people paid to see the lunatics. Ellen and Peter and Stanley went with their mother to visit her there every Sunday with a packed lunch. Lilly died in Bedlam and was buried in its grounds in an unmarked pauper's grave, a little shapeless pine coffin dropped unattended into the lime-rich earth. 'Of course, Bedlam's the Imperial War Museum now,' said Uncle Peter, 'so you couldn't have put a stone up if you wanted to.'

All of this seemed very black to Tom and me, very black indeed. Of course, we weren't capable of understanding all the details I've given here, these have had to be researched afresh, but I do remember the strong impression it made on Tom and me, and having the word 'pauper' explained to us set in our minds that that was what we were, and if the robbers didn't return the prayer book, we should have to be buried at the Imperial War Museum, which sounded a violent place indeed.

After all these stories and recollections, which had been Peter's attempt to take Ellen's mind off things, a sudden silence fell as Ellen stared towards the door.

'You don't think he'll come here looking for us?' said Ellen, and she jumped up from the table and ran to the window. 'We should have been watching the street, he's bound to know where I've gone.' Cynthia began to look worried as well; it hadn't occurred to her that he might turn up and make a scene. 'There's no telling what he'll do,' said Ellen. 'You don't know what he's like, he's got no respect for property. What'll I do if he comes, where can we hide, he's like a thing possessed when he's had a drink.'

'Perhaps you'd better fit another lock,' said Cynthia.

'No,' said Peter, 'he won't look no further than the Dog and Bucket.'

We went back into the living-room where Ellen stood by the window, flanked by Cynthia. We were so frightened that we couldn't concentrate on the television.

Frank did not come, but for the duration of our stay we were nervous about the carpet and of getting in Cynthia's way. Ellen tried to please but she was over-enthusiastic about the washing-up and smashed things, and when she was depressed she couldn't eat and Cynthia would say, 'Is there something up with my gammon?' – a line of conversation with which we were familiar. We spent the day walking around Wimbledon or sitting on the settees while *Listen with Mother* was on the radio.

The situation was hopeless. Ellen didn't have a change of clothes and the money that was remaining after the car had been broken into had gone. Tom and I had put it shilling by shilling into the sick donkey's collecting box on the bar (coaxed as we were by the fact that the little wooden donkey on the top lowered its head each time). Ellen had tried to get it out but was worried about Peter walking in and catching her with a knife in the slot. After a week in their house there was nothing to do but to go back to Prospect.

CHAPTER XIV

In which Frank discovers that we have run off and we return to Prospect and witness a terrible and final event

The rain that had destroyed the peafield had also cleared the haze and the stormy atmosphere of the preceding days. The streets were clean and crisp and the leaves on the young hydrangeas in Frank's garden sparkled as he swayed on the front step and fell into them. The 'Bucket had installed an electric pump to cope with the new chemical beer and Frank and Clancy had been helping the landlord to test it. They'd felt it to be unfair on the new beer to dismiss it out of hand without a reasonable test. The effect of the rain on Prospect was in exact opposition to the effect of the beer and although the air smelled sweet, Prospect was at an angle.

Frank got out from the hydrangeas and began an exhaustive search of his pockets for the front door key. Why on earth they designed the heads of keys to resemble pennies Frank couldn't fathom, and since he only had

pennies left in his pocket it was, finally, to a rather
smooth and slightly bent specimen bearing the head of
Edward VII that he resorted and attempted to force it
into the lock. After a second fall into the hydrangeas,
Frank discovered the key in the turn-up of his trousers,
but then, alas, he lost the lock, and inadvertently dropped
the key through the letter-box, in his enthusiasm to get to
the toilet. Being drunk on a doorstep and needing a
slash, with the key on the other side of the door, was
enough to make Frank, or any man, vow never to drink
at lunchtime again. He could see the key through the
letter-box moving slowly side to side on the swaying
carpet.

'Ellen,' he called, 'open the door, open the door, I
need a Jimmy Riddle.' Silence returned from the house.
He decided to climb the bolted back gate, and, by
standing on the old rabbit hutch, the door of which the
buck had kicked off, he got in through the kitchen
window. Standing in the sink, and breaking a plate, he
looked around the empty house.

'I'm home,' he called, 'I'm back,' and a severe attack
of hiccups made it imperative that he get out of the sink
and on to the draining-board, which was at an angle he
reckoned to be level. From the draining-board he managed to get a delicate footing on the Burco boiler, and
from there gained the safety of the floor. Treading beans
into the front room carpet he crossed the hallway to call
up the stairs, where he presumed Ellen would be, probably hiding with us behind the bedroom door.

His first thought when he found that we were not there
was that the house had been burgled and his wife and
children carried off. He took himself upstairs, two steps
up and one step down, and lay face down on the bed.
He pulled the pillow over his head to block out the shafts

of sunshine. The room moved so much, and there were
so many little quills sticking out through the pillow case,
that he couldn't sleep. He banged hard on the wall and
called for Clancy, but Clancy was sleeping soundly on the
other side. Frank didn't wake until mid-evening. He
fancied he could hear the television on downstairs. In
fact it was Clancy's wife, Did, who was attempting to
wake her husband next door. Because of the new beer,
pints were on offer all week at the Dog and Bucket, and
the brewery had sent several bewildered young girls,
done up as buxom serving wenches, to support the launch.
It was all too much for Frank to resist. We had chosen
the wrong week in which to run off. The walls and
furniture alone watched as Frank placed a stockinged
foot delicately on the bedroom floor; his plan: to sneak
out of the house without being heard. He went to particular pains on the stairs, carrying his shoes and shooshing
himself at every creak. He would not normally have been
so coy had he not been planning to spend every opening
hour among the promotional wenches from the agency in
Croydon, and the half-price ale. He clicked the front
door shut and scuttled down the path, remaining unshod
until he reached the bottom of the 'sac.

Similarly when he returned pie-eyed he snuck into the
house and eased himself into the edge of the bed, careful
not to disturb Ellen, who was not there. In the morning
he presumed that Ellen was shopping and that we were at
school. He stuck his head under the tap and took a cool
draught of Prospect's water into his mouth to rehydrate
his kidneys and his liver. Even the skin on his face had
gone tight, his hands were blotchy from the beer, he had
a dull ache in his back and the smaller veins in his nose
had been rising subtly, evening by evening, to give him a
red and shiny rozer.

Remarkably, because of Frank's itinerary, it was three days before the empty drawers and photographs missing from their frames made him realize that we had gone. He stopped creeping about the house and stood still completely.

He went next door to see Clancy. 'You'll never guess what's happened,' he said.

'What's that?' said Clancy.

'Ellen's run off with the kids.'

'Yeah I know,' said Clancy.

'You know?'

'Did told me days ago. I thought you knew, I wondered why you hadn't said. Everyone saw her go. She waited for you to go down to the 'Bucket and then she went off with her brother in his car, taking the kids and the suitcase.'

'I know she's taken the suitcase,' said Frank, 'I've seen all the fluff on the bedroom floor that's come off the top of the wardrobe.'

'Are women worth all the trouble?' asked Clancy, after shutting the kitchen door so that his wife could not hear him.

'I just don't know,' said Frank, 'they're beyond me. They have minds of their own sometimes.'

Clancy suggested that they ought to go to the pub to drink off the calamity, but Frank declined. 'No,' he said, 'I'm going to sit in the house in case she comes home.'

Frank went back home. He was still a little shaky from the excesses of his drinking and he felt nervous and weak. He sat down in an armchair to have a think. Having a think was a terrible ordeal for Frank and he always approached it with all the seriousness it demanded. He could generally put off the meat of the think for some time, by calling for silence from us, or demanding that the room be put in order, before he could put his mind to the problem in hand. The house's being quiet, as it was on this occasion, deprived him of his necessary preliminaries and he found it difficult to begin. He lit up a cigarette and positioned an ashtray at arm's length. He so placed it that the smoke wouldn't blow in his face and distract him. He sat like Lincoln on his monument. He began to think about his own childhood and how he disliked and feared his father; about how his father would box with him, on a Sunday afternoon after the boozer had shut, and if he cried out how his father would hit him harder. He remembered Ellen as a child, and how her father had seemed so much nicer, and how he'd been playing cricket in the court and struck her on the head with the ball. He took out his wallet and pulled out of it an old photograph. Journeyman photographers would regularly come into the courts of the tenements and call all the children together, an event which caused great excitement. The photographer arranged all the kids he could find into neat rows, like cricket elevens, on the tenement steps. Then, when the photo had been printed up, he'd knock on the doors and sell the prints to the parents. Frank laid the photograph on the arm of the chair. There was Billy Higgins with his one-legged brother Ernest, behind them Eileen Clarke and Lizzy Issacks, and the two Morris sisters, one of whom was boss-eyed and looking in the wrong direction, and next to them, and directly in front of Frank himself, was Ellen, with a woolly hat pulled down over the bruise on her forehead.

Frank couldn't bear the empty silence of the house. He couldn't think. Over the remaining days of our absence in Wimbledon, Frank sat like this many times. He made no attempt to come to Wimbledon himself. He couldn't think of anything that he could say to bring us back. He sat with a stubby pencil making a list of all the things he had ruined and done wrong in his life. He wrote it on a piece of cardboard and placed it on the arm of the chair.

Being born
Playing hookey
Not sitting for certificate
Moving down
The drink
Blake's Mill to be knocked down for a carpet w.house
Throwing weight around
Owe Clancy £2

We came home on Saturday, at eleven at night, in Uncle Peter's car with our Uncle Stanley coming along too for the ride. We were happy to be going back and were looking forward to seeing Frank. When we arrived he was sitting in his armchair. He was pleased to see us and smiled and giggled nervously. Ellen said nothing to him. Peter stood in front of him, flanked by Stanley, and began the speech that he had prepared in his mind at the traffic lights on the way.

'I have people come into my shop, Frank,' said Peter, 'I have them banging on my door at two and three in the morning. They plead with me, but do I give them a bottle? No!' Peter paused, satisfied with his rhetoric.

'You're in the wrong business, mate,' said Frank.

This, Peter found facetious and his hackles rose. 'There's a demon in that bottle, Frank, you think you're drinking the drink, but the drink is drinking you . . . it's drunk your marriage, it's drunk your children, it's drunk your furniture . . .' (the new sideboard had been sent back).

With this the worthy licensee paused long enough for Frank to say, 'It's none of your business.' Peter assured

him that it was while Stanley went upstairs to our bedroom to look for our cricket bat. When he came down
Ellen pushed us into the kitchen and shut the door behind
us. We wanted to know what was going on. If we were
going to play cricket could we join in?

Stanley took over from Peter in the speechmaking.
'You're way out of order, Frank,' he said, and whacked
him around the head with the cricket bat. There was a
stunned silence and then we heard Frank groan. We
rushed to the front room door. Ellen tried to bar our
way, but she was weak with fear. We heard more cracks
of the cricket bat and then we got into the room. We saw
our father lying on the floor, moving slowly, holding his
head with his hands through which we saw the blood
seeping. Stanley placed the bat on the top of the television
set. Ellen went back to sit in the kitchen. We didn't walk
too far into the room, presuming that Stanley would hit
us with the bat as well.

'We were playing and there's been an accident,' said
Peter. We couldn't understand what he meant.

Peter and Stanley began to discuss what they should do
next.

'He's got to be taught a lesson good and proper,' said
Peter.

'He has,' agreed Stanley.

'We should take him out and put him in the only place
that's fit for a woman beater.'

'The gutter,' said Stanley.

'The gutter,' agreed Peter, 'but I think we'd better go
to the next turning.'

'Good thinking,' said Stanley, 'but we don't want to
have to lug him far. What's that turning with the tree?'
Stanley asked me.

'Geranium Walk,' I said.

'What's the gutter like there? – I mean, it's not all parked cars, is it? There will be some space? – because it's terrible round here for parking now.'

'It is!' said Peter. 'It is!'

'Right then,' said Stanley, 'you take the feet, hey up!'

When they returned Uncle Peter was white and shaky and he offered Stanley a nip of brandy from his flask. It was many years since he'd taken part in such an exploit. He'd also begun to worry about the legal implications of what they'd done to our father. 'Don't you think we'd better lose that bat?' he said to Stanley.

Stanley picked it up. 'Here, Tom,' he said, 'make yourself useful and go and put it in a hole in the garden for me.'

Tom looked up at him slowly. 'No,' he said. 'You took it, it's your bat.'

Stanley looked at Peter indignantly. 'I gave them that for Christmas,' he said, 'I'll get them another.' He turned to me and gave it to me. I remember the exact weight of it in my hands.

'You've got a shovel, or a trowel, have you?' asked Uncle Peter.

'Yes,' I said, knowing that my bucket and spade were still by the back door from when we came back from Newhaven. I was quite numb to the dark and took the bat to the farthest corner of the garden and left it in what would be called on television 'a shallow grave'.

When I returned Peter took another nip of brandy. Ellen took us upstairs to bed while the two brothers stayed in the living-room, in case he should come back. They had waited a long time to get him back for hitting their sister with the cricket ball.

CHAPTER XV

In which we are alone with our mother and the house is fortified against burglars but a surprising turn of events turns up to surprise us. The Pascoes are introduced

Timbuctoo was very quiet now. Its garden flourished and its doors stayed on their hinges since there was no one to fall into the flowers or slam the doors until the frames shattered. Ellen removed the Timbuctoo sign from the gate. The new quietness was so strange to us that we found it unsettling. Ellen was always on the alert for strange noises and signs of intruders. For the first few weeks we were frightened that Frank would return; that he'd come crashing through the front door without warning, all boozed and blasting. Once we had adopted the habit of being like nervous gazelles, sniffing every breeze for lion, we found we could as much relax out of it again as they could. If the dustbin-lid fell in the garden, or a tile slipped from the roof, Ellen dashed us all up the stairs in fear, where we all got into her bed and pretended to be asleep.

'If the burglar gets in the house make out we're all asleep or he'll murder us,' she told us. Many times we heard the burglar rattle the pane in the kitchen, and had to miss the end of *Space Patrol*, and we'd hear him creak on the stairs, and slowly creep on the landing, especially after the heating had been turned off and the house was cooling. There had been a spate of burglaries on the estate. Every night Ellen would tour the house checking the bolts and the windows. She heard reports of people nearby having their gas meters broken into and it worried her greatly. The Gas Board had made matters worse by putting out an edict to the effect that subscribers would have to bear the cost of any raided meters themselves. This was to discourage the tradition of raiding one's own meter when times were tight. On the whole people felt the accumulation of so many shillings and sixpences, under their own stairs, too much of a temptation to resist. Frank, in his time, had experimented with various methods of obtaining warmth without charge. He felt it to be a basic human right and had drilled a hole in a sixpence and fitted it with a length of wire so that it could be retrieved after it had registered in the slot. The ingenuity of this device, however, proved insufficient, he jammed the meter with it and the gasman had to come to mend it.

There was very little in Timbuctoo to attract the burglar. Ellen had no jewellery of any worth, and never any spare cash, and the old television sets were too heavy and cumbersome to be easily portable – but this shilling eater under the stairs was always there, Ellen felt, as a risk to our security. A risk which had been greatly increased since Prospect had been declared a smokeless zone and all the houses fitted with gasfires.

'They watch the house,' Ellen told us, 'and if they see you've always got the fire on they think to themselves, "Oh there must be a pretty penny in their meter, we'll do them tonight."' This meant that we very rarely had the fire on at all. Then, in order to dissuade our surveillors, Ellen bought a small, nasty-smelling, paraffin heater and placed it near the window in easy view.

We began to construct a very vivid picture of this demon in our minds, a man who was half human and half ice. We lay in bed at night frightening each other with stories about the ice-burglar, as we called him. Tom told me that in every house he'd burgled he'd chopped off the mother's ears. I told Tom that in every house he'd burgled he'd tied the people up and set his scorpions on them. If we heard another noise, we decided, we would all go out into the garden and dig the cricket bat up and kill him with it.

When we were walking in the street with our mother and a man happened to look at her she always froze, saying afterwards, 'I wouldn't mind betting it's him and now he knows we're out of the house.' Such an event having occurred Ellen would do her shopping very quickly, forgetting all the essential items. No local man was exempt from her suspicions. Mr Bannister always seemed to be trying to get a good look into the house, as did the milkman, and as for the doctor, under whom she was for her nerves, he had ample opportunity during his housecalls to make an assessment of people's possessions.

When the gasman came, to perform the miracle of the resurrection of the burned shillings, the relief in our house was enormous. We were fascinated by his delicate operations. We watched as he broke the seal, pulled out the metal box, cleared Ellen's table and laid the silver out so that not one coin stood upon another. The dexterity of his fingers in counting amazed us. The coins flew from the table-top as soon as he merely pointed his finger at them, and formed themselves into neat ranks of twenty in the palm of his hand. Pound by pound he piled them up, confirming for us the great risk we had been under. His fingers were blackened by the coins and made to shine so that every line and cut glistened.

At the conclusion of his collection the gasman would make Ellen a rebate from his stock of shillings. Somehow the hungry meter overestimated how much money it actually needed to keep us in heat. Ellen received twelve to thirteen shillings back from him. This money was always an unexpected windfall which would mean a treat that day as well as the fact that we'd click lucky for some of the shiniest shilling pieces. We considered these more valuable because of the way they made the gas burn brighter when you put them in the slot.

Our relief was shortlived, however, as we became aware that the silver-store was building up again. Ellen followed the activities of the burglar in the *Orpington and Kentish Times*. One day she read that he'd hit a place in the 'sac, the Dobsons'.

'The Dobsons,' said Ellen. 'I wonder why he's picked them? I mean, they keep themselves to themselves. You rarely see her at the shops, and when you do she hasn't got two words to say about anything.'

We puzzled over the Dobson mystery. Why had they suddenly been thrust into the forefront of the local drama? They were lucky to have escaped with their lives.

'They must have something,' said Ellen, 'something of value. That's probably why they've kept themselves to themselves for so long, but it hasn't done them any good has it?'

'No,' we said, 'it hasn't.'

Whenever the Dobsons passed our house, with their tragedy-stricken faces, Tom and I ran to the window shouting, 'Mum, Mum, there they go!' We'd all hide behind the nets and watch them pass.

'If it had happened to me, I wouldn't go out, I wouldn't leave the place unattended,' said Ellen. 'I expect they're on their way to see the police, they're helping them with their enquiries.'

From the day that Ellen read about the Dobson raid she redoubled her efforts to fortify Timbuctoo. She decided that we needed new bolts to the doors, and window fasteners front and back. She bought the things but shattered the window frames banging in screws with a hammer. Ellen wasn't on terms with Clancy and Did, since they had been cronies of Frank's, and so she went to see our other neighbour, Danny Pascoe, to ask if he could help her with the bolts.

Danny was always very friendly to us, and we liked him. 'You can't be too sure these days, I've just fitted something similar. My wife is sick with worry,' he said to Ellen.

'So am I,' said Ellen. 'It's like living through a nightmare with no man in the house.'

'These people know what they're doing,' said Danny.

'People?' said Ellen. 'You think there's more than one of them?'

'Oh yes,' said Danny, 'these types operate in a gang. They don't wait until you go out these days, they burst in, robbing and raping . . .'

'Oh no! I don't know if I like the sound of that,' said Ellen, deeply shocked to hear her fears confirmed. Now, she couldn't relax until Danny had thoroughly fortified the house. Ellen became quite friendly with Josie, his wife, and if anything ever needed doing in our house she'd send Danny round to fix it.

'She's lucky to have a good man,' said Ellen, and we all reflected on how the same had not been so for herself. We became very fond of Danny; he taught us to climb up his legs and over his head – something which we were delighted to do. We loved it when he was in our house, or digging in our garden, but when he went back to his own house we'd get upset, and cling on to his legs. We'd cry when he had gone, and sometimes stood with our lips against the wall calling for him through the brick. He made Ellen feel more secure as well; he had promised to dash round if he heard screams, an offer for which she was very grateful.

It was an even greater shock, then, when Ellen opened up the local paper to find an article reporting the capture of the burglar, red-handed, breaking the seal of Have-a-Go-Hero Eric Baldwin's meter. The burglar was Mr D. Pascoe of Clover Gardens and he'd been sent down for six months.

'No wonder he came in to do all those jobs,' said Ellen. 'He was waiting to see if we bought anything worth pinching.'

We were mightily shocked and confused by his arrest. We weren't having a lot of luck with men, we concluded. We had to face the fact that one is always let down by the 'dults.

When Danny got out of prison we watched his every movement. Ellen was too nervous even to hang her washing out in the garden. 'Well he could just reach over with a stick and pull them off the line,' she said. She took the milk in quickly too, 'because you mustn't put temptation in the way'.

Timbuctoo was now as secure as the Old Lady of Threadneedle Street: one needed to be an escapologist simply to weed the garden. She even fitted a bell to the gate, and left buckets of water in the hallway and on the stairs at night. She kept a bottle of bleach and a pot of pepper by her bed to chuck at him if he came in. All the new bolts, however, did not entirely work to our advantage for one day we came back from the shops and Ellen had lost the keys. We sat on the front steps for a while, and then, finally and in desperation, she went and knocked on Danny's door.

'Um, Mr Pascoe . . . Danny . . .' she said, 'I've done a silly thing.'

'Oh yes?' he said.

'I wonder if you can help me out.'

'Of course, love, what is it?'

'Well. I've lost my keys and I've gone and locked myself out. I can't get back in because of the bolts you put in for me.'

'Oh dear me,' said Danny, and he chuckled.

'And I wondered if you knew anything about . . .' Ellen flushed, '. . . I wondered if you could advise me?' she said.

Danny smiled. 'Just let me go and get a tablespoon,' he said and disappeared back inside his house.

Ellen looked at us and repeated the word 'tablespoon'. We repeated it as well, to endorse the fact that we'd all just been made party to criminal secrets.

Danny came over to Timbuctoo and with two small taps he made the front room window fly open. He climbed through and opened the door to us.

'I needn't have splashed out on all them bolts,' said Ellen.

'No,' said Danny, and he laughed.

CHAPTER XVI

In which we are lied to by our mother on the draining-boards and we swap transfers with Kacky Fanakerpan and our mother is hoist with her own petard

We were sitting on the draining-boards, either side of the sink, having our bath, when Ellen said, 'I'm going to send you back to your real mother one day, and then you'll be sorry.'

'You are our real mother,' we replied.

Ellen shook her head slowly from side to side. 'No,' she said. 'Your real mother is Mrs Fanakerpan, I've only been looking after you.'

We were terrified of Mrs Fanakerpan. Being sent back to her was a worse prospect than having our hands fried by Mrs Rubbidge. Mrs Fanakerpan lived in a house by the woods, which was enough in itself to suggest that there was something dark about her. Whenever she walked in the street with her husband, he'd walk on one side of the street and she on the other. At intervals she'd shout at him and he'd respond by giggling in the manner of a simpleton. Such had she reduced him to. If we were sent back to her the same would happen to us. Woody Lane, where they lived, had been intended by the architects of Prospect to replace the woods themselves. Only half the road was ever built, because of watershed problems, and the Fanakerpans were left jutting, at the end of a half-finished road, into the remaining undergrowth. Our real mother had a high bony nose and long matted hair which shone with grease. There was no doubt that she was a practitioner of the black arts, and all the Fanakerpans dressed poor.

Every street on the estate had a family like this: as well as the 'rowdy lot' there was also the 'simple lot'. The gardens of these families were overrun with weeds, bedsteads and old back boilers. They had a talent for amassing wheel-less prams and rain-hardened sacks of cement. They fought nature with stolen paving slabs. They ricked their backs and were laid off work. They managed to make their houses look decrepit and fit to be condemned even though they were no more than eight years old. Countless children ran in and out. There were broken windows patched with cardboard. Sometimes the people in the simple house would be thrown out and moved to one of the new, and much hated, tower blocks. It was as if these houses were reserved by the authorities for such tribes for no sooner had one simple or awful lot been moved out than an equally simple and awful lot replaced them. It must have been that the houses fell into such a bad state of repair that only the most desperate would take them.

Whenever Tom and I were playing in the street with Charlie and Mrs Fanakerpan came along we would run away like the wind. We'd give no explanation to Charlie but run and lie panting behind the greenhouse. Not a very good place to hide.

The Fanakerpans' son, Christopher Litchwood (Fanakerpan was Ellen's invention), was in our class at school. He looked like a boy who, in his grandfather's time, would have been shoved up grand chimneys. He wore long, khaki shorts, cut down from some of his dad's National Service kit, and he wore them every day. It was because of these shorts that the class called him Kacky. It wasn't only the extraordinary shorts that made him so appealing as a target, there was a whole list of things:

His ginger hair
His freckles
His picking of dandelions (known to us as wet-the-beds)
His odd nose (from which he derived continual sustenance)
His lack of underpants
   Simmer all ingredients for six to seven years. Season with eczema and spots, add a pinch of congenital rickets and bind in bones. Serve in outsized shorts to peer group.

At playtime he would mooch around the litter bins. No one would associate with him, except to smash his head against the wall if he spoke to us. Shortly after Ellen had made her announcement to us while we were on the draining-boards the teacher was late one day and the class began to pick on Kacky. Barry got him upside down into the pencil-shavings bin and Charlie spiked his hand with a compass. Kacky cried out. We felt very badly about it. Tom told Barry to stop and I pulled Charlie away and disarmed him of the compass. We helped Kacky, sobbing, out of the pencil-shavings bin. Barry and Charlie were dumbfounded when we told them to say that they were sorry. The whole class looked on, but how could we explain our turnabout? Kacky's place was with the shavings, why should the unison of twins suddenly say otherwise?

We shuffled uncomfortably. We looked towards Kacky, who was crouched on the floor holding his bleeding hand, and went over to him.

'He's our brother,' said Tom.

'Yeah,' I said. No one looked more surprised at this than Kacky himself. The teacher arrived and we went back to our places, revealing no more of our thoughts than this one, enigmatic, statement. When we were in the playground at break he smiled at us. We didn't know what to do, so Tom showed him his Superman transfers which that morning in the school toilets he had applied to his hand, and I showed him mine.

On our way home from school that evening we passed the Fanakerpans' house and saw Kacky sitting on the step. As we marched past he called out to us, standing up and pulling leaves off a shrub as he spoke.

'Where do you get them transfers then, out of corn-flakes or what?' he asked.

'What if we do, Kacky?' said Tom.

'I've got lots anyway, and better ones too,' he said.

'No, you haven't, you haven't got nothing,' I said and immediately felt guilty.

'Do you want to swap anything?' he asked, undaunted by our coldness.

'Might – might not,' said Tom. 'What have you got?'

'A war medal,' said Kacky, coolly. Tom and I looked at each other. We didn't know whether to believe him or not.

'Do you want to swap me transfers for it?' asked Kacky. We did. Very much we did.

'Might – might not,' said Tom.

'Yeah,' I said. 'Our transfers are valuable.'

'Let's have a look at this medal, then,' said Tom.

'It's indoors,' he said and began walking toward the house. We remained where we were, we didn't want to go anywhere near Mrs Fanakerpan in case she decided to ask Mum for us back.

'Are you coming then?' asked Kacky. We walked a little up the path.

'What are you scared of?' he asked.

'Nothing,' said Tom, 'we ain't scared of nothing.'

As soon as he'd gone into the house we stopped. We heard Mrs Fanakerpan shouting at him. 'What are you doing back in the house when I told you stay in the garden?' We heard him get a whack round the ear. We felt sorry for him. When he came out of the house he had welts on both sides of his face, one from his mother's hand and one from his father's, with the outlines of their fingers in red.

'What did you get hit for?' asked Tom.

'I dunno,' said Kacky, 'but I got the medal.' Although there was a tear on his cheek he was smiling and he didn't acknowledge the pain at all. His mind was on the transfers.

We looked at the medal and weighed it in our hands. It was a service medal from the First World War.

'Do you want to play with us?' we said.

'Do you want to swap me transfers for this?' said Kacky.

'Might, might not,' said Tom, holding out for the best deal possible. 'Do you want to come and play round our house?'

'Don't mind,' said Kacky.

When we got to our house with him we dashed up the path very quickly and pushed him through the gate into the back garden. We were worried that someone from our class would see us fraternizing with a Fanakerpan. We left him in the back garden while we went in to get our transfer doubles. We brought them out with a bowl of warm water. He had a look at them and liked them.

'All right, give us that medal then,' said Tom. He gave it to us. We soaked his transfers off the paper for him – he didn't even know how to do it – he rolled up his sleeves while we applied monsters, heroes and rockets to his arms and hands. He looked them over with pleasure, holding his arms at all angles.

'How long do they last?' he asked.

'Forever,' we said, 'they're indelible.'

We told him to wait in the garden while we went in to get Mum's Bluebell to shine the medal.

'I want to go to the toilet,' he said. We knew this was only a ploy to get in and see our house.

'Well you can't come inside,' we said. 'Mum doesn't allow.' He didn't say anything. When we came back he was squatting behind the greenhouse. We were shocked.

We'd never seen him so happy as when he got his transfers. He'd been the only boy in class who hadn't got any. All of our mates had made their mums change over to Coco Pops. The Fanakerpans probably didn't even have breakfast.

Mum opened the kitchen window and said, 'There's some cake on the table for you.'

'We've got to go,' we said to Kacky, 'Mum's calling us in.'

'You can bring your friend too,' called Mum. Tom and I looked at each other; Mum obviously didn't realize who it was we had with us. He couldn't believe his luck and he came in, making straight for the cake, the largest piece. As he sat at the table he stared around the room, looking at it as if it were a palace. Mum spoke to him.

'And what's your name?'

'What?' he said.

'What's your name?' repeated Mum.

'Christopher,' he said.

'Oh, that's a nice name isn't it?' said Mum.

Kacky shrugged his shoulders and looked at his cake. 'I dunno,' he said. He picked up the crumbs of chocolate from his plate and looked up to see if there was any more. We heard *Blue Peter* start on the television and we all went in to watch it. Kacky sat right up to the screen.

'What are we going to do?' Tom whispered in my ear.

'I don't know,' I said.

'What if he goes mouthing off at school that he's been in our house?'

'He'd better not, or else!' I said.

'Here, Kacky,' said Tom, tapping him on the shoulder.

'What?' he asked.

'You'd better not tell anyone at school, or anyone ever, forever, that you've been in here.'

'Why?' he asked.

'Or else . . .' said Tom.

'Or else what?' asked Kacky.

'Because,' I said.

'Because what?' asked Kacky.

'Because you'd better not or else,' we said together.

'I might,' he said.

'If you do, you know what we'll do,' we said.

'What?' We wished he'd stop asking these obvious questions and simply accept the threat like he would normally at school.

'We'll take the transfers back,' said Tom.

'But they're indelible,' said Kacky.

'So what? That don't mean we can't saw your arms off, does it?'

'I'd still tell,' he said.

'If you tell anyone you've been in here,' I said, 'we'll tell everyone, including our mum, that you did a crap behind our greenhouse.'

'All right then,' said Kacky, and returned to watching the television.

After the programme Mum wanted to Hoover and so she shooed us all upstairs into our bedroom. While we were showing him our airfix Spitfires Tom noticed that the transfers were beginning to crack on his hands already. We began to feel bad about the medal, especially since the inscription running around it read PTE C. LITCHWOOD, which was probably his grandfather.

Tom whispered to me, 'I don't think we should keep the medal, it's not fair.'

'I know,' I said, 'we ought to give it to him back.'

When we gave it to him he looked a little confused. 'But I give it to you,' he said, 'those transfers are valuable.'

'No they're not,' I said, 'they're not valuable like your medal, look they've started breaking up already.' Kacky looked at his hands, and as he pulled his sleeve up he scraped off those that were on his arm. He stared at them and his lip quivered.

'Don't cry about it,' said Tom, in the most compassionate voice I'd ever heard him use.

'No,' I said, 'there's no use in crying about it. We'll give you some more.'

'But I gave the medal to you,' he said. We knew that by this he meant that he wanted us to have it because we saved him from the pencil-shavings bin, and because he wanted to be our friend.

'You can get them out of Coco Pops, anyway,' I said.

Kacky looked up, the red welts still on his face. 'My Mum won't let me have them,' he said. 'She don't let me have nothing.'

We felt so sorry for him that before we knew what we were doing Tom had said, 'If they keep making you sit in the garden you can come and live here. Our mum would look after you, wouldn't she, Rich?'

'Yeah,' I said. 'Our mum wouldn't mind, she'd definitely look after you. She's not our real mum anyway,' I added, 'but she looks after us.'

'I don't think my mum's my real mum,' said Kacky, 'and I know my dad's not my real uncle.' We were all pretty confused about our exact positions. 'Can I live here, then?' he asked after a while.

'Yeah,' we said. We stayed in the bedroom and when it got to about seven o'clock I went downstairs to see if there was any juice on offer.

'Is that boy still up there with you?' asked Mum.

'Yeah,' I said.

'What's he doing, moving in?' said Mum.

'Yeah,' I said and Mum laughed. When I went back upstairs I said to Kacky, 'It's all right, I've told Mum you're moving in and she says it's OK.'

We all came back downstairs again to watch a last bit of telly before bed. At eight o'clock Mum turned to Kacky and said, 'Don't you think you ought to be going home? Your mummy will be getting worried about you.'

'No she won't,' said Kacky.

'Well I think it's time you were going, anyway.'

'But you said he could stay,' I said.

'Yes, I know,' said Mum, 'but only for tea. It's eight o'clock now, I'm going to have his mother banging on the door.'

'But he's moving in,' I said, 'you're going to be his mum.'

Ellen raised her eyebrows, dropped them again and then raised them a second time.

'You know *who* it is,' said Tom, 'it's Kacky Fanakerpan.'

'Oh, my gawd,' said Mum, and sat down laughing and shaking her head.

When she explained to us about her lie we were furious and began to shout. The funnier Mum found it the more cross we got. We were angry with Kacky too, for getting into our house under false pretences; but worst of all we felt stupid. Kacky just shrugged his shoulders again and took himself out of the front door, accepting his life as a series of unwarranted blows.

We never believed anything Mum said to us when we were on the draining-boards again.

CHAPTER XVII

In which we seek a new father and launch a campaign to marry our mother off to the rentman, and then the milkman, but Ellen subscribes to a marriage bureau and Mr Norman Spanish comes into our lives

'My Decree Nisi has come through,' declared Ellen from the hallway as she went to the door one morning. She sailed up the stairs in a great flutter of skirts like a galleon.

'What's a dickie nizzi?' said Tom. We gazed up the stairs.

'I dunno,' I said, 'the postman brought it.'

The other post, a letter and a free gift we had sent away for, still lay on the mat, abandoned in the excitement.

'What is it, a parcel or what?' said Tom.

'Something off the catalogue,' I said.

Ellen came back down the stairs. Her cheeks were flushed and she had affected a strange wobble to her head. We guessed that the wobble was directly related to the discovery of the dickie nizzi on the mat. Suddenly she went very quiet and sat down. No sooner had she sat down than she jumped up again and all the springs in the settee boinged.

'Well that's that,' she said, and wobbled her head again, furiously. We didn't like to admit that we didn't know what was going on so we sat quietly. Presently she said, 'I'm going down to the box to call Uncle Peter.' This meant that it had to be something of great importance and our curiosity increased to such a degree that we began

wobbling our heads as well. As soon as she went out of
the door we dashed up the stairs to her bedroom. We
had heard her shut whatever it was in the drawer by her
bed. We slowly slid the drawer open but all we found was
a dull buff envelope. We had a look inside it at a grey
folded document but found it uninteresting; it was some
kind of bill or insurance policy. We shut it back in the
drawer. The dickie nizzi was never explained to us but
there was a definite and discernible change in Ellen. She
sat quiet for periods, walked around the house and
brushed her hair wildly.

We were sitting on either side of the sink, in our
usual places on the draining-boards, having our Saturday
morning bath when Ellen made a second declaration.
'Now that my Decree Nisi has come through I'm going to
look for a new husband.'

She looked at each of us to judge our reactions to the
news. We wobbled our heads.

Prospect wasn't ideally suited for the task. Beer had
begun to be sold in cans which the men took home, there
was no cinema or dancehall. Rows and rows of family
units with no spaces between for single people.

Tom and I lay in our beds and discussed her chances.
'She could put an advert in the paper,' suggested Tom.

'I hope not,' I said. 'They never stopped coming round
when she sold the pram.' We pictured the scene after
such an advertisement: hopeful but sad-looking men, with
bunches of wilting daffs, hovering in the front garden,
trampling the plants and peering in through the windows.
We supposed we'd have to lead them in, one by one,
saying, 'Well this is her, what do you think?' like we did
with the pram, and Ellen would set them impossible tasks
to complete. Whoever was successful would win her hand.

We wanted nothing but the best for our mother, and

bearing in mind that he would become our new father, we decided to be of as much help as we could. We drew up a shortlist of the two most eligible candidates: 1. *Mr Bannister, the rentman*: Mr Bannister was just about the most important man we knew. When he collected the rent he often spoke to Ellen and seemed to like her. He looked very dashing in his beret. He had a lot of money. 2. *Gerry, the milkman*: Gerry was very good at whistling. He could drive. We wouldn't want for milk. As well as selling milk he'd also begun to sell little bottles of fizzy orange on the side. We were very keen on this new line and a ready supply, always on tap, would be a good thing for the future, we felt.

We told our mother all of this but she didn't seem to listen. We decided that if it was to come about we would have to give it some help. The next Monday, when Mr Bannister called for the rent, we were waiting by the garden gate to catch him before he knocked. Our intention was to get him into a good mood, and maybe mention that he ought to marry our mother.

'Hello, Mr Bannister,' I said in my best voice.

'Hello, Mr Bannister,' said Tom in his. He smiled at us and we at him. The three of us smiled for a good few moments and then he said, 'How are you getting on, kids?' and we said, 'All right,' casually adding, 'so is Mum; she's getting on with the washing and tidying up the house. She always keeps it nice and she cooks lovely dinners.' Mr Bannister laughed.

'It's very nice to see you,' said Tom.

'Thank you,' said Mr Bannister and he laughed again.

We watched from the gate as he knocked and as the door opened.

'Oh no!' said Tom. 'What's she got her curlers in for? She's going to ruin her chances.'

When Mr Bannister came back down the path Tom and I stood in his way.

'Mum's curling her hair,' said Tom, by way of explanation.

'It looks lovely when it's all curly,' I added.

'I'm sure it does,' said Mr Bannister, laughing, and he went on his way.

'I don't reckon he'd have been any good anyway,' said Tom, sneering. 'All he does is laugh all the time.'

We set our sights on Gerry, the milkman. We didn't want a repeat of the curlers episode and we were worried that he'd come early when Mum was still in her dressing gown.

'We've got to get it away from her,' said Tom. We got up early, took the robe from behind the bathroom door and hid it in the radiogram. Then we sat at the kitchen table and set about writing a note which we placed in the empty bottle on the step and which read:

> Dear Milky
> come in for a cuppa
> Mrs Stone

As far as we were concerned the thing was practically in the bag and we could already see ourselves in our page-boy suits and our mother all in white sailing to the church on the milkfloat. We watched from the garden again but this time we hid ourselves behind the hydrangea, happy that everything was all set up. He picked up the empty bottle from the step, took out the note and read it. He hesitated for a moment and then he knocked on the door. He had to wait quite a while because Ellen was running around the house looking for her dressing gown. He got more agitated the longer he waited. He shuffled about on the step and then he turned to the hydrangea where we were hiding and said, 'Is your mum in?'

'Yes, yes, she's coming, don't go away,' said the hydrangea. Gerry read the note again and smiled uneasily towards us. Ellen opened the door. Our hearts sank. She was wearing nothing but a purple towel. 'Why couldn't she have put her nice dress on?' we thought.

Gerry looked from side to side as he asked for his money, doing all he could to avoid looking at her. He fiddled with his blue and white apron, adjusted his cap from time to time and dipped his hands in and out of his money pouch. 'Three and six this week, Mrs Stone,' he said.

'Oh, right,' said Ellen and picked up the money from the hall table. 'Please excuse the way I'm dressed . . .' said Ellen, '. . . I couldn't . . .'

Before she had finished her sentence Gerry grabbed the money and dashed back down the path shaking his head. Ellen turned towards the hydrangea. 'Come on you two,' she said, 'I've told you not to jump out on people from behind there.' She pulled us indoors. 'Where's my dressing gown?'

'We dunno,' we said, 'maybe it fell in the radiogram?'

'He shot down the path sharpish. I don't know what he must have thought,' said Ellen.

We were very near to giving up. It was beginning to look like we'd have to wait until we were grown up and one of us was old enough to marry her. This was a perfectly acceptable idea to us except for one point: it would not provide either of us with a father now. We had set our hearts on a new one. The subject cropped up in all our games and bedtime talks. We'd already told our classmates, and most of the neighbours, that our mum was practically married. We'd described our new father in full to Charlie and even reported on the circuses and fairs that we'd been taken to by him, and we'd shown Charlie two lollysticks as proof of ice-creams he'd bought us. As far as we were concerned Ellen was too deep in to back out now.

We were sitting on the draining-boards and Ellen made a third announcement. 'I've joined a club.'

'What club?' we asked.

'A marriage bureau,' said Ellen. We puzzled over this, it sounded like a large piece of unfolding furniture.

'People fill in their details and you write in and they match you up with someone with the same details and then they write to you and you write to them and then you meet up somewhere, under a clock,' Ellen explained. This gave us a much clearer picture, a marriage bureau was a big writing desk. With all the letters involved we could see why mum was getting one.

Ellen received her first letter and she was so excited she read it out to us in her best voice:

Dear Mrs Stone,
My name is Malcolm Davis and the Matchmaker Marriage Bureau has given me your address. I am 36, divorced, and my interests are in cycling, photography and travel. Could I visit you on Saturday the ninth of the month, at, say, seven-thirty?
Yours faithfully,
Malcolm M. Davis

'Well, what do you think?' said Ellen, 'should I write to him and say yes, OK?'

We were very glad to be consulted. We were frightened that the bureau would exclude us from all the excitement, so we said 'yes'. Ellen was very pleased. On the Saturday of the ninth we threw ourselves into hoovering the house, advising Mum on her dress and deportment and spreading plate after plate of fishpaste crackers. It was all so romantic.

We pressed ourselves against the window pane for an hour, and when finally we saw Malcolm M. Davis approach the house we whooped and shrieked with excitement. Ellen pulled us away from the window, licked the corner of her handkerchief and washed our faces. This was the worst kind of washing in the world, like a mother cat with its kittens; it was worse even than the draining-boards, because the hankywash always happened at times of great excitement when two boys would rather be running round and round the room in ever widening circles singing signature tunes. We put up with it, however, because we knew that we came as part of the lot and because our mother had us firmly caught by the elbows.

When Malcolm M. Davis walked into our front room our excitement was at such a pitch that we were stuck to the floor with our mouths wide open and our heads wobbling. Ellen pointed to us and said, 'And these are my two boys, Richard and Thomas.'

Malcolm Davis shook our hands, which thrilled us as we had never had our hands shaken before. Then he said, 'I've a little girl, Alice, by my first, and two boys, Billy and Darren, and one of seven by my third, and a little one from my fourth.'

This stopped our heads wobbling good and proper. We were all dumbfounded by such a profession of progeny. We'd never heard anything like it. There was no doubt in our minds that Mr Malcolm M. Davis was an experienced applicant. Ellen was frantically trying to put some picture of his domestic arrangements together in her mind. Were the two boys Billy and Darren also of the first like Alice, or perhaps of the second? Or were they extra-numeral, being of no marriage at all? As for ourselves, we weren't sure that we wanted to join such a roll call, but the seven-year-old by the third disturbed us – had he simply forgotten its name? And how little was the girl, Alice? If the seven-year-old was by the third, Alice would hardly be so little; the last thing we wanted was a big sister. And how little was the one by the fourth? The second to last thing we wanted was a baby.

'Well,' said Ellen, not quite sure what to say, 'perhaps you'd better sit down.'

'Thank you,' he said and sat right in the middle of the settee, leaving Tom and me to share the remaining armchair. Ellen ran his letter through her mind.

'So you've travelled a lot, have you?'

'No,' he said, 'I haven't. I just put that on the form and in the letter because I thought I'd better put something. It said put three things.'

'Oh,' said Ellen, and the conversation, or at least the attempt at one, floundered.

'I've moved house a fair bit though,' said Davis.

'I suppose you have,' said Ellen.

He was a stocky man with pale, nervous hands which spent the whole time tugging at his trousers and fiddling with his fly zip. He pulled at his collar too, so that it rose high up his neck, his tie practically knotted over his chin. He fiddled with his socks, which he had gartered up to his shins, and he pulled his cuffs down over his hands. It was as if he were trying to disappear altogether.

'As a matter of fact I don't have any interests at all,' he said after a while.

'Except cycling,' said Ellen.

'No,' he said, 'that's my brother Eric, he's the one with

the bike. You'd like him. He's been inside but he didn't do it. I don't have time for interests . . .'

'Neither do I,' said Ellen, 'so we've certainly got something in common there.' We were very relieved that at last they'd found some common ground. 'Not with keeping the house straight, and the twins here,' she added.

He took a short, expressionless glance at us and then a much more interested look around the room. 'It's a very nice home you have here,' he said.

'Oh, thank you,' said Ellen, excited.

'I'm in digs,' he said, 'but I want to get out.'

Ellen continued on the subject of her home which seemed to interest him. 'I haven't got much, really. I could do with a new Burco, or even a refurbished one, but my husband, my ex-husband, was no good. He drank . . .' Ellen looked over to us. 'He was a bad lot, their father.'

We didn't like this. Why should we get the blame? We didn't like the idea of a perfect stranger knowing all our business, even if he was going to be our father.

Ellen offered him a fishpaste cracker but he refused, saying that they made him chesty. We took against him for that. Together with this he kept having to go up to the toilet informing us on each occasion that he had a bladder like a sieve. We didn't like this turn of phrase, we felt it lowered the overall romantic possibilities of the meeting. Whenever we felt sure that he wasn't looking at us we'd catch Mum's eye and shake our heads slowly from side to side.

After an hour we were sent upstairs to play but we couldn't think of any games. We used the time to fold and lick stamp hinges in case we should one day get some stamps for our collection. Within thirty minutes we heard

the front door shut. We went down and he had gone.
Ellen was a little shaken.

'Well,' she said, 'he sat there all that time doing nothing
but fiddle with himself and not making any conversation
to speak of and then all of a sudden he makes a lunge at
me. That's when I showed him the door.'

'You didn't like him, did you?' we asked.

'No, I didn't, did you?'

'No,' we said, 'we don't want that one.'

'I reckon he was only after getting out of his digs and
moving in here.'

We were very relieved and we told Mrs Rubbidge and
Mrs Pascoe all about Mum being lunged at.

Ellen was courageously undaunted by the unfortunate
episode with Malcolm M. Davis and she wrote to the
bureau requesting another contact. Within a few days
another letter arrived. She read it out to us. We were
feeling pretty professional about the whole thing now and
reckoned we would be able to tell from the letter alone
whether it was worth granting the man an audience or
not. It was from a man in Basildon New Town, printed in
a very small script and, appropriately, on blue Basildon
Bond notepaper.

Dear Mrs E. Stone,
   Allow me to introduce myself a little because the Marriage
Bureau has kindly passed your name on to me as we match up
in what we're after since I am a widower of forty-two, a young
forty-two, and I work in a light electrical company which
manufactures a wide range of quality products such as pen
torches and thermostats. So I've got a head on my shoulders all
right. I'm in the dispatch and since my wife passed on two years
September have put in a lot of overtime I can tell you. So I've a
bit in the bank. Like you I'm teetotal I also preserve steam and
Hornby 'O' gauge and I shall be down your way in your vicinity
at about six o'clock on Sat twenty to watch the *Flying Scotsman*

go through and I wouldn't mind killing two birds with one stone, all being well with the railway. I did have a car on the road but it's in dry dock now for two months Tuesday last. They don't hurry themselves do they? Anyway, you can't beat the train. So shall I say a provisional seven on the date above if I do not hear from you or get a line I will think this is all OK and come. I am looking forward to meeting you acquaintance.

Yours, as ever,

Mr Spanish (Norman)

We were all very impressed by the letter. He would obviously be much more adept at conversation than the unfortunate Malcolm Davis. We all wondered if he was Spanish.

'A Spaniard!' said Ellen. 'I don't know what the 'sac will say.'

Tom and I hoped he would arrive in his bullfighter's clothes. 'When is he coming, when is he coming?' we asked.

'Tonight, it says tonight, all being well with the railway. I'll have to get everywhere straight. You'll have to help me.'

'We'll do the hoovering,' I said.

'Yeah,' said Tom, 'and you go down to the hairdresser's and have a perm.'

Ellen ran her fingers through her hair and shook it. 'Do you think I should?' she asked. 'Do you think my hair looks a sight then?'

'Yeah,' we said, 'get a perm.'

'Right,' said Ellen, almost crumpling the wonderful letter in her hand. 'I'll buy myself a box of home perm from Woolworths and then I might be able to stretch to a new rigout.'

We threw ourselves into spreading fishpaste crackers again and arranged them romantically on a best dainty plate while Ellen got herself into the new rigout upstairs. When she came down she spun in the front room to show off the dress to its best advantage. It looked so wonderful, all purple with red polka-dots, that we hoped she'd get the chance to spin again when Norman Spanish arrived. The only thing that worried Ellen was that with the new perm she might look fast. We assured her that she didn't look fast but that the combined effect of the perm, the red and purple dress and the fishpaste crackers would be irresistible to a Spaniard.

Norman Spanish arrived at seven on the dot, undisappointed by the *Flying Scotsman*. We were upstairs in our bedroom having been told to: 'Stay upstairs and be quiet and no sneaking down for a glimpse.' We spent the first hour pacing up and down like expectant fathers. We lay on the floor a couple of times and listened through the ceiling. We could hear the burble of Norman Spanish's conversation interspersed with our mother's giggles. When Ellen came up to the toilet she pushed our bedroom door open.

'How's it going?' we asked.

'All right,' she said, 'he's very nice, more like fifty than forty-two, but he's very nice: he's English, he's eaten all the crackers . . .' With this she darted out again.

'Well, he's eaten all the crackers,' said Tom.

'Good,' I said.

At nine o'clock he left to watch the *Flying Scotsman*, back from Dover, go through again, and to catch his train back to Basildon. Ellen sat in the armchair and read over his letter again.

'What did he look like?' we asked.

'Well,' she said, 'he had brilliantine in his hair, which I don't really like – you can see where it's marked the back of the settee – but it did set his face off. He wasn't a big man, nine stone he said, but more like eight; look, you can see where he was sitting and he didn't make much of a dent.'

'Is he coming again?' we asked.

'Yes,' she said. 'Next Saturday, and this time you can sit in and meet him. In three weeks' time we might all go down to his caravan at Selsey Bill, if he's managed to get the Calor gas rigged up.'

We jumped up and down with excitement. We talked about nothing else all week. On Wednesday a little card, with a picture of an engine on the front, arrived from Norman. Ellen was thrilled and she read it out to us. Norman had covered every inch of the card with his tiny script.

Dear Mrs Stone,
   Just a line to say didn't we have a lovely and nice evening Sat twentieth and the beautifully prepared biscuits were most acceptable I will have to treat you to a real slap up nosh shortly you'll be pleased to know I got home safely and with no injuries changing at Blackfriars as I said I would without too much of a wait on the platform. I am looking forward to seeing you again Saturday next and meeting your two boys whom I've heard so much about already. I wouldn't be surprised if you see me in the same suit of clothes again. These dry cleaners don't hurry themselves do they? But I think it's well worth the extra to turn yourself out spruce.
                                        Yours sincerely,
                                        Norman (Spanish)

'And he's looking forward to meeting you two,' said Ellen, 'that's good. I thought having you two would put them off.' We couldn't understand this at all – surely having us two made the prospect of marriage to Ellen even more appealing.

When Norman Spanish arrived, again promptly at

seven, we were lined up for inspection, having had our hankywash, and our hair stuck down – not unlike Norman's – with Ellen's lacquer. We had pinched and pulled our cheeks to make them rosy and we prepared ourselves to shake hands. But Norman Spanish crossed straight to the crackers. 'You don't expect a buffet on a suburban line,' he said, 'but it would be nice, wouldn't it?'

'Oh yes,' said our mother. 'Have you not had a good journey then?'

'Oh, I mustn't complain, but the state of the carriages since they did away with the third class, it's something chronic. In future I shall travel first, it's worth the little extra to be in comfort and not in squalor.'

Ellen agreed and went to boil some water for the tea. We were a little disappointed that Norman Spanish wasn't in his bullfighting outfit but nevertheless we were happy when he turned to us to speak. 'Do you two travel by the railway much, then?' he asked us.

'Yes,' said Tom, 'we went to Brighton.'

'What sort of time did you make?' he asked.

'I dunno,' said Tom.

'Two hours fifty, as a rule,' he informed us. 'But Brighton, dear me it's full of these Mods and you can't get a decent plate of cod any more, can you?'

'No,' we said, 'you can't.'

'And as for the front, what about the paintwork?' We didn't know about the paintwork. 'They spend all that money on bulbs and then let the paint peel. It doesn't make sense. I shall drop them a line about it. Do you think it makes sense?'

'No it doesn't,' we said.

'You never want to have any dealings with Basildon Council,' he said, changing track. 'What would you do in my position? I removed my hedge. Well, you don't want to have to be cutting it every five minutes, do you? What do they want me to do now? They want me to put it back in again. Well, I've made a fire and burnt it. I told them to get their paving slabs patched up first before starting on me about a blinkin' hedge. I've always been my own man. Well you've got to be nowadays, haven't you?'

'Yes,' we said, 'you have.'

I fancy that Norman had not had the same close contact with children that his predecessor, the unfortunate Malcolm Davis, had.

Ellen came back in with the tea.

'You all seem to be having a rare old time,' she said.

'Oh yes,' said Norman, 'the boys have been telling me all about Brighton, how you can't get a decent plate of cod down there any more.'

Our mother looked rather surprised at this but smiled nevertheless, and marvelled that we should come out with such things. She wondered where we had 'got it', herself always having praised the wet fish of the south coast.

'Well, here we are again.' he said, slapping his thighs excitedly. It looked to be an invitation for our mother to sit on his lap, which indeed it was. 'I said in my note I'd be in the same suit of clothes, didn't I?'

'Oh yes, thank you for your lovely note with the engine on it,' said Ellen.

'Well, I've always known how to do things properly,' said Norman. 'When it comes to things of this nature you've got to know how to conduct it with dignity or else it's just smutty, and I don't like smut.'

'Oh, neither do I,' said Ellen, 'I switch the set off as soon as it comes on!'

'I had a very decent letter from my bank manager Tuesday,' he said, 'advising me of my premium.'

'Oh lovely,' said Ellen.

Norman reached for another couple of crackers. 'Oh, I've a tidy sum all right, a tidy sum. I was the apple of my mother's eye until her legs went varicosed.'

'Oh, I'm sorry to hear that,' said Ellen.

'Well it's all right. It makes them get irritable. No son could expect to be the apple of the eye once they go varicose. It'd be tempting fate.'

We watched Norman Spanish in awe. He seemed to know about everything. We were particularly impressed by the sheen of his brilliantined hair which was as shiny as the elbows and the seat of his suit. So the conversation went on, the greater part of it unintelligible to us, but the general gist we understood to revolve around the achievements, the charms and the investments of Mr Norman Spanish, resident of Basildon New Town, Essex. At nine o'clock he left, having devoured all the crackers and a round of spam sandwiches with mustard, and having plucked up the courage to seal his departure with a peck on Ellen's cheek. Although his teeth were, by his own admission, unreliable, he carried the peck off to the satisfaction of all and left Ellen waving furiously on the step. Off he went into the night to change at Blackfriars (into what we didn't know) leaving an air of electricity in one small household on the Prospect estate.

Ellen decided to get herself another new rigout for the next great visit of Norman Spanish. She couldn't really run to it but she dipped into the holiday money and the Christmas fund. She went to the new boutique which had opened on the parade, and which she termed 'the booty-queue', and was talked into trying on a red and white Hawaiian-style dress. She knew it was a little loud but she was feeling confident, and anyway having tried it on she felt she was obliged to buy it. She was swirling for us

in the dress when another letter arrived from Norman.
Ellen, in excitement, read it out to us:

Dear Ellen,
   Thank you so much for the other lovely evening we had the
other evening at which I enjoyed meeting your two boys don't
they shoot up these days? Before you know where you are
they're in long trousers and getting interests beyond their years.
I got home safely despite the street lighting and the chronic
state of the pavements it's a disgrace. The bureau have sent me
the particulars of another lady like yourself who suits my
particulars as well so I shall be off again on Saturday to look
her up, wish me luck, I will keep you posted. I hope this letter
reaches you as it leaves me.

                                          Norman (Spanish)

   Ellen sat down and flattened the new frock on her lap.
She bit her lip. 'I don't understand it,' she said. We
weren't sure whether we should cry or not. 'I will keep
you posted! I should coco, Norman Spanish!'
   With this she went into the kitchen to bang the dinner
plates about in the sink. At intervals she put her head
around the door to issue statements like: 'You'd have
thought he'd have said to me do you fancy a film or some
eats!' and 'All he did was sit there and munch through
cracker after cracker.' And finally, after shouting from
the kitchen, 'Eleven and six he's cost me for this horrible
frock,' she came in, switched the television on and sat
down with some knitting.
   As promised, Norman kept us posted with his affairs.
A week or two after his letter announcing his intention of
visiting another lady, another letter arrived.

Dear Ellen,
   As promised here's a line. Well I saw a Mrs Beasley the
other evening but to be perfectly honest with you she wasn't all
her details made her out to be. I spent fourteen shillings on a

fish and chip supper for the two of us but it was money thrown
away I think. Have you had any luck? Let me know if not, I'm
seeing a lady in Sidcup next Saturday and on the following Sat
I've put my name down for some overtime because there's a
rush on with abroad but the Sat after that I'm in your neck of
the woods and could probably just fit you in then.

N. Spanish

Ellen was infuriated by the letter and she threw it out
of the window. 'He didn't buy me no fish and chip
supper!' she shouted. Ellen didn't reply to the letter of
course but nevertheless another arrived shortly after.

Dear Ellen,
Well some people! The Sidcup woman was a disgrace, said
her interest was travel but could she so much as make it to the
kitchen to boil a kettle? – No she couldn't. All in all it was a bit
of a wash-out I'm not struck on Sidcup anyway. I had to give
my right arm for a sandwich at the station. I should have known
from the tone of her letter that she'd be a dead loss but once
you've paid twenty guineas to join you might as well give it a
go. Had any luck yet? I might be down your way Sat next if one
I'm working on falls through.

Yours.
Norman (Spanish)

Norman Spanish became a byword in our house for
anything that was no good or broken. When the sole
came off Ellen's slippers she said, 'They've norman-
spanished on me,' and threw them away. Ellen no longer
felt like 'giving it a go' and she decided to cut her losses
and write to the bureau saying that Norman Spanish was
not the type of man she was looking for and that she'd
like to be removed from their register.

Dear Mrs Stone,
Thank you for your letter. We are sorry that you are dis-
satisfied with our service, and the calibre of our gentleman

admirers. Several other ladies have written to me on the subject
of Mr Norman Spanish and you'll be pleased to know that I've
struck him off.

Yours,

pp

This was retribution enough for us.

'He needed striking off,' said Ellen, but we did feel a
little sorry for him. He was just a sad little man, the only
glamour in his life being a dash of brilliantine and the
opportunity to meander all over the Southern Railways
region, at the weekend, in the guise of a suitor to lonely
women and fatherless children. Norman Spanish stuck in
our minds – a shabby figure, relegated to the ranks of the
struck off: the negligent anaesthetists, the incompetent
doctors, the defrocked vicars, and the dishonourably
discharged guardsmen. Ellen went off the idea of romance
and began to think of herself as a widow, her task in life
to bring up fatherless twins. Tom and I felt shabby among
our peers, turning our heads to the ground whenever we
heard the awful phrase 'broken home'. We felt as if we
had been struck off too.

CHAPTER XVIII

*In which we run away but come back again to find another
turn of events which greatly affects the course of our lives
for the remainder of the novel, and possibly beyond*

Ellen's health began to deteriorate along with her spirits.
People seemed to be forever stopping her in the street to
tell her that 'children need a father's hand'. Ellen's heart
began murmuring so heavily that she woke in the night

feeling as if she'd fallen down the bed. We listened to her telling Mrs Rubbidge that her heart was missing beats, she could feel it when she lost them. We were universally acknowledged to be twice the handful of non-twins, and responsible for those missing beats. It was very unfair.

There was a terrible scene, and scowls for days, after we set fire to the landing curtains. 'You'll be sorry when you've driven me to my grave,' said Ellen. We were sorry now. We were sorry as soon as the polyester fabric caught into a blaze – we'd only intended to singe the very edge of it, just a little.

Misfortunes befell us uninvited, cups fell from our fingers now that we handled the china, and our new white sandals sank and were ruined when we tried to bail out the water from the lavatory. We were at the age of walking into calamity and the sum and total of it was that we became the handful as prophesied.

Ellen announced that she was run down. At first Tom and I thought that she'd been hit by a car, but no, nothing so exciting, she was just run down.

'I just don't understand it,' said Ellen. 'I just don't know what I'm doing wrong. I'm doing everything the way I always have; I boil the water, I even warm the cups, I'm using the best pot but I just don't seem to be able to make a decent cup of tea any more.' It was true, it was all true, somehow the power had left her. When we made the tea, even though we broke some of the cups, the tea was always fine. 'I don't understand it,' said Ellen, 'I just don't seem to be able to make a decent cup of tea any more. It's got no strength and no refreshment.' Ellen made a dozen pots a day but it all went into the sink because the leaves would not yield to her. We decided to run away from home.

It was difficult at first to agree upon a place to run

away to. Tom favoured the back of the shops because there were lots of cardboard boxes to jump on and I favoured the park because they were putting in some new swings and the builders had left a pile of sand.

'It's no use living in the park,' said Tom, 'we only get beaten up over there.' This was true. Finally we hit on the allotments. This idea seemed perfect because we would be able to live in one of the sheds and whenever we were hungry we could just pull food out of the ground. We packed up the basic essentials we felt we would need: some drawing pins, elastic bands, plasticine and the Christmas decorations. But when we got to the allotments we found that all the sheds were locked up and the cabbages had seen too many caterpillars come and go, the runner beans were only halfway up their poles and the radishes were woody.

'We can't live on this,' said Tom, 'let's go home, have tea and run away again.'

'Yeah,' I said, 'let's.'

When we got back there was an ambulance at the bottom of the 'sac. The back of it was open and we joined the other kids standing around to see the excitement. We wondered if someone had really been run down. After a while we got bored and decided to go home and get some biscuits. When we got to the gate we saw that the front door was open. We ran up the path. The house was full of people. A nurse, in blue uniform, was peering at a snap of Tom and me which was in a little frame on the mantelpiece; Mrs Pascoe, still in her apron, was folding up a nightdress to put in a paper bag, and her husband, Danny, was securing the windows. Two large ambulance-men sat in the armchairs, one resetting his watch and the other utilizing the time to remove the hairs from his nostrils. We couldn't help but stare. Doctor Woodle was standing beside the settee on which our mother lay. We ran through the crowd to her, she opened her eyes, looked up and said, 'They're here.'

'We've been waiting for you,' said the doctor. 'Your mother is not at all well and she has to go into hospital.'

'Can we ride in the ambulance, then?' we said.

'No, I'm sorry you can't,' said the doctor, 'you are to go with a lady who'll be here in a minute.'

Ellen began to cry. The nurse flew into action. She put her hand on her forehead, timed her pulse and told her not to get upset. 'They will be all right, won't they?' said our mother, 'or I'm not going.'

The ambulancemen got up and moved in on her, unfolding a metal contraption as they did so. They lifted Ellen into it so that it became half chair, half stretcher and they carried her out of the door. We followed behind with Danny. All the neighbours had turned out to watch. The women shook their heads as if they were not surprised by the procession as it travelled down to the open ambulance. I touched the edge of the thick red blanket that was tucked around her. 'Red is for blood,' I thought and could think of nothing else, but there was no blood, only a whiteness in her hands and face. I expected her to fight them and to scream but she just lay with her eyes staring upwards at the sky. She kissed us goodbye and was lifted into the ambulance. It was just a touch of lips.

We stood on the edge of the kerb between Danny and the doctor watching the ambulance drive away. We felt that maybe everyone was cross with us for going to the allotments, and for being the cause of the missing beats, we wondered where our mother had gone, and when she would come back. I turned to Danny. 'Mum will be coming home again, won't she?'

'Yeah, of course she will, kid,' said Danny.

'Will she be home tonight?'

'No, not tonight.'

'Tomorrow, then?'

'Soon, she'll be home soon, but not tomorrow.'

We had not really begun to worry until we heard the bell start on the ambulance as it turned the corner. The noise of it frightened us and we began to cry for the first time. Danny took us back to the house with an arm around each of our shoulders; we were shaking with sobs.

Very shortly the lady that Doctor Woodle had told us about arrived. They talked together in the hallway. 'They're in there with one of the neighbours,' said the doctor. 'They've been quite brave but the shock is setting in. I think we'd better get them out of the house and settled as quickly as possible.'

'Leave them to me,' said the lady.

'Hello there, children,' she said as she came into the front room. 'My name is Miss Barnes.' We stared at her. The house still seemed full of people and we were confused.

'Now, your mummy isn't very well . . .'

'We know that,' said Tom, 'we saw her go off.'

'She has to have a rest in a nice bed at the hospital.'

'She could have a rest here,' I said, 'we'd do all the cooking.'

'I'm sure you would,' she said, 'but I'm afraid it isn't possible.' We watched as she sat down and folded her hands on her lap. She was elderly and she spoke very slowly so that we would understand her. She had a flat briefcase and we wondered what was in it. 'Now I'm going to take you to the lady who is going to look after you,' she said.

'What lady?' asked Tom. Miss Barnes looked nonplussed for a moment and then opened her briefcase and began searching through the pieces of paper.

'The lady is called Mrs Goody and she has a lovely house with two nice beds all made up for you and a little boy of her own called Billy, with whom I'm sure you'll get along, won't you?'

'We ain't going,' said Tom, stamping his foot and then sitting down resolutely in the middle of the carpet. I joined him and we folded our arms just as we did at school assembly on the gymnasium floor. 'And we ain't going to get along with no Billy!' shouted Tom.

'Listen,' said Danny to Miss Barnes, 'we've got a room they can have. My wife and I would be happy to look after them.'

Miss Barnes looked surprised. 'Are you immediate family?' she asked.

'No, but we only live next door, it'd be the same for them for school and everything.'

Miss Barnes nodded her head, it seemed a good idea to her.

'Can I have a word with you, Miss Barnes?' said the doctor. Danny looked up at the ceiling in exasperation. The doctor and Miss Barnes came back from a short conference in the hallway.

'I'm sorry, Mr Pascoe, I can't possibly consider it under the circumstances,' said Miss Barnes.

'What right have you got just to push these kids about? They know me, what do you think I'm going to do, teach them to nick the Crown jewels?'

'I am The Authority,' said Miss Barnes, 'and they are assigned to my care.' She turned to us and said, 'Have you got your things packed?'

'Yes,' we said and showed her our paper bag with the drawing pins, elastic bands, plasticine and Christmas decorations inside.

'I think you might need a little more than that,' she

said and she took us upstairs to collect our school things and our pyjamas. We didn't need any toys she said, there were already toys where we were going; Billy would let us play with his.

'We ain't playing with no Billy,' said Tom. Tom hadn't taken to Billy at all.

They had to force us to leave the house and we were led out to a car. Miss Barnes drove us away. We were shocked to see an elderly lady driving and it confirmed in our minds that she was possessed of unnatural powers. The car was small and grey with a dashboard which Miss Barnes had made herself by stealing children's tortoises and bashing them flat. The back seat, where we were in custody, had piles of green forms upon it, which we expected to have to fill in at some stage. She drove at such a steady pace that it was as if we sat inside an immobile, resolute tortoise, and our little house was being dragged away from us, and Danny and Mrs Pascoe, and Charlie who stood bewildered on the verge, were being struck by the unearthly powers of The Authority.

The wealth and the better houses of Petts Wood moved towards us and the dark cover of the pine trees lining the private roads moved over us. We turned into the gravelled drive of a mock-Elizabethan semi-detached with bits of bright red wood slapped cosmetically on to its frontage. Miss Barnes opened her door and extended her grey fleshy neck into the air. She folded forward her seat and ushered us out on to the gravel. 'Now she's a very nice lady and you're to call her auntie,' said Miss Barnes, as she walked us up to the door. She pressed the doorbell and set off a peal of cathedral chimes.

We were unsure about calling someone we didn't know, 'auntie'. The peal of chimes ended but there was no answer at the door. Miss Barnes tried again, and then she walked across the lawn to rap at the window. The heels of her shoes sank in the grass and she complained. 'This is terrible,' she said, turning to us, 'the nice lady must be out.'

'Good,' said Tom, 'I hope she stays out.'

'She knew we were coming, I telephoned her. We shall have to wait in the car.' We returned to the car, which was still sitting happily in the driveway, chewing the plants. We sat for some time. Miss Barnes sifted through pieces of paper, Tom and I tried to uproot some of the leather from the seats.

After half an hour Miss Barnes drove us to the Welfare Office. We had never been in a room with so many telephones before, and she sat us, beside her desk, on swivel chairs. We didn't like these chairs at all; whereas in happier times we would have merrily spun ourselves round on them until we were sick, now we associated them with our plight. We reckoned they were for the use of people who were crippled in some way; also, our feet didn't reach the floor, which perturbed us greatly.

Miss Barnes sifted through cards in a box-file and made a succession of telephone calls, none of which was satisfactory. We began to prepare ourselves for a night in the Welfare Office. There was a lot of activity all around and we heard talk of other children in similar situations to ourselves. A young woman came in to see Miss Barnes and talked about a child she'd removed from its parents and had taken to the hospital. We wondered if we might go to the hospital as well, and live there with our mother.

As the afternoon drew on the office emptied and we still sat on Miss Barnes's swivels with our little suitcase by the door. The events of the day ran through my mind. I wondered how Mum was and what the hospital was like. I thought about Danny and couldn't understand why we didn't go to stay with him. I wondered if the nurse had remembered to put the paper bag with the nightdress into the ambulance. I wondered if the ambulanceman had managed to get all the hairs out of his nose, or if he'd tugged so hard at them that he'd given himself a nose bleed and had had to be admitted to hospital himself, in his own ambulance.

'Right,' said Miss Barnes, finally, 'we're off again,' and she led us out to the grey and tortoiseshell car. We drove to another house, this time on the estate, and were led up to its door, again being instructed to call the lady auntie.

'How many aunties have we got?' asked Tom. Miss Barnes said that she hoped we were going to be good boys. We shrugged our shoulders. It depended. A woman opened the door. She was wearing a turquoise housecoat and three or four children peered out at us from behind her back and between her legs. We didn't like being stared at and we liked it even less when the woman said to Miss Barnes, 'Oh no, I can't take two.'

'But I did say on the telephone,' said Miss Barnes, 'that there were two of them.'

'Yes, but you didn't say twins,' said the woman. 'I've had twins before, and as I said to you then, Miss Barnes, I will never again, because they're nothing but trouble. You obviously didn't make yourself clear on the phone. I'll take one but not the other.'

'Oh no, I couldn't split them up,' she said. 'Can't you take them just for tonight?'

'What are they?' asked the woman, looking us up and down, 'maltreated, broken home or what?'

'Their mother's gone into hospital for a short while.'

'Short while? That's what you said once before and I had them a year.'

'Just for tonight?' pleaded Miss Barnes again.

'Hospital . . .' said the woman thoughtfully. 'They're not going to fret are they?' She looked at me and saw my lip quivering. 'They're going to fret,' she said, resolutely. 'I've got two fretters already. No, I'm sorry, twins are nothing but trouble. How old are they?'

'Just nine,' said Miss Barnes.

'Oh no,' said the woman, 'not nine, difficult age, they're a handful.'

I looked up at Miss Barnes, I was about to cry. We'd tried to be brave, as we'd been told to be, all afternoon, but there were limits. I didn't want to cry in front of the other children staring through her legs so I pulled at Miss Barnes's skirt and said, 'Please, miss, can I sit in the car?'

'See what I mean,' said the woman, instantly, 'nothing but trouble.'

With this I began to cry quite loudly, I was so overcome with shame.

'Oh dear, oh law, listen to the noise of it, look at the ugly face it's pulling,' said the woman triumphantly.

Miss Barnes was beginning to wonder if the woman was entirely suited to the employment she gave her, but she was desperate to get us placed, and pleaded on our behalf one more time. 'Look,' she said, 'you can see how upset they are – their mother's in hospital. Couldn't you just give them some tea and I'll collect them tomorrow? See how you get on with them?'

I watched her head as it swayed from side to side. 'Oh no, I don't think so,' she said, 'I'm low on milk.'

Miss Barnes led us back down the path. I was sobbing and clinging on to her legs, Tom walked independently behind us and kicked the heads off all the tulips.

CHAPTER XIX

In which we go to live with Mrs Bagbourne and we meet Mr Bagbourne who is most sympathetic to our plight but has possibly had a drink

'It'll have to be Mrs Bagbourne,' said Miss Barnes as she put us into her car again. This time the tortoiseshell Hillman was a mere formality; we drove only three or four streets to the new house. We got out and stood on the pavement, looking towards the house. There were wheelless prams and backboilers in the front garden, and a broken window patched with cardboard.

'We're going in there?' asked Tom.

'Yes,' she said, hesitating, 'come along'; but we drew back and tried to return to the car.

'Let's not have any silliness,' she said, and prised us, like limpets, off her Hillman Imp.

Miss Barnes had put a hat on for this trip to give herself greater authority. As we walked up the path the little feather, which stuck out from the front of the hat, swayed from side to side as if expressing Miss Barnes's disapproval. 'I must insist that Mrs Bagbourne does something about this untidiness,' said Miss Barnes.

'Yeah,' said Tom, 'it's a mess.'

Encouraged by this we marched up the path in a workmanlike fashion. The door, which was marked by the scratching of dogs and the kicking of kids, was on the latch, so we went through.

'Mrs Bagbourne! Mrs Bagbourne!' called Miss Barnes, 'are you in?' Mrs Bagbourne approached us in the hall.

There was no bulb in the passage and she loomed out of
the half light so that all we could make of her distinctly
was her smell, a mixture of Marmite, beef extract and
what we later found to be gin.

'Who is it, duck?' called this bronchitic voice of Mrs
Bagbourne.

'It's me, Miss Barnes.'

'Oh hello, love, what can I do for you?'

Miss Barnes explained that she was in a tight spot with
two short-stay children. She was sorry she'd given her no
warning. She hoped she would take us in nevertheless.
Her feather twitched against the light of the open door.
Gradually Mrs Bagbourne's features became apparent in
the darkness.

Mrs Bagbourne agreed immediately and conducted us
around the stacks of cardboard boxes into the front room,
which was also poorly lit, the curtains being drawn. The
only light in the room was that which came through the
gap between the pelmet and the sag line of the drapes.
Mrs Bagbourne tugged them open a little and the light
cut through the dust and debris of the room like a sword
and shone full in our eyes. We were like two little actors
in their first matinée blinded by the spots. We stood close
together. When our eyes became acclimatized and finally
we saw her, we were at last able to appreciate fully her
enormous bulk as she eclipsed the sun. She had long
black hair, tied in a pony tail, and she wore a great green
cardigan with lavatory paper, in assorted colours, flowing
from its pockets. Every now and again she would take up
one of these pieces, thrust it into her face, and impersonate a trombone to the life. When the paper returned to
the pocket freshly dampened, it would invariably work its
way loose and fall to the carpet to join the rest of the
roll.

'Well it's nice to see you, dear,' she said to Miss Barnes, 'how are you keeping? – still battling through?'

'Yes, thank you,' said Miss Barnes.

Mrs Bagbourne swung towards us to look us over. 'These are them, then, are they, then?' she asked.

'Yes, this is Richard and Tom,' said Miss Barnes.

'Oooh, I don't know how I shall tell them apart, they're like peas in a pod.'

We went and sat quietly on a settee which had been unfolded into a bed. We looked around at our new home. There were two babies in a cage by the fire, roasting. They were naked but they'd attempted to dress themselves in what appeared to be little strips of red silk. We later found this to be jam, and awfully sticky. Miss Barnes looked toward them. 'I'm about to bathe them,' said Mrs Bagbourne.

Another child of about four years was putting a puzzle together on the floor. We could hear others in the back garden breaking something up with great enthusiasm. Miss Barnes stood up and walked over to the blazing coals and, as discreetly as she could, placed the fireguard, which was flying grey underwear on all its masts, in front of the fire.

'Now you're sure you can take another two? I'm sorry it's such short notice,' said Miss Barnes. We watched the little feather continue to flutter after she had finished speaking. It was like a little exotic bird which had been snared in paradise and now found itself in a badly run pet shop in south London.

Mrs Bagbourne eyed us up and down and repeated her amazement at our identical appearance. 'Well, they are only short stay, aren't they, duck?' she said. We wondered why Mrs Bagbourne continually referred to Miss Barnes as a duck. Perhaps it was something to do with the feather.

'Well . . .' said Miss Barnes, leaving a long pause in response to whether we were short stay or not, '. . . I'm sure their mother will soon be well.'

'Not if she's gone to the General, she won't,' said Mrs Bagbourne. Miss Barnes coughed loudly.

'What did she mean,' we wondered, ' "not if she's gone to the General"?' Who was this? What General? Was she being cryptic, did she really mean God? Rachel Purnell's cat had gone to be with God, but we found the fur, and one of its ears, in the road. 'When will we be going home?' we asked.

Miss Barnes turned to us and said. 'Why don't you both help little Jeremy with his puzzle?' We did as we were told. We squatted down next to little Jeremy on the smelly carpet. The puzzle was about pigs and cows. We could have done it in two minutes but Jeremy wouldn't give us any of the pieces. When I managed to get a piece that he was sitting on he bit me. We listened to the two women talking.

'About that business with Brian, how is he now?'

'Well he's very good, Miss Barnes, but he's still playing me up.'

'Mmm, well, did you try putting a biscuit under his pillow at night?'

'No, I didn't want to mark the sheets.'

'Well try it, it'll just let him know that you're his mother.'

We later discovered that Mrs Bagbourne's own son, Brian, had grown violently jealous of the fostered children. I don't think there could ever have been a more falsely grounded jealously. We listened to all we could about Brian, dreading that he would attack us, but Brian was a quiet boy who stayed out in the garden most of the time. At night we could hear him singing in bed, he had the most beautiful voice and sang in the church choir.

We got up from the puzzle and wandered a little round the room. It was very drab and smelled of babies and long-boiled vegetables. There were no ornaments or trinkets but instead there were piles of papers, magazines and envelopes. Mrs Bagbourne had never thrown anything away. There were even milk bottles. 'What sort of person,' whispered Tom to me, 'keeps milk bottles in the front room?' We shook our heads, we had really come down in the world now, and we knew it; we had been farmed out to an 'awful lot'. We may as well have gone straight to the Fanakerpans.

'Miss Barnes?' said Mrs Bagbourne.

'Yes, Mrs Bagbourne?' replied Miss Barnes.

'Umm . . . for twins, I do get paid as I would for two normal children, do I – they don't count as one?'

'Oh yes, it's the same rate,' said Miss Barnes and the little feather twitched uneasily as if they shouldn't be discussing the financial aspect of the enterprise in front of the actual children. We didn't realize that these people got paid to look after us, we thought they did it out of their love for children.

'And what about a clothes allowance for them?'

'Well I don't think that's necessary; they have brought their own things with them; I don't think they need anything, I don't know.' She leant down to us. 'Do you need any new clothes, school things, anything like that?' she asked.

'Yeah,' said Tom, 'we need snakebelts.'

'Snakebelts?' replied Miss Barnes, astonished.

'Yeah, everyone's got them,' said Tom. They were the cheapest belts on the market, a simple length of elastic secured at the waist by a clasp in the form of a snake. They were the best thing in the world for keeping up oversized hand-me-downs.

'I don't think you really need belts,' said Miss Barnes. Her feather sprang down level with her eyes and bobbed up and down as if to say, 'These children request the most peculiar things.' We didn't get our snakebelts, even though they would only have cost the ratepayer a few shillings and made us feel a great deal better.

'And their mother's in hospital is she . . . and there's no father around I suppose?' asked Mrs Bagbourne.

'No,' said Miss Barnes, again hesitating. She looked to see if we were listening, and whispered, 'No, there's no father.'

'About visiting this mother of theirs,' said Mrs Bagbourne. 'Am I expected to traipse over there with them?'

'Well, it would be nice if you took them on Sunday.'

'Yes,' said Mrs Bagbourne, blowing her trombone into a piece of toilet paper, 'I would, but I don't want to make the other children jealous.'

'It would be nice if you could.'

'Well, we'll see,' she said.

As Miss Barnes made to leave we moved close to her, hoping that she would say, 'Oh, stuff this, kids, I ain't leaving you here in this mess.' But she didn't, she simply looked back into the room as if she were thinking, 'I don't like this but what can I do? We simply can't get the homes for all these children.'

There was a divorce boom on Prospect with which our misfortune happened to coincide. The Welfare wasn't really ready for it. As Miss Barnes drove off in her car her little feather looked down at her and said, 'You think that if you take slum families out of London and put them in nice new houses the divorce rate will drop. On the contrary, Miss Barnes, the reverse is true, the reverse is true.' Miss Barnes was forced to agree with her feather.

The real horrors of our new home began as soon as Miss Barnes had gone.

'Right,' said Mrs Bagbourne, in a voice much shriller than she'd employed before, 'we'd better get you two sorted out. Follow me upstairs and we'll see about your bedding.'

We followed. The stairs were cluttered with all manner of debris, beaten-up books and lengths of material. We could barely see because, again, there was no bulb in the socket which hung, shadeless, from a filthy dark ceiling. The stair carpet was loose because the rails had come away and I fell. Mrs Bagbourne didn't even turn to see if I was all right. Tom helped me up. The wallpaper was torn at two levels, one where she had brushed against it with her enormous bulk as she went up and again at the level of the younger children. She pushed the door to our room open with difficulty because a great heap of things was leaning against it. There were two cots and a narrow bed with dirty green blankets. There was a terrible smell. She saw us turn our noses up.

'Bit of a hum in here, is there?' she asked.

'Yes,' I said, 'there is a bit.'

'There is a lot,' said Tom.

Mrs Bagbourne looked around, blew her trombone into more toilet paper and said, 'I'm going to have to see the doctor about my sinuses. I bet Jeremy's been in here and pissed again.'

Tom and I looked at each other, embarrassed – 'Fancy using language like that in front of children,' we thought.

'Right,' said Mrs Bagbourne, her business with her nose completed, 'the pair of you can start clearing the things off the bed.'

'Whose bed is this, then?' asked Tom.

'Yours,' she said, 'one of you at one end and one at the other.'

'Can't we have our own beds?' said Tom. 'We're nine.'

'Oh yes, certainly, and where's my Brian going to sleep, in the garden? I was fifteen before I had my own bed. You mustn't make any noise at night because Jeremy's in that cot and the two babies are in the other. Don't you forget that I know about children, I know all your tricks.' She went back downstairs and left us to tidy up the room.

'I don't like it,' said Tom.

'Neither do I,' I said, 'it's horrible.'

'Is she going to change these sheets? Look, they're wet.'

We stayed up there, in the dust and the stench, for an hour before going down again when she called tea.

All the other kids came in from the garden, about six in all, not including Brian, Jeremy and the jam babies. Brian and Mrs Bagbourne had their tea in the kitchen. The rest of us had Marmite sandwiches in the front room watching *Looney Tunes* on the television. We didn't eat ours because, as Tom said, 'It looks like she's spread the bread with shit,' which we thought it was. After tea all the others tore back out into the mud and twisted metal that was her back garden. None of them had spoken to us and they were all younger so we stayed in the house.

We heard the front door, which was always on the latch, open wide and a man walked in, muttering. This was Mr Bagbourne. It was a shock; we had had no idea that there was a Mr Bagbourne. He was as large as his wife, the width of his trousers alone amazed us without the rest of him, which loomed large over Tom and me as he swayed in the doorway. His arrival seemed to surprise

Mrs Bagbourne as well because she stood up abruptly from her place in front of the television and said, 'What the bleeding bloody hell are you doing here?'

Mr Bagbourne did not reply but swung his legs, one after the other, until he reached the settee where he lay down. He coughed deep down in his chest and raised his head a little to say, 'I'm not a well man. Any cider in the house?'

We stood, mesmerized, as his arm reached out, flapping about in the air for something. He grabbed Tom's arm and held it tight. Tom was petrified.

'Brian,' he said, in a sorrowful way, 'go down to the shop and get me a couple of bottles of cider.'

'That's not Brian,' I said.

'For goodness sake, Alf,' said Mrs Bagbourne. Mr Bagbourne looked up at me, opening his eyes one at a time as if they were stuck with glue, and then he looked at the boy whose arm he had and let go of it as if it had suddenly got hot.

'Coo blimey,' he said, in disbelief, 'there's two of them!' Mrs Bagbourne blew her nose. 'You'd better make it four bottles of cider!' he bellowed. Tom rushed away from him to the other side of the room. 'What's the matter with you?' he shouted at Tom, sucking in the saliva that had caught in his whiskers, 'and you?' he shouted at me. 'Running away from your own father?'

'You're not their father,' said Mrs Bagbourne.

'No, you're not,' I said, squeezing the words out in terror.

Mr Bagbourne looked dumbfounded and he shuffled his elbows under his ribs to lift himself up from the couch. He stared between us, blinking heavily, then he turned to his erstwhile wife and shouted, 'Not mine? NOT MINE?' Mrs Bagbourne tried to speak but his arm was already up in the air in a declamatory fashion. 'Not bloody mine? Then whose? Whose?'

'You've pickled your brains,' said Mrs Bagbourne.

Little Jeremy stood up from his puzzle to watch and came into the old drunk's focus. 'And what's this one?' said Mr Bagbourne.

'Just go, just bloody get up and go,' she said.

The other kids came in from the garden to see what all the noise was about, all the kids, that is, except for Brian, who knew better. They filed in and stood around the room like the dumb animals at the Nativity. Bagbourne surveyed them in astonishment. His vision was limited: there was so much clutter and so many children in the room, and so much cider pickling his brains, that he had to take the scene by instalments, uttering gasps of disbelief at every juncture. Finally his eyes lighted on a small black boy who approached him. He shook his head and turned away to see another child standing behind him.

'I've only been away six months,' he said, and with this he shut his eyes firmly, refusing to see any more.

'Open your eyes,' screamed Mrs Bagbourne.

'No,' he said, in a deep voice which gurgled in the phlegm of his chest.

Mrs Bagbourne knew that this shutting of his eyes would result in unconsciousness, and it did. She pulled at his jacket and he wobbled slightly, but it had no effect.

'Help me to pull him off the settee,' she said. We began to pull at him and the younger kids joined in, tugging at his fat fingers and his hair, like the Lilliputians moving Gulliver. Suddenly he rolled off the settee and crashed to the floor, still unconscious, while we scuttled backwards to avoid being crushed.

'Well, we've got him off the settee,' said Tom, 'now he's on the floor.'

'I can see that, Little Lord Fauntleroy,' said Mrs Bagbourne.

'Well, how are we supposed to get him out of the door?' asked Tom.

Mr Bagbourne began to snore. It seemed to involve his whole body, the great heaving sound beginning in his feet and rippling and wrenching its way up the length of his body until it erupted, lava-like, from his open mouth.

'He's sleeping like a baby,' said Mrs Bagbourne. A wet patch appeared on his trousers. She turned to the Lilliputians and sent them back into the garden. 'Why don't you go and play in the street?' she said to us. We went and sat on the kerb. As we went out of the front door we saw Brian sitting on the stairs with his head in his hands quietly singing a hymn.

We sat on the kerb for a while, picking up lolly sticks and dropping them down the drain. We watched a line of ants come across a lump of bright pink bubble gum; they couldn't decide whether to walk round it or drag it back to their hole; we watched as some of them got stuck to it and had to be pulled off by others who invariably got stuck themselves. Normally we would have stamped on them but on this occasion we felt sorry for them. We saw Mrs Bagbourne come out of the house with a shopping bag; we got ready to catch it but she simply said, 'I'm going down the offy, don't get dirty, ducks.' Where were we going to find dirty ducks?

We went back into the awful house by the back door. Mr Bagbourne had stopped snoring and lay, with his eyes closed and quivering, in the middle of the room on the circle of carpet that had been worn down to the glue by the constant dramas. We crept past him, watching his eyeballs moving under the lids with great fear and fascination. His eyes opened. We were fixed to the spot. 'Oh! oh!' he shouted, as if frightened himself, 'who is it?'

'It's Richard and Tom,' I said. 'We've been out in the street.'

He looked at us quizzically; he could remember parts of what had gone before but not enough to be able to piece it all together from his position on the floor. He lifted his head; it looked like an awfully heavy thing to have to keep lifting. He was embarrassed by our finding him in the middle of the room, on the floor. 'I must have blacked out,' he said, pathetically, 'while changing the light bulb. Hot sweet tea, that's what I need – put the kettle on.' We didn't move. Mr Bagbourne continued, 'Mrs Bagbourne, my wife, has taken you in has she?'

'Yes,' I said.

'She's a good woman like that, all heart. I go away for a bit, I come back and she's taken in half the bloody estate. Where's your own mother?'

'She's ill in hospital,' we said.

Mr Bagbourne heaved yet more of his weight into the air so that he was almost sitting. There was a look of deep sympathy on his face and he stared sorrowfully at us. 'She's ill?' he asked.

'Yes.'

Mr Bagbourne rubbed his hand on the carpet for comfort. 'Oh that's terrible,' he said, almost singing it. 'How long's she been in?'

'All day,' said Tom. Mr Bagbourne removed his hand from the carpet and covered his eyes with it. We stood in our most waif-like, abandoned, miserable stance, fishing for his sympathy.

'And how old are you?' he asked, still with his hand over his eyes to express sorrow.

'Nine,' we said, pitifully, hanging on to the word for as long as we could.

'Nine years old and all this trouble,' he said, looking at

us again and gently smiling. 'What about your dad, can't he look after you?'

'No,' I said, 'he ran off. He doesn't care about us.'

Mr Bagbourne adjusted the whole of his body on receipt of this news. He raised his thick arm and banged it down on the threadbare carpet in disgust. His cheeks grew red with indignation. 'Run off?' he said. 'Your mother's ill in hospital, you're only nine, and he runs off, just like that, and he leaves you. He leaves two little boys with no one in the world, no one to wipe their noses . . .' and with this he wiped his own nose, 'no one to take them to the seaside,' and then he stretched out his own hand towards us and thumped it down on each of our heads in turn, 'you poor bloody little mites, bless your cotton socks. I've never heard anything like it. I don't know what this world is coming to, do you, eh?'

'No,' said Tom, 'we don't know.'

Mr Bagbourne fell back, like a dead weight, on the carpet, shutting his eyes. Within an instant he sprang up again. 'Tell me what's getting better? You can't, it's getting worse!' he said.

'Much worse,' I said.

'It has, it has,' he shouted, agreeing with me. 'You want to join the RAF, they'd look after you,' he said.

'We're too young,' said Tom. In receipt of this Mr Bagbourne shook his head violently from side to side and gave himself a sudden and terrific headache. We presumed that it was his brains swilling around in the pickling vinegar which caused him to howl out. The howl rose and fell for a few moments and then it slid back into recognizable words. 'Your mother's ill . . . father's run off, and the RAF won't have you.' He shook his head again and it produced the same effect. He seemed to be using the pain to express his great distress at our plight.

'We've been at the Welfare all afternoon,' we said.

'Horrible was it?' said Bagbourne as if he knew from experience.

'Worse,' we said. 'And now we've ended up here, and one of the kids has pissed in our bed.'

'Life,' said Mr Bagbourne, thumping us each on the head again, 'isn't all beer and kittens.'

We agreed.

'And your poor mother's on her last legs, and now you've got my wife, Mrs Bagbourne, to contend with.' Mr Bagbourne began to cry. 'Just looking at you standing there so miserable makes me want to weep,' he said, weeping. We began to get uneasy. 'Bloody governors,' he said and grabbed us suddenly in his arms and sobbed. We were worried that we'd get wet, if not by the tears then by the pee. He squashed us against himself. 'I don't know what I'm going to do,' he said. 'I just don't know where I'm going to turn,' and he buried his head in my chest. At length his head flew up again, he sniffed back his tears, and sucked some more out of his whiskers and said, quite brightly, 'I know what you could do with, hot sweet tea. Go and put the kettle on, kids, and we'll see what we can do to cheer you up.'

When we came back in from the kitchen he was asleep on the settee, deep in a nightmare which made him snuffle and snort and whine. We went over to the television and changed the channel to the BBC. *Blue Peter* came on, which cheered us up.

CHAPTER XX

In which we go to school and struggle with our tables in the shortest chapter of the book

Miss Graterex was already calling the register and collecting the week's dinner money when we walked late into her classroom. It was the first Monday after we had been moved to Mrs Bagbourne's. She and her husband had been snoring soundly when we woke and left the house breakfastless and unsure of which way to walk to school. We had walked along the same streets several times, rather like our parents had done when they first came to Prospect. As we entered the classroom all the faces turned towards us. They regarded us with suspicion.

'Why are you late?' asked Miss Graterex.

'We came the long way round,' said Tom.

'Well, now you can take the short way round to your desks and sit down,' said Miss Graterex, angrily.

We went to our desks. Our teacher proceeded steadily through the alphabet and eventually came to our names. She invited us to approach the desk with our dinner money. We did not move.

'What have you done with it?' she asked, 'spent it on the way?'

We didn't know what to say so Tom said, 'Yes.'

Miss Graterex now looked very angry indeed, and every eye was on us. 'Stand on your chairs and put your hands on your heads,' said Miss Graterex. This was the most severe punishment that Miss Graterex meted out, save standing outside the headmaster's door. Generally

she used it at the end of the day when the class had been
unruly and she could bear no more. Never had this, the
most severe of penalties, been prescribed so early in the
day. The class silently gasped. We stood on our chairs.
Barry Foster fixed his eyes on the clock. For most pupils
about two minutes elapsed before they began to cry and
Miss Graterex called them down again. Barry was a tough
customer and held the record of four minutes. We were
determined not to cry. We had been on the chairs for
four minutes when the class assembly turned to prayers,
and although most were peeping through their fingers at
us, we stood resolute. After the Lord's Prayer Miss
Graterex called us down. We returned to our seats in
triumph. Miss Graterex sat opening the letters on her
desk, while we copied down the date and the spelling list
for the day from the blackboard.

> apple
> bed
> cat
> donkey
> egg
> fish

Miss Graterex came across a note from the headmaster
informing her of what had happened to us.

> goat
> house
> ice
> jelly
> knot
> lasciviously

'Tom, Richard,' said Miss Graterex, 'why didn't you
say you were on free school dinners?' and she smiled at

us apologetically. 'Will you come up to the front please?'
We walked up to her desk. 'You should have told me
that your mummy was ill. I'm so sorry I made you stand
on the chairs . . .' and she patted our heads '. . . you silly
boys, I didn't know . . .'

We wished she'd not found out. We were much happier
letting the class think we had stolen the dinner money. It
was the likes of Kacky Fanakerpan who had free school
dinners and received with resignation the special book of
orange tickets, enough to last a term. Any self-respecting
mother, as our own was, finding that she was too short of
cash to pay, would send a note to say that her child was
going home to dinner. Anything rather than put the child
through the indignity of Welfare. We hung our heads in
shame. Barry Foster sniggered and Charlie turned away
embarrassed. Miss Graterex compounded the situation
by making a speech to the class about how everyone
ought to be nice to us while our mother was in hospital
and how things weren't going to be easy for us. It was ten
times harder not to cry from shame at this point than it
was on the chairs. We returned to our seats, our minds in
a flurry.

> One nine was nine
> two nines were nine
> three nines were ninety-nine
> four nines were nine nine nine.

Also we were nine.

CHAPTER XXI

In which we are branded delinquents by the Bagbournes and are betrayed into the hands of the state

The second Saturday of our residence at the Bagbournes' dawned. Mrs Bagbourne was thrashing at the sheets and her voluminous undergarments in the bath. The hooks and the press-studs scratched against the enamel of the bath like lobsters dropped into a boiling pot. We picked up our white shirts, which were dirty brown at the collars and cuffs, from the chair at the end of our bed and carried them to the bathroom. 'Please, Mrs Bagbourne,' we asked, 'it's Sunday tomorrow, can we wash our shirts?'

'Don't tell me you go to Sunday School?' she said.

'No,' we said, 'but Miss Barnes said we could visit Mum at the hospital on Sundays.'

Mrs Bagbourne threw her corsets in the tub and turned around. 'Miss Barnes says?' she said. 'Then Miss Barnes ought to take you.'

'But we didn't see her last Sunday and Miss Barnes said we were to visit on Sundays because that's when they let children in.'

'Do you know how much it is on the bus?' said Mrs Bagbourne.

'No,' we said.

'Do you think I'm rolling in it – it's ninepence.'

'Mum's got ninepence,' said Tom, 'she'll give it to you when we get there. She'd give you more than ninepence, probably.'

Mrs Bagbourne retrieved her corsets and began removing their bones and piling them up on the soap-rack, making it look like an elephants' graveyard.

'If we had some powder we could do our shirts in the basin,' I said.

'Oh all right,' said Mrs Bagbourne, 'give them here, they can go in with the rest, and if they don't come up clean I'll boil them in the Burco.' We surrendered our shirts to her.

'And can we go to the hospital tomorrow?'

'Yes, all right,' she said, 'but I don't want no scenes when it's time to come back.'

We agreed not to make any scenes.

'Haven't you got any little friends you can play with and get out from running under my feet all the time?'

'Yes,' we said, but we had not. Charlie and Barry had disassociated themselves from us, partly through embarrassment and partly through fear that our condition might be catching. We spent the Saturday wishing the hours away until the next day.

We talked to Mr Bagbourne in the afternoon when he came back from the pub. He was always chatty for about half an hour before he fell asleep in front of the wrestling.

'Mrs Bagbourne's taking us to the hospital,' we told him, happily.

'Mrs Bagbourne's taking you to the hospital?' he repeated in his astonished bellowing voice.

'Yes.'

'Poor bloody mites, bless your cotton socks,' he said, thumping his fist down on the little black boy's head. 'Your mother's in hospital and now you've got to go in as well. I thought you was looking peaky. I said to Mrs Bagbourne you was sickening for something. I said to her you was ever since you had that bout of hiccups between you. It's always the first sign.' He shook his head and, as an expression of the frailness and uncertainty of the human frame, he gave out a long, low, belch, and then repeated it shortly after, there being two of us.

'We haven't had hiccups,' said Tom.

'You haven't?' said Mr Bagbourne.

'No,' we said.

'What, not never?'

'No,' we said.

He shook his head in ever greater disbelief.

'No wonder you've come down with something then, it's all been building up. It's gases. They build up in the guts from Mrs Bagbourne's cooking, and then wallop, it hits you like a truck. You want to learn to belch. It's the finest thing for your health. That's how I've got by all these years.'

'Mum tells us off if we burp,' said Tom.

'Tells you off?' said Mr Bagbourne, outraged. 'You're down on your luck, no home to go to, your mother's in hospital and all she can do is tell you off for having a belch? There's no justice is there?' We agreed that there was no justice.

'We're not supposed to burp at school either,' I told Mr Bagbourne. I knew it would surprise him, and it did.

'They expect you to learn?' he said. 'How can they expect to cram your head full of facts when your belly's full of gases?' We agreed; perhaps this was why we weren't doing well with our lessons lately.

'Here,' said Mr Bagbourne, 'have a mouthful of cider and I'll teach you to belch.'

We didn't like the idea of drinking out of his bottle but we took a swig each, working on the principle that if we caught anything from the bottle it would be cured by the belch that followed.

Mr Bagbourne taught us to belch. Tom was better at it than I was, he could get a rise and fall to it and emit three in a row as Bagbourne commanded him. Mine took a long time to come and when it came there was very little gas in it, I felt. It was agreed then, with Mr Bagbourne, that if he could not make it to the hospital himself to teach our sick mother to belch then Tom was now ably equipped to teach her in his stead.

Sunday morning came with Jeremy howling and throwing things around the bedroom and with the jam babies in rebellion with their sodden sheets. Mrs Bagbourne had put a roof over their cot, made from an old banister rail, and they had made themselves even more secure by tangling up their pale, sticky limbs in the sheets. Mr Bagbourne still lay semi-conscious on the settee with the little black boy sharing, where he had collapsed after the exertions of the belching lesson. Brian, his chorister son, still remained scarce. All we knew of him were the words of the Twenty-third Psalm which he sang in his bed at night. He would sing it through several times and then suddenly it would stop, and he'd be asleep.

We went and got our white shirts from the line; the collars and cuffs were still damp, but we put them on so that we would be ready to depart for the hospital at any moment. We looked among the piles of debris for some paper and set about making get well cards for our mother, colouring them in with crayons. Mine showed the ambulance that she went off in and included a little scene detailing the ambulanceman's nosebleed. Tom's showed a patient having his leg sawn off while biting a bullet. We knew that our mother would be thrilled with them.

At three o'clock a Shirley Temple movie came on the television which entirely absorbed Mrs Bagbourne and no one was allowed to speak. She loved films with children in them. Immediately it was over and Mrs Bagbourne had finished wiping her eyes with toilet paper we asked, 'When are we going to the hospital?'

'Well, we can't go yet can we? Not until Mr Bagbourne is back from the boozer to keep an eye on the others.' It was miraculous that however difficult it was to wake Mr Bagbourne, his eyes always opened sharply at five minutes to opening time. Bagbourne himself commented on it, praising Mother Nature for his internal clock. Why we had to wait for him to return we did not know; he was unable to do anything but piss on the floor and pass out. We were the only ones who enjoyed his company and we would be at the hospital. We tried to take our minds off the non-return of Mr Bagbourne and our diminishing chances of seeing our mother by strapping Mrs Bagbourne's enormous brassières to our heads and playing a game of Vikings. Finally we returned to our room and watched the blowfly bashing itself against the pane. We didn't come down for tea and Mrs Bagbourne wasn't worried to come and get us in case we went on about the hospital.

So the days went on and weekends followed the same pattern of promises on the Saturday and disappointments on the Sunday. Brian began to lose his resentment of us as he saw that we kept out of his mother's way and made few demands on her love and affection. One Friday night when he came home after choir practice he spoke to us. We were astonished. 'Can you two sing?' he asked.

'No,' we said, wisely.

'I'm singing a solo in the Passion,' he said. In his hand he held his anthem, a flimsy sheet, worn at the edges, which had been handed down from chorister to chorister ever since the church had been built in 1960. He was evidently proud of it for he held it like a telegram in front

of him. We imagined what it must be like to sing in a
Passion. It must be very noisy, and rather like Frank
Ifield when he yodelled. We weren't sure he was ideally
suited for it; his singing in the night was so soft and
sombre: one little tuneful voice entirely out of place in its
surroundings. Neither of his parents showed any interest
in his singing at all. The music teacher from the school
had arranged for him to join the choir to get him away
from his parents. It was odd that on the one hand people
were trying to get Brian out of his home situation, while
other people were sending us to it. Miss Barnes and her
feather were constrained by circumstance.

Brian was not an angelic-looking boy rather he was
big-boned with the stature and the bearing of an appren-
tice. His voice, when he sang, was an unlikely product of
his lungs; wheezing and whooping would have been the
more likely outcome. It was entirely different from his
speaking voice. It was as if someone had kicked a bucket
and produced the clear sound of a bell. We longed to
have his gift.

'Do you know any anthems or psalms?' he asked. We
thought for a moment.

'We know the "Hippy Hippy Shake",' we said.

Brian stopped talking to us and walked over to the
table where he laid his sheet of music down in a space
that he had cleared for it. He sat beside it at the table for
the rest of the evening while the television blared and
Mrs Bagbourne yelled in her manly voice at Jeremy and
ourselves. She seemed to dislike the jam babies as much
as us, most likely because like us they were trouble.
Sometimes their cage would get pushed too near the fire
and she would have to spend half an hour rubbing
germoline ointment on their blotchy bodies while they
wriggled and screamed. They were a great inconvenience.

At eight o'clock Brian complained of a headache and took himself to bed and sang his anthem through from memory. We could just hear snatches of it in the short gaps between the advertisements. We looked at the sheet of music lying on the table and tried to comprehend the tangle of signs. It fascinated us, like someone speaking a foreign language.

A few days later, when we were sitting out in the street, we heard screams coming from the house. We thought perhaps Mrs Bagbourne had finally roasted the jam babies and so we ran into the house.

It wasn't the jam babies, they were lying at the bottom of their cage. Brian was in a rage and was hurling the papers, the boxes, the milk bottles – the general detritus of the front room, against the walls and at his mother. Brian's anthem had been lost. By the grate we could see a couple of little crotchets and a few minims lying in some ash. In the gloom of the poorly lit room she had mistaken it for the *Daily Sketch* and had lit the fire with it. Brian was in a frenzy. How could he explain to the choirmaster that he had lost what he imagined to be so precious an object, as if he had allowed the music itself to be destroyed while it was in his charge. His rage surpassed even Mr Bagbourne's rages and the paddies of the jam babies. Brian ran out of the front door, fell on the kerb, cut his knees, but stood up and ran on again, until he was out of sight.

'Well how am I supposed to know what's his music and what's the newspaper?' said Mrs Bagbourne. 'Anyway, I'm sure I didn't do it. Have you two been lighting fires again? I wouldn't be surprised if it was you, you've got no respect for my Brian's things.'

Brian returned but he was moody for several days. On

the Friday night of his next choir practice Mrs Bagbourne said, 'Aren't you going up the church?'

'No,' he said, 'we haven't got a practice tonight.'

Saturday between eleven and three-thirty generally saw the house briefly reprieved of the presence of the Bagbournes. The younger children were in the garden, we were in the kitchen. Brian came in. 'Do you want to see something?' he asked.

'Yes,' we said. Brian went over to the oven and pulled down its door. Inside an assortment of long-forgotten baking trays and prehistoric baked potatoes were welded to the side with grime. It had a lining which would have been more appropriate to a stomach than an oven; and then a very ancient stomach of a creature which thrived in the sewers. It was a gruesome cavern unused to light. Mrs Bagbourne was not given to baking things, she lacked Mr Bagbourne's internal clock, and there was no timer on the oven either. What we ate was either from a tin or was fried out of a packet. There was no doubt that by the time a piece of meat or quantity of boiled mince reached the table no amount of forensic research could establish the species of animal from which it had been taken. Her culinary skills were founded on a basic mistrust of the slaughterhouse and the butcher. Each cut she re-slaughtered and re-butchered. Food-poisoning was entirely out of the question unless it came from the water or the fat. The high likelihood of the latter was the only interest which our food retained.

We gathered together with Brian to gaze into the oven. Brian reached up to the controls and we listened to the hiss of the gas as it blew the grease out of the jets. 'Can you smell it?' he asked.

'Yes,' we said. It was an acrid smell that, although unignited, burned our throats and nostrils.

'We have to put our heads inside and breathe in as much as we can,' he said. It was a pathetically popular way to do oneself in, as long as the shilling didn't run out. We were well aware of the consequences, but we went along with it, pleased in part that Brian had included us and at the same time not really believing that we should die. We were inquisitive, just as we had been when our teacher had warned us about inhaling solvents and we had hunted high and low in her stockroom for glue to see if she was right.

It was not a simple business, breathing in the gas. First no results were immediately apparent and second it was very difficult for all three of us to get our heads in the oven at the same time. At one point Tom and I forced Brian out and he complained. 'It's my turn now, you've had enough,' he said, 'it's my shilling pocket money.' We wished we had not spent our shilling pocket money on sweets and lucky bags. He put his face back into the oven to breathe in more.

When Mrs Bagbourne returned Tom and I had tired of gassing ourselves. We were helping Brian by holding his head inside the oven, under his own direction. Mrs Bagbourne pulled us both away, pinching our arms and pushing us to the floor. She dragged Brian out into the garden.

'Brian's n'arf going to cop it now,' said Tom.

'I know,' I said. But Brian didn't cop it, he was cradled in his mother's arms for the first time in years while she sobbed and slapped him. She returned from the garden, slapped us as well and pushed us up the stairs and barricaded us in our room with a chair against the door. She went to the telephone box to call Miss Barnes.

It was a fortunate turn of events for us we thought. As soon as we told Miss Barnes how we'd not been to see our mother she would no doubt feel pity for us and take us straight away to the hospital in her tortoiseshell Imp. Miss Barnes arrived, the feather in her hat fluttering and a moleskin jacket rising in two high, padded, mounds on her shoulders. We were sitting by the gate, behind the jam babies' cage.

'Oh, I'm so pleased you're here, Miss Barnes,' said Mrs Bagbourne in a voice that used more breath than speech and gave the impression that she had just suffered a terrible shock.

'So what has happened?' asked Miss Barnes.

'Well, I'll start at the top,' said Mrs Bagbourne, 'because I don't want to leave anything out. I want you to get the full picture of what's been going on here since you brought these two. I hope you don't mind me being frank but that's the way I am. I call a spade a spade.' Having established this, Mrs Bagbourne laid her first spade on the table: 'Well, first, I catch the two of them stealing the washing from the line and parading up and down the street in my brassières.'

Miss Barnes looked over to where we sat. We couldn't deny it.

'Now I said to you when you first arrived, Miss Barnes, that it would all depend on Brian. It's not fair to him, my having to give so much attention to these two when I'm his mother, and I said to you, didn't I, that if they upset him they'd have to go? Well they've done nothing but be full of spite and nastiness all along the line. First they throw his song what he has to sing up the church on the fire, and now he won't show his face at the practice for fear of what the vicar will say, and then they eat the biscuit that you, yourself, told me to put under his pillow.'

It was true, we had taken the biscuit, but Brian never ate them and we had given it to one of the jam babies to stop it crying all night. Miss Barnes shook her head at us disapprovingly. Mrs Bagbourne continued: 'And now this, this really takes the biscuit . . .' She shook her head as well and beat her chest, and blew into her toilet paper.

'Now they've done what?' asked Miss Barnes.

'They've tried to gas him in the oven.'

'Surely not!' said Miss Barnes, taken aback.

'Surely they have,' said Mrs Bagbourne. 'I came in and caught them not half an hour ago, both holding his head in the oven, and him trying to get free, but what could he do against two of them all filled up with spite? Smell – you can still smell the gas in the room even though I've opened all the windows. I've had to lay Brian on his bed, he turned blue.' Miss Barnes sniffed the air and nodded. Smelling the gas for herself confirmed that what Mrs Bagbourne had said was true. In the silence created by their sniffing Miss Barnes heard the soft, pathetic voice of Brian, lying on his bed upstairs, singing the Twenty-third Psalm. She looked at us with cold, penetrating eyes. We had seemed such timid, sweet children when she had first taken us to her office. Had we turned vicious out of jealousy, or was this just what she should have expected from estate children all along?'

'They're difficult children with a vicious streak and I'm sorry but I won't have them under my roof.'

'I can see,' said Miss Barnes, trying to understate the situation for the sake of simplicity, 'that it's not working out.' At this point Mr Bagbourne returned, and greeted Miss Barnes heartily. Mrs Bagbourne told him the whole story, and we sat through it all again, with all three of them looking towards us as each of the crimes was described. At the conclusion Miss Barnes announced her intention of taking us away there and then. Mr Bagbourne applauded her.

'After all I've tried to do for these kids,' he said, 'it makes you want to spit. Doesn't it make you want to spit, Miss Barnes?' Miss Barnes nodded briefly, unsure of whether this was her exact desire. '. . . to go back to your office and spit,' reaffirmed Mr Bagbourne. 'Of course, I said to my good wife right from the beginning that this was how it was all to end up. But you, you're too good-natured, it's a crying shame. I knew right from the first time I clapped eyes on them what kind of sort they were. I've tried to be a father to them. I came back as soon as I heard my wife had taken in twins because I thought "well, if anything needs a father it's twins", if not two. What do they do? They spit in your face!' As Mr Bagbourne said this he spat in Miss Barnes's face fully to emphasize the point. 'And my own son,' he continued, 'the blood of my own loins, lying up there at death's door, his face all blue, his little legs shaking, his little heart barely pattering. Two minutes longer with his head in and he'd have been a stiff. What is it? I ask you, Miss Barnes, what is it?' Miss Barnes didn't know, so Bagbourne told her: 'It's nearly a tragedy. He's not a well boy in any case and I wouldn't be surprised if this wasn't the last straw. The least he'll have is brain damage, gas ain't the best thing for you. I bet he's dead by the end of the week. I'd lay money on it, mark my words, I bet he's dead by the end of the week. It makes me want to spit.' With this he stamped his foot, slapped his hand against the table and belched again, but fortunately for Miss Barnes, who was shielding her face with her hands, he didn't spit. 'You've tried your best, Miss Barnes,' he said and laid his hand reassuringly on her shoulder. 'You mustn't blame yourself. You went round there when their mother was ill straight away, like a shot, didn't you?'

'Yes,' she said feebly, gradually sinking lower as Bag-bourne emphasized his points by banging her on the shoulder as if she were a tent peg.

'You went round there and you rescued them out of the goodness of your heart. How long have you been helping children may I ask?'

Miss Barnes was sinking lower under the weight of his arm, and she was very embarrassed. 'Well,' she said, 'I suppose six months.'

'Six months!' said Mr Bagbourne in astonishment. 'Six months!' he repeated to his wife as if she had not heard it. 'That's more than what you'd get for murder these days. It's a calling. Can I ask you, Miss Barnes, do you consider it a calling?'

'I suppose it is.'

'And so you heard God's voice one day, calling, and you said "yes Lord", and you've served for six months, rescuing poor little mites who haven't got no other bugger to turn to. You deserve a medal. You went round there, rescued these kids and what happens? They spit in your face. It's a disgrace. Why isn't something done about it, that's what I want to know, when they spit in your face.' Although Miss Barnes was prepared for the spray of saliva that Bagbourne produced whenever he said the word spit, she had sunk so low as a result of his tent-peg banging that it missed her face this time and caught in the feather of her hat. The feather bowed low and dripped. 'And now you've got to take them back, and you do it willingly, you're a saint!' he said. 'Women like you ought to have monuments when you're dead, if not special words on your headstone. When I look at the world and I see all the good that's done, all the medicine and the welfare, I despair, don't you, Miss Barnes?'

'I do,' she said, and from her crouching position she

began to slip out from under his arms and to move toward us, gradually straightening herself up.

As she led us out to the car, with a tight grip on our shoulders, Bagbourne stood on the step shaking his head and beating his hand on the door. 'She came and rescued you out of the goodness of her heart like Florence Nightshade,' he called after us, 'she should have a medal, but what does she get? You tell me that! It's disgraceful!'

So the car pulled away and we left the house of the Bagbournes quietly and in disgrace.

CHAPTER XXII

In which we arrive at Crab Apple Road, a meal is eaten and a sausage is lost, and in which, as in other chapters, it rains

There were children's homes on the estate, built at the ends of the longer roads. They were made to the same design as the ordinary houses but they were bigger and because of this they looked rather strange. They were more like the model homes, the small artisans' dwellings, which were built in the nineteenth century under the patronage of Albert, the prince consort.

It was as if they had an invisible inscription, carved in roman lettering around the eaves:

ERECTED THROVGH PVBLIC SVBSCRIPTION IN THE FIFTH YEAR OF THE
REIGN OF ELIZABETH II FOR THE RELIEF OF WAIFS

Their front gardens were larger than those of the other houses so that they were set farther back from the road.

Whether the planners had built them knowing that the Prospectors would die or divorce, or whether they had moved out whole communities of children along with the slum clearances, I don't know; I suspect the latter.

Ordinary children crossed the street when they passed such places; it was bad luck to step on a cracked paving slab outside one. The inmates were not to be fraternized with. One of the homes, The Crab Apple Road Home, was infamous, it was reserved for especially difficult children, known to us as 'linquents. When Miss Barnes's car stopped outside The Crab Apple Road Home we hoped that she was just making a visit there along the way. When she pulled the front seat forward, to allow us to get out, we held firmly to the leather upholstery of the back seat. Miss Barnes explained to us how she was perfectly happy to stand there all day, and that, since we could not drive and had nowhere to drive to, it would make the whole thing a great deal easier if we just quietly followed her. Still we clung on to the leather seat. Miss Barnes explained how in time we would get hungry, sitting there, and then we would starve, and since she had eaten a great more in her lifetime than we had then we would die before she did and she would simply go and get a sandwich. And that would be that. This made no impression on us either and we began to look out of the window. She took a deep breath, adjusted her hat and informed us that if we were not out of the car by the time she had counted five then she would go and get the uncle from the home to pull us out. Miss Barnes counted as far as six, and then as far as seven, before she accepted that we were not going to move, and before she faced the simple fact that if she went to get the uncle we would run off.

'If you come with me I'll let you have one blast each

on my hooter,' she said at last. Tom and I looked at one
another, and then at the bright red button at the centre
of the steering wheel. Tom pushed it first, and then I
pushed it and we followed Miss Barnes up the path,
running through the sheeting rain.

The houseparents, Mr and Mrs Wallis, were quite
young and well spoken. They showed Miss Barnes and us
into a small office just off the passageway.

'This is Richard and Thomas Stone,' said Miss Barnes.
'I have had to remove them from their foster parents. I'm
sorry to land this on you but I do feel that they would be
best suited here.'

'I see,' said Mr Wallis, understanding that some event
had taken place which had put us in the category of
disturbed children.

'You do have room?' asked Miss Barnes.

'Oh yes, we can put them in the end dorm with the
Wheelan boy, we're perfectly happy to take them. I
gather there's been some disturbance has there?'

'Yes,' said Miss Barnes, turning to us. 'Richard and
Tom here have a few things to learn about getting along
with other children.'

Mr Wallis looked at us and smiled. 'And why is that,
Richard and Tom?' he asked.

'We held somebody's head in the oven,' I said.

'The son of the foster parents – jealousy,' Miss Barnes
informed him. The faces of the Wallises grew serious.

'Do you want to talk about why you did this?' he
asked.

'No,' I said.

He turned to Miss Barnes. 'Will there be a special
Care Order issued?'

'I shall file a report and we'll take it from there, but in
the meantime if you could keep me posted on their

resettlement I'd be grateful. Their mother's in hospital, the father's no longer around and they haven't adjusted. They desperately need a normalizing environment.'

'Too right!' said Mr Wallis, nodding his head earnestly. Behind him, on the shelves, were lots of books. Mr Wallis turned to us again. 'Now, Richard and Thomas, I want you to understand a few things right from the beginning. We are just like a big family here with lots of brothers and sisters. We don't allow any jealousy or any fighting, we're all here to help each other along. Mrs Wallis and myself have helped many children like yourself, there's nothing you can try on that we don't know about . . .' With this he patted a book that lay on his desk and which was entitled *Rebuilding the Delinquent*. 'You are to think of Mrs Wallis and myself as your mummy and daddy while you are here, and I'm sure we'll get along just fine and any naughty things you've done in the past we'll just forget.'

We were nervous but reassured. They looked like nice people, but it was difficult to think of them as mummy and daddy when they sat on one side of a desk with us on the other and, in any case, at the conclusion of the interview we were instructed to refer to them as Uncle and Auntie.

Miss Barnes left and we were led into a large kitchen-cum-dining-room where all the other children, twelve in all, were sitting waiting for their evening meal. It seemed like a formal occasion, Christmas or a birthday, except that there was no festivity. There were only blank faces to greet us, and a few complaints about our having held up the meal, as Uncle introduced us to them.

As soon as the sausages and mash appeared on the table there was an explosion of noise like the roar at the track when the dogs are released from the traps. Terry, a

boy of about fourteen years old, purloined the ketchup
bottle and refused to give it up until Uncle took it from
him and commanded that it be passed around the table in
an anti-clockwise direction. We were unsure what he
meant, never having passed anything in this kind of way
before, and so we were nervous about what to do when
the bottle came to us. Dolores, a girl sitting two places
away from Terry, was told off next. She had attempted to
get all of the sauce out of the bottle and on to her plate.
Auntie ordered her to put it all back again with her knife.
Reluctantly she began putting it back in the bottle,
deliberately slopping most of it on the table. Her sausage
looked like a victim at the centre of a dreadful accident.
A collision with a pig, perhaps.

Uncle looked over at us and could see that we were
perturbed by it all. Appearances did not match up to the
description we had been given of everyone helping each
other along. Uncle flicked through the textbook chapters
in his mind and opened on a paragraph entitled 'humour-
coercion'. 'All right everyone, settle down, Auntie's food
isn't that good!' The delinquents laughed as Auntie play-
fully struck her husband on the nose. We smiled and
relaxed a little. Uncle spoke to me: 'What's that up there
on the ceiling, Richard?' I looked up at the ceiling. I
couldn't see anything up there. I looked at the lampshade,
it was yellow with black dots. I studied it for some time
but couldn't think of anything to say about it, so I looked
back to Uncle, who was still smiling. I expected him to
tell me what I should have noticed, and when he didn't I
looked down to my plate, embarrassed. *My sausage had
gone*. My face flushed, I'd been made a fool of while I
was looking at the lampshade. I felt awful. I wanted my
sausage. It had been a large pink one with a split at
each end where the sausagemeat was crispy. I had been

shovelling the mash into my mouth expressly because I was saving my sausage until last. Without the prize of the sausage at the end of it I wouldn't have eaten the mash. It wasn't as if I'd even been able to make it more palatable by the addition of ketchup. The boy sitting next to me had deliberately screwed the cap on so that I couldn't get it off. Food's an enemy and the table a torture to the young. I began to cry. I sobbed and shook so violently that as I gripped the table, all the knives and forks rattled.

'It's all right, it's all right,' said Uncle, 'I've got it, I've got your sausage.' At this I sobbed even louder. I would have expected it from one of the delinquents, but why had he taken my sausage? Why had he taken against me so soon? What had I done wrong? Why hadn't he picked on Tom instead? 'It's all right, it's here, see,' he said, and I looked up to see him reveal it, speared on the end of his fork, from under the table. This was not the sort of thing we would have done at home. Ellen regarded it a moral crime to play with food when it's paid for by the Welfare. He reached over to me and waved the sausage in front of my mouth for me to bite it, but I couldn't. In the end Tom had to eat it in my stead.

After tea we went with the other children into a large room marked with the word 'lounge' on the door. There were boardgames scattered everywhere, and dice and markers down the backs of all the chairs. None of the furniture matched, it was all from house clearances. We sat on a short settee for two in the bay of the window. We looked out at the pelting rain, which was somehow soothing. It reminded us of that best of days, the rainy Saturday, when all plans were cancelled and the family stoked up the fire and played games.

On the walls of the lounge there were pictures, some

of which had been scientifically crafted so that they were in three dimensions and winked when you walked past. There was one of Jesus, surrounded by sheep, which looked disturbingly like a photograph. There was one of a boy, sitting on a step, with trousers ragged at the knee and pearl-like tears rolling from his oversized eyes. At several other stations of the house, the hallway, the landing and the stairs, there were similar pictures. One showed a group of three, an elder sister clutching two little boys to her skirts; before them were the wheelmarks of a cart in the muddy road and, in the rut, a dead kitten, its eyes shut tight and one paw pointing peculiarly in the air. These pictures greatly disturbed Tom and me. Unlike the prints with which you would furnish a room, these pictures were a constant thief of our eyes and the more we looked at them the more we saw. You can probably imagine the picture that hung above my little iron bed: a group of people in Victorian dress standing before a fireplace observing the pale body of a chimneysweep's boy being brought down from the stack.

Tom and I sat together on the short settee for quite some time before any of the delinquents spoke to us. They simply stared from time to time.

Being the most senior it was Terry who at last came over to us to conduct the formal interview on behalf of the delinquents. 'Are you orphans or what?' he asked.

'No,' we replied.

'Where's your dad?'

'He's gone,' said Tom.

'Dead?' asked Terry, hopefully.

'No, he ran off,' I said.

'What about your mum, is she dead?'

'No,' we said, 'she's in the hospital.'

'Dying is she?'

'No,' we said together.

'She might,' said Terry, hopefully.

'No she won't,' we said.

'But she might,' persisted Terry. He seemed to be very keen to prepare us for the worst. This must have been the helping each other along that Uncle had mentioned.

'But she might not!' I protested.

Terry looked around the room at all the other delinquents and addressed them. 'Who has had a mum go into hospital and die?' he asked. Everyone instantly put their hands up. 'There you are,' he said triumphantly, and with this he punched me in the stomach so that all the air left my lungs and I sank to the floor. Tom picked me up and sat me back on the small settee. We didn't make a sound.

Next, Dolores came over to us. By hitting Terry as hard as he had hit her she had become a kind of sister to him. 'Do you want me to show you the table-tennis room?' she said. She seemed to feel sorry for us and we were glad.

'Yes,' we said, and we got up from the settee. She led us out of the room and down the passageway, talking about the ping-pong tournaments that they held. We were very glad of her kindness. We reached a door at the far end of the passage which was bolted. Dolores drew back the bolts, threw the door open and in an instant had pushed us through it and bolted it behind us. The door did not lead to a table-tennis room; it led out into the darkness of the garden where the rain soaked us as suddenly as if the night air was a solid wall of water. We stood confused for a moment and then ran around the house until we found the front door. We stood and knocked. Uncle opened it to us and we were let in. We were so wet that Auntie came at us with huge bathtowels and rubbed our hair furiously.

'You obviously weren't reckoning on the rain,' said Uncle. We went to say that we had been pushed out of the door but Dolores appeared in the hallway and we remained silent. 'Well, let's hope this'll be the last time you try anything on like this. We'll talk about it at tomorrow's session,' said Uncle.

All in all it had not been one of our better days.

CHAPTER XXIII

In which our mother is disappointed with us and in which the reader sees a little of our lives at Crab Apple Road

We came down to breakfast the next morning, which was a Sunday, and sat at the table, amazed at the size of the cornflakes box. A dozen eggs lay frying in a great silver pan as if a flock of chickens had flown over and been surprised by something. A machine for making toast rotated above the grill and Mrs Wallis was pouring tea from an urn into a tray of cups. 'I thought you'd at least be wearing your best clothes,' she said.

We looked down at the table and shrugged our shoulders. We seemed not to be able to do anything right once we'd been marked down as delinquents. We chewed our cornflakes slowly and dared not reach for an extra spoon of sugar to liven them up when the milk had made them soggy. After breakfast we went into the lounge, with the others, and sat on the chairs, arranged in a circle for the session.

Mr Wallis came to each of us in turn to talk through

our problems. We were a fairly average bunch of delinquents all in all, none of us mass murderers or enemies of the state. Terry had already been in the home for four years, having been brought in at our age after a succession of petty arsonings and attempts on his own life. Dolores had spent three and a half years in The Crab', done for shoplifting and running a protection racket in the Guides. Her father, who managed the local working men's club, had found her unmanageable. Next in the circle was Tim O'Sullivan, the boy who had screwed down the lid of the ketchup; three years in The Crab' for breaking into cars and trying to drive them away. Joan Scanlon sat beside him, she looked a great deal older than her eleven years and was sitting reading *Winnie the Pooh*: two years in The Crab' after knifing her babysitter. And so he went round the room: Micky Finch, Mark Wheatley, Julian Green, Humphrey Barclay, Paul Keegan, Micky Richards, and finally us, Richard and Thomas Stone, ten years old: wearing women's clothing and attempted murder.

'How do you feel you're settling in here?' asked Uncle.

'Don't know,' I said.

'What would you most like to achieve in life?' asked Auntie.

'To go home,' said Tom.

'Why do you think you found it so difficult to get on at Mrs Bagbourne's?' asked Uncle. We looked at all the other kids who were staring at the floor and picking holes in their chairs.

'Don't know,' we said.

Mr Wallis left it there; no doubt we would open up in time and he'd be able to lead us to face our problems and difficulties. It was a strange experience for us, like a public confessional. The other delinquents were so used to it that they not only rattled off all their misdemeanours and problems very quickly and efficiently but frequently pre-empted Uncle in his psychological judgements. Terry was in his element. Most of the dreadful things he said about himself were invented and designed merely to impress the others. He had a kind of understanding with Uncle; if Terry said that he'd murdered the milkman then Uncle would have to believe him or else Terry might really do something.

Sometimes Terry would turn directly to Mr Wallis and ask, 'And what about you, then, are you coping?' like a chimpanzee mimicking its keeper.

'Yes, thank you, Terry.'

'Still having feelings of aggression towards me?'

'Some feelings of aggression, yes, but I've managed to contain them so far.'

'It's not me you want to hit, it's yourself.'

'I don't want to hit you, Terry, you've got to get used to the idea.'

'You didn't even want to hit me when I sliced up the new sofa?'

'Yes, I wanted to hit you then.'

'How's your sex life?'

'Very nice, thank you, Terry.'

After the session was over Mr Wallis came and spoke to us. 'Those pullovers are a bit scruffy, I thought you'd be in your best clothes today.'

'That's what I said to them at breakfast,' said Mrs Wallis.

'We can't have your mummy seeing you like that. She'll think we're not looking after you,' said Uncle, laughing. Both our mouths fell open.

'When are we going to see her?' we asked.

'After lunch. Visiting time is two o'clock, isn't it?' said Mr Wallis.

'Yes,' we said.

'That is the time you go?'

'Oh, yes!' I said.

'We've never been,' said Tom.

Mr and Mrs Wallis looked at each other in a way that suggested, for the first time, that maybe we weren't the delinquents we'd been made out to be.

Mrs Wallis walked us to the hospital; it wasn't far, she said, and the walk would do us good. We knew that we'd be late because of this, arrive after visiting hours and have to walk back again without having seen her and without having even been on a bus. We hadn't been on a bus in ages.

When we got to the hospital, however, we were twenty minutes early and had to wait for a bell to sound before we could go into the ward. During this time Mrs Wallis took us into the visitors' cafe where we not only had lemonade and biscuits but she gave us the money to buy a quarter of a pound of black grapes for our mother. We were so happy that we jumped up and down in excitement and had to sit and hold our breath for forty seconds to calm ourselves down.

When the bell sounded Mrs Wallis led us to the ward and to the first cubicle in which our mother lay. Mrs Wallis stood behind us. We walked in quietly. She lay in white and pink sheets surrounded by all manner of mystical apparatus. Outside her window we could see the old hospital tree. It had grown so large and sprawling that its branches were supported by dozens of metal crutches to prevent them from crashing through the frail roofs of the prefabricated wards. The tree blocked out a great deal of the light, and sticky bandages were wrapped around its trunk to discourage beetle. We couldn't decide who looked the more poorly, the tree, or our mother.

Slowly she opened her eyes and saw us. We held out the quarter-pound of grapes.

'Hello, Mum,' I said.

'Hello,' said Tom. She didn't say anything for a while but simply moved her lips and then she said, 'Who is it?'

'It's us,' we said, 'Richard and Tom.'

A tear came rolling down her cheek very slowly; we watched as it glistened on her pale skin, like oil on marble, and then as it suddenly disappeared, soaking into the sheet at her chin. 'They've had to put you in a special home, they told me,' she said weakly.

'Yes,' we said, 'but it's all right.'

'It's not all right . . . I've never been so ashamed . . . why couldn't you be good boys while I was in here? Miss Barnes came to see me last night . . .' As she said this our hearts broke and all the happiness we had in seeing her at last disappeared like the glistening tear. She turned her face into the pillow, 'First Frank, now the two of you; I knew you'd take after him. You've let your mummy down . . .'

We were near to tears, and Mrs Wallis put a hand on each of our shoulders.

'We've brought some grapes,' I said.

'I'm nil by mouth,' she replied.

We stood for a few moments and then Mrs Wallis began moving us toward the door. 'Come on,' she said, 'let's have another lemonade and go home.'

'We don't want to go home,' we said.

'Your mother needs her rest, she's tired,' she said.

We left the room and walked sobbing, gripping on to Auntie's skirts, out of the ward. The woman in the next cubicle must have thought Ellen had just died.

When we got back to the home we put a brave face on it. We told the others that our mother had given us the bag of grapes, which I still had tightly gripped in my hand, to share with everyone. The grapes caused great excitement, especially after Terry discovered that he was expert in spitting the pips at me and Tom.

We sat for the rest of the evening, bemused and lifeless. We didn't talk to each other about what had happened, but each of us brooded apart, feeling that the small hopes we'd had for a change in our prospects had gone. Mr and Mrs Wallis were especially soft spoken when they talked to us. Mrs Wallis tried to explain about how our mother was on drugs and that she wasn't herself.

'What's wrong with her then?' asked Tom. 'She only went in because she couldn't make a cup of tea.'

Mrs Wallis smiled. 'No,' she said, 'it's a little more serious than that.'

'What is it she's got?' I asked, knowing that she knew because she'd spoken to the sister as we left the ward, and I'd seen them shake their heads.

'Your mummy has something growing inside her that they're trying to get out,' she said.

'What's growing inside her?' I asked.

'Well it's like a kind of plant, growing up her spine,' she said.

Tom thought for a moment. 'Is it a runner bean?' he asked.

'Yes,' said Auntie, 'it's something very like a runner bean.'

It must have begun that day she collapsed on the peafield. We were glad that at last someone had told us exactly what was wrong with our mother.

Mr and Mrs Wallis were very worried about us. It was difficult to predict how disturbed children, such as ourselves, would react. They sat in their office until late at night reading up all their books on delinquents with hospitalized parents. They watched us closely for days, expecting us to produce phantom cancers, or maybe try to injure ourselves to get into the hospital, but we quietly went about our business, rarely smiling, saying little, empty inside, no comfort even to each other.

CHAPTER XXIV

In which we ask to go to the cinema, and Mr Bumble makes a brief appearance to thwart us, and in which we are unhappy

Barry Foster, Charlie Rubbidge and Joey Morris were charging about the playground waving their arms in excitement, playing a new game.

'Come on,' said Barry to us, and he began to tick like a clock and open his mouth wide. He tried to bite us. This wasn't something Barry usually did, usually he kicked. 'You've got to run,' he said. 'I'm the alligator that swallowed the clock.' We didn't know what he was talking about.

Charlie Rubbidge ran up to us with his index finger strangely curled. 'I'm Captain Hook, aaaaaargh aaaaaargh!' he said and then stopped and looked at us puzzled. 'Haven't you seen it?'

'Seen what?' we said.

'You mean you haven't even seen it?' said Charlie.

'What? What? What?' said Tom, in frustration. He got only the blankest look as if he were the most uninformed boy in the world. Charlie ran off, chasing all the other kids in tandem with Barry as the alligator.

We went and stood by the bins. Joey ran by and we caught his arm. 'Joey, what are you playing?'

'Peter Pan,' he said. 'Haven't you seen it?'

'We're going tonight,' we said quickly.

'Well, you'd better, it's coming off tomorrow; my mum's taking me again.'

The whistle went and we got into lines to walk back into class. Tom and I looked at one another. 'Do you reckon they're going to take us but they're keeping it as a surprise?' said Tom hopefully.

'Yeah, I expect so,' I said.

When we got back to the home that night we went into the lounge. Dolores was working on her chair, cutting the seat with a penknife, Terry was breathing on the window panes, the others were mooning about. I went over to Dolores. 'Here, Dolores?'

'What?'

'You know this film *Peter Pan*, do you reckon they're going to take us to see it?'

'I dunno,' she said.

The other kids looked up, one of them said, '*Peter Pan*, are we going?'

'We dunno,' we said.

Terry came over. 'Why don't you ask Auntie?'

'Why me?'

'Because I said so, that's why, shithead.' Everyone seconded his motion.

I sank down on the little settee wishing I hadn't mentioned it. Just before tea Mrs Wallis called Tom and me to go and do our kitchen duty. We disliked this, not because it was a chore but because the kitchen was so daunting. At home we had practically lived in the kitchen but this one had a stone floor and all the pots and pans were of an enormous size.

I poured the powdered potato that Mrs Wallis had measured out into a large silver pot and, when the hot water was put in, stirred it. I stirred for ten minutes imagining myself to be a prisoner on an island doing thirty years' potato making. I made myself miserable looking into the yellowish sludge. My mind dwelt on the gloomy lives of ragged boys shut up in the poorhouse with tyrannical, cyst-ridden masters; it dwelt on the whip, the meagre food, the morsel saved, the agonizing death in the night of one's poor, starved brother; and best of all the grief cut short by the necessity of working on the treadmill with bleeding feet – sometimes no feet at all. I got so carried away with these fictions that whenever Mr or Mrs Wallis came into the room, I'd jump in terror and cower in the corner. I resolved to eat only a portion of dinner so that I could get that empty feeling inside and imagine myself to be suffering greatly.

On one occasion Mrs Wallis had found me tied to the washpost in the garden. 'Who tied you there?' she asked.

'I can't tell you,' I'd said nobly, but I'd done it myself in order to imagine being flogged. Great tears would roll down my cheeks and, catching them in my hands, I would look up to heaven, pleading:

> 'Oh God, why must we suffer?
> Let me die, oh let me die!
> Let us shrink up and die
> in horrible agony,
> me and my brother.'

If anyone came out into the garden I'd stop quickly, wipe my face, and make out I was talking to someone over the fence in the next garden.

I finished stirring the instant potato.

'Thank you,' said Mrs Wallis when I carried it over to her. I should have asked her then and there about the film, but I didn't, I left it until we were all at the table. It took me some time to summon up the courage. I looked up at Mrs Wallis. She could see that I wanted to say something. Terry prodded me with his foot and Dolores tapped her knife on the table.

'Please, Auntie,' I said, opening my eyes as wide as I could, 'can we go to the pictures?'

'What? What!? WHAT!? Oh my goodness, Uncle, did you hear that?'

'What was it, my dear?'

'Husband, dearest, I beg your pardon but Richard Stone has asked for a trip to the pictures!'

'The pictures? Do I understand that he has asked to go to the pictures after he has already been watching the television, after he has had all that the British Broadcasting Corporation has to offer lavished upon him?'

'He has indeed.'

'And does he want to go alone, or does he intend the whole house to participate in this jamboree, this lavish bunfight, this outrageous beano at the ratepayers' expense!?'

'I think he intends it for the whole world, honest I do. I'm quite overcome.'

'The whole world in one great picture palace perhaps? Is this what the boy wants? Ah! – even from a child's mind such a notion of wickedness and depravity! And what is it he wants to see at the p i c t u r e s?'

'*Peter Pan*, Mr Bumble, *Peter Pan*.'

'*Peter Pan! Peter Pan*! He flies does he not?'

'I am informed that he does.'

'And other improbable tricks no doubt. Allow a boy to fly, ma'am, allow a boy to fly and he'll be up to all the mischief in the world within the hour! Is this child's mind not stuffed with enough nonsense already?'

'I think it has been amply stuffed with nonsense, Mr Bumble.'

'In that case, IN THAT CASE – we had better knock a bit of it out of him! Richard! Fetch me THE POTATO LADLE!'

'What's on?' said Mrs Wallis.

'*Peter Pan*,' said Tom and Terry together.

'Oh lovely,' she said. 'Perhaps we could go tomorrow.'

'It comes off tomorrow,' I said, pitifully.

'I'll ask Uncle if there's enough in the kitty.'

Mrs Wallis retired with Mr Wallis, after tea, to their private sitting-room. We all listened at the door. They discussed the trip. Mr Wallis had some reservations. He talked about a boy who had seen it from a home in Sydenham and come home thinking he was Peter Pan. We heard him laugh as he said, 'I can just see it now: it's the middle of the night and there's children leaping from every window shouting "Tinkerbell!" "Tinkerbell!" '

'Oh it's such a shame,' said Mrs Wallis. 'I think they all wanted to see it.'

Our hopes lifted a little at this but then Mr Wallis went on to say, 'I dread to think what Terry will get up to when the lights go down.' That seemed to put an end to it and they went on to talk about something else.

I went up to bed. It had been important for us to see the film. Mr Wallis's speech upset me. He seemed to think we were all disturbed, we were all odd. I lay in bed and assumed the position of crucifixion. I was soon asleep.

CHAPTER XXV

In which we meet Hibedyhoy Harold and make plans to run away to join the fair and, also, in which a present is given to Miss Graterex and there is a shoot-out

During the days preceding the Whitsun Bank Holiday the streets of Prospect were filled with ancient and brightly painted trucks and caravans all heading for the recreation ground. We stood in the street watching them all day and in the evening we all crowded at the lounge window to gaze out towards the rec'. They were testing the lights on the attractions.

'Auntie, Auntie!' shouted Terry, 'the big wheel's nearly up,' and he smiled at us all. We all kept Mr and Mrs Wallis posted on the progress of the fair. We began to speculate about the rides and the stalls.

'I'm going on the rifle range,' said Terry. 'I'm an ace shot. I shot a cow once when I was out hunting with my dad.' Nobody said anything; if Terry claimed he shot a cow, then he shot a cow, no one would argue.

Tom, however, was in slightly better spirits than usual and such a claim was far too much for him to allow. He turned to me. 'We've only ever managed a pig, ain't we, Rich?' I didn't answer.

Terry jabbed him in the ribs. 'I didn't ask you to pipe in, did I?' he said.

The most exciting thing about the fair, apart from the attractions, was the effect it had at school. There were lots of new children, from the fair people, and when they arrived at the school and were divided among the classes it was a great distraction. We envied them, naturally, because they travelled with the fair and could, probably, have as many free rides as they liked. This meant that no one would speak to them. They were so far behind in their education that they had to be put with children much younger than themselves and added to this they used to fall asleep because of being up so late taking tickets or guarding the lot.

As well as the fair people themselves there was quite a community of gypsies who followed the fair to work the rides. It was a gypsy boy who came to join our class, much to our delight since we would no longer be at the bottom of the social pile. His name was Harold and within five minutes of being in our form he had already gained the new name of 'Hibedyhoy Harold', which he didn't seem to like much but which he suffered with grace. He sat down at the front with us. We were all quite intrigued by him because he had dark Romany skin and wore long trousers; he had a little gold earring in his left ear and a red paisley cravat tied loosely at his neck. When he told Miss Graterex that he had his own goat and he'd have to go back at lunchtime to move its post and chain, we were all absolutely astonished by him. When milktime came he dashed to the front to get his little bottle of milk out of the crate and then when he'd finished it he asked Miss Graterex for another. This was even more astonishing than the goat-moving. We did everything we could not to have to drink our milk. Even though the little bottles were quite cute and we were given a straw, we didn't like the idea of drinking without a cup. Mum would never have let us do it at home, and Auntie would hit the roof. In wintertime the milk was even worse because it would be frozen. The crate would be balanced precariously on the radiator but although some of the milk became warm it never entirely thawed out in the middle.

Hibedyhoy Harold's father had told him to listen to everything that the teacher said and to learn as much as he could before they moved on. Harold was very keen to comply and so when he went to Miss Graterex for a third bottle of milk and she said to him 'you'll turn into a cow' he looked very greatly disturbed indeed and said 'will I?' Nevertheless his appetite for milk was of great advantage to us: sitting next to him as we did meant that we could slip him our bottles to drink. Through this profitable interchange, we and Hibedyhoy Harold became friends. When we were in the playground he taught Tom and me how to suck vinegar out of the vinegar-vein plants that grew on the edge of the playing-field, and how to record our voices on to rubber bands, by stretching them and speaking very close. We found all of this of great use because we were seriously thinking of leaving the Home, forgetting about our mother, and going to live wild, like the cats at the hospital and our buck rabbit that kicked the doors of the hutch sooner than be eaten at Easter. Barry and Charlie, who didn't talk to us any more, informed us that we'd catch nits from him, and Barry said that Harold smelled. This couldn't be denied, we did sit next to him after all. Hibedyhoy Harold was rather upset by such a blunt statement of fact, but Tom leapt to his defence by declaring it to be a 'country smell'. Harold was thrilled by this. He'd wondered what it was himself.

On Bank Holiday Monday, after a week of aching anxiety, Uncle and Auntie took us to the fair, en masse, with a stern lecture on the way. Mrs Wallis walked in front, with we delinquents behind her in twos, and with Mr Wallis bringing up the rear reminding us of the serious rules that applied to pleasure as we went. 'No one is to go running off when it's time to come home. You will each be given enough money for five rides and when that's used up you're not to come asking for more,' he said.

Tom and I chuckled to each other. 'Five whole rides,' said Tom with excitement. It was more rides than we'd ever had on anything in our lives, excepting Miss Barnes's Hillman Imp, of course.

The fair was probably a very shabby one, but there was the smell of candy-floss and Wrestlers' hamburgers and enough light bulbs to make us feel as if we were in Disneyland. The five rides had sounded a great deal but although Tom and I had been very prudent in our choices – one go trying to win a teddy bear and three goes on the dodgem cars – within twenty minutes we were down to our last ride. I elected to go on the ghost train but Tom said it wasn't worth it, it was sissy and in his opinion it wouldn't be scary at all. Tom went on the octopus because it wouldn't spoil his evening if he happened to be sick on the last ride. He left me to go on the ghost train by myself. I got into the carriage and waved to Tom and the Wallises as it started up and banged through the skull-shaped doors. It was very dark inside. The first frightening thing was a large lobster whose eyes lit up. I was not impressed. Various cardboard witches appeared and taped screams gave the impression to people outside that the punters inside were having a good time. When the ride was over and my carriage came out Mr and Mrs Wallis looked at one another. I was not in my seat. As the ride had entered a patch of pitch darkness some wet string hung from the ceiling had dragged across my face. I had screamed, panicked and jumped out of the carriage. Consternation grew outside the ghost train as the small crowd realized that a child had fallen out and was missing.

People demanded that the electricity be turned off, which served to plunge me into complete darkness. I wandered around for a good ten minutes trying to find my way out; eventually I emerged, to cheers, very white in the face, from the door where I had gone in.

While Mr Wallis was explaining to me what a stupid thing I had done by getting out, our attention was caught by a rumpus at the rifle range. We looked and saw Terry with a gun pointed at the owner. He had paid for six shots with a .22 rifle and, having failed to win a prize on the first five, had saved the last shot with which to hold the man up.

'Somebody get the police! For gawd's sake get the Bill!' the man was shouting.

'Shut up or I'll shoot, shithead,' said Terry. Mr Wallis ran over, with us hard on his heels, hoping that Terry would shoot. The rifle man had his hands up and we were very impressed with Terry's professionalism.

'It's OK, it's OK, everybody calm down, he's with me,' said Mr Wallis, and he turned to the man with his hands up and smiled. 'I'm sorry about this, Terry gets a bit over-excited.'

'Over-excited?' said the rifle man. 'He's about to bloody murder me!'

'Now come on, Terry's not going to murder anyone, are you, Terry?'

'The kid's a lunatic, just because he didn't win a prize he holds me at gunpoint.'

'Well, did you try explaining that he couldn't have a prize if he didn't hit the target?' said Mr Wallis, reasonably.

'I would have thought that was fairly obvious from the start,' said the man, his arms beginning to wave a bit above his head. Quite a crowd was gathering. Terry was in his element. 'Just shut up, the pair of you, or I'll blow his brains out!' he shouted.

Mr Wallis seemed thoroughly unperturbed but the rifle man went into a frenzy. 'The kid's crazy, look at his eyes, he's going to kill me.'

'If you don't mind my saying,' said Mr Wallis, 'I think you're in the wrong business. It's only a pop-gun anyway. Now come on, Terry, put the gun down.'

'It's a .22,' said the rifle man, 'it'll blow my brains out.'

'Don't tell him that,' said Tom. The crowd laughed.

Mr Wallis got serious. 'Now come on, put the gun down or this'll be the last time I bring you to a fair if you don't know how to behave.'

'Hand over the goldfish,' said Terry.

'You missed,' said Mr Wallis, 'you don't get a goldfish; you've got to learn that about the world, you've got to come to terms with it.' It was all rather like one of our sessions sitting in the circle of chairs.

'All right then, I'll shoot the tank and nobody will have any,' said Terry, turning to Mr Wallis. As he turned so the rifle man grabbed a gun for himself and aimed it at Terry's head. 'OK kid, put it down. I'm a better shot than you.'

Terry put the gun down. Mr Wallis thought it was about time we left the fair. I got the impression that they had both thoroughly enjoyed themselves.

There was no doubt about it that on this evening the punters, chiefly myself on the ghost train and Terry on the rifle range, had been more entertaining than the fair itself.

The next day at school we began telling Hibedyhoy Harold that we were going to leave the home and travel like he did. Harold hadn't been used to striking up friendships so quickly; he had a gentle, simple manner which we liked, and when he said we could live in his caravan we were overjoyed. We accepted the offer immediately. We secretly packed a few things that evening in our satchels, and we stole some curtain rings to use as earrings when the time came.

We were sitting in class a couple of days later, copying from the blackboard, when the door opened and there was great excitement when suddenly a large ruddy-faced man in ramshackle clothes appeared and knocked very politely on the door after he'd opened it.

'Class sit quietly,' said Miss Graterex. Hibedyhoy Harold got to his feet, looking disappointed.

'Excuse me, Miss,' said the ruddy-faced man, holding his hat in his hand and flapping it in the air as if he were used to being bothered by flies, 'Um . . . excuse me, interruptin' lessuns an' all, but the rozzers 'ave bin down.'

'Rozzers?' said Miss Graterex.

'Policemen,' said Harold, explaining the term.

'Yes,' he said, 'with Billdozers and tractys and no warnin' . . .'

'Oh dear me,' said Miss Graterex.

'. . . turnin' over the 'vans, diggin' up the site . . . we're movin' on.'

'Oh, I see,' said our teacher. 'Harold, you may pack up your things and leave with . . .?' She looked towards the man.

He made a swipe at some more of his flies and said, 'Um . . . Mr Rowlindsun, that's the name . . .'

'With Mr Rowlandson.'

Mr Rowlandson knocked the door with his hat and added '. . . the boy's father.'

'Yes.'

As Harold walked away from his desk Mr Rowlandson

crossed over to Miss Graterex and said, 'I'd jus' like to, um, well say a big thank you to you, Miss . . .?'

'Graterex.'

'Yes . . . Miss . . . thank you for teachin' the boy up a bit, it's much apprishiated by us travelin' people, and, praps we'll see you again come spring for a bit more . . .' Then Harold's father produced an enormous bottle of scent from his overcoat pocket and gave it to her.

'With much gratitood,' he said. Miss Graterex didn't quite know what to do, she quickly put it on her desk. We began to clap and the rest of the class joined in, because we had done this when one of the teachers had left and had been made a presentation. Miss Graterex looked moved and embarrassed by turns and tried to quell us by flapping her arms up and down.

'Thank you,' said Harold, in his soft voice. 'I've tried to learn everything what you said, and I won't drink no more milk.' A small tear came to our teacher's eye and she brushed his hair with her hand.

Mr Rowlandson smiled and bobbed from side to side. 'I 'ope he's bin no bother,' he said.

'Oh, no, no, a very good boy,' said Miss Graterex.

Harold's father beamed with pride. 'Educasion's a good thing,' he said and turned with his arm around Harold to lead him out of the door. The class was overcome with emotion. Tom and I stood up to leave with them.

'Sit down,' said Miss Graterex, softly, 'sit down.' We carried on with our copying from the blackboard. She sat behind her desk sharpening pencils, wiping her eyes and shaking her head from time to time whenever she looked at the bottle of scent.

Tom and I sat in class wishing that the door would open again and our own father would be there saying, 'Excuse me, Miss Graterex, but I've come to take the boys.' Where he would take us to we hadn't thought, but we looked towards the door all the same.

CHAPTER XXVI

In which we go on holiday but we are found to be wanting at the table-tennis table, also in which several children are sick on a coach

The skies brightened and the summer holidays came but we were still in the Home and there was no sign of Mum leaving hospital. The Welfare decided to send all the children from the homes in Prospect to Devon where we would get the benefit of the fresh air.

We travelled in a green Dormobile van, leaving Mr and Mrs Wallis behind and under the charge of two welfare workers, Dave and Sue. The road was one of our arch enemies. We dreaded the annual school trip when, because of it, everyone in our class would be sick. There were still very few cars on the estate and none of us had been broken in to the combustion engine. There were several remedies for the dreadful sickness. The worst was the little pink pill because it was marketed expressly for the purpose. It tasted sweet – but not candy sweet, it had an acidic, poisonous sweetness. It had to be taken twenty minutes before the journey, and, as soon as it hit the tongue you felt sick, and no coach in sight. All the children heaved as it did its unnatural work of drying out the stomach and turning the tongue to leather. The second method was to cram yourself full with dry bread. This was supposed to stabilize the stomach and stop the swishing about. All it did was to make the act of being

sick even harder work. The third, and most bizarre
method, was the static chain. People believed that if a
length of chain was suspended from the rear bumper so
that it trailed on the tarmac, static would be released
from the vehicle and sickness prevented. Before we set
off in the Dormobile, Dave and Sue took us all around to
the back to show us the chain.

'There we are,' said Dave, reassuring us. 'Everyone
seen the chain? Now we're not going to have any sickness
are we?'

'No,' we all said, but some of us brought up our little
pink pills as we mounted the Dormobile's step. We
couldn't quite make out Dave and Sue. Dave was wearing
jeans, not the sort of thing we were used to, and he had a
pink shirt. We'd heard about pink shirts before. One
day, before Mum had gone into hospital, she had come
back in from the shops and said, 'You'll never guess
what. I was walking along the street and I saw a man,
well if you can call him that, in a p i n k shirt!' It was a
great novelty.

We had never travelled anywhere as far away as Devon
before and we became worried after an hour on the road.
How would we ever get back? Sue could see that we
were upset and began to talk to us. 'Have you ever been
to Devon before?' she asked.

'No, but we've been to Wimbledon,' said Tom.

'Oh,' she said in an interested way, trying to draw us
out, 'and what did you think of Wimbledon?'

'I don't know, we were only kids,' I said to end the
conversation. I didn't want her to ask any details about
our broken home.

All of us, except for Terry, were sick by Guildford. I
was feeling fine until Dolores was sick all over the back
of my seat.

'If you want to throw up,' said Dave, 'tell me and I'll stop the van, it's no bother.' We were intrigued by the expression 'throw up'; we'd never heard it before and we thought he was probably swearing. We had heard from the television about the swinging sixties and this was probably it. After about eight 'throwing up' stops Dave gave out paper bags.

We stopped for lunch in the New Forest. The air, and the excitement of picnicking off liver-sausage sandwiches, revived us.

Terry had been laughing at us all the way but over lunch he began to grow green. Dave asked him if he was all right. "Course I am,' he said, and fell to his knees. We all cheered as he threw up his liver-sausage and a bit of apple got stuck in his throat. We had to pay for this pleasure of course; as soon as he recovered we all got hit and he sulked the rest of the way and kicked the back of Dave's driving seat.

'Terry, will you stop that please?' said Dave.

'What?' said Terry.

'You know what you're doing.'

'No I don't.'

'Do you want me to crash this van?'

'Yeah.'

We stayed in a girls' school three miles from the sea. It seemed a long way to drive not to get any nearer. It was a huge white place; the stairs went this way and that through a maze of classrooms, dormitories and corridors, but everything was as uniform and heartless (with everywhere the oppressive smell of hockey boots) as only a house which has become a school can be. Our dormitory was crammed full with hospital-type iron bedsteads. After seeing this place we prayed that we would never be sent to a public school. We went to bed that night to the sound of eerie gulls. We imagined how unhappy the girls who had been sent there must be and we felt a certain sympathy with them. I could hear Tom sobbing under his sheets.

'Go to sleep, Tom,' I said, 'we'll go to the beach tomorrow.'

'I want to go home,' he said and, sobbing, added, 'my elbow hurts.'

The worst days of the holiday were those on which it rained and the organizers provided entertainment for us all. There was a table-tennis tournament, between all the homes. Dave said that we all had to take part in it because Mr and Mrs Wallis would be so proud when we came back with the inter-home trophy. This notion appealed to Terry and Dolores and they threw themselves into it with serious enthusiasm, going first in the doubles. Having been in the Home for many years they were experienced players, and Dave and Sue cheered them on, glad to see that they were doing something legitimate for once. When the time came for Tom and I to play, however, Terry's mood began to change. Table-tennis was not our game. No matter how we swung our bats the little ball was never able to find them. Terry couldn't bear the disgrace and he walked up to the table and took the ball.

Dave intervened. 'Now, Terry,' he said calmly, 'we aren't going to win if you remove the ball, are we?'

'Ain't going to win anyway with Laurel and Hardy here, are we?' said Terry.

'Well at least you can let them try.'

'Give them a bat six foot wide maybe they'll hit it,' he replied.

We stood there nervously pulling the rubber bobbles from our bats.

'Terry, this is a holiday,' said Sue. 'It's the fun of taking part. Now put the ball on the table and let Richard serve – it is your service, isn't it, Richard?'

'I don't know,' I said. 'What's a service?' Terry looked up at the ceiling and then placed the ball on the floor and stood on it. It gave off a slightly acrid smell as the gas inside escaped.

'I don't know what you're trying to achieve by that,' said Dave, stepping nearer to the table and looking up apologetically at the spectators.

'To break the bloody ball,' said Terry in reply, and he came over to me and took my bat.

'Give Richard his bat back,' said Sue.

'Yes, just return it,' said Dave.

Terry looked at them coolly and then smashed the bat down on the table so hard that he broke the net and the bat split in two.

'This display is getting you nowhere, Terry,' said Dave, in a deep, controlled voice. Terry kicked the leg of the table and the whole thing collapsed flat on to the floor, catching Dave's leg as it did so. It made a terrible bang and we covered our ears. 'I think you'd better leave this tournament,' said Dave. Terry walked out of the room and into the courtyard outside. Dave followed him out. 'You miserable little bugger,' we heard Dave shout, and watched from the window as he kicked Terry in the back.

We couldn't help feeling that Uncle would have handled it all so much better.

CHAPTER XXVII

In which I get a bang on the head and I have tea with my mother

Terry found a golf-club, when we got back from Devon; not the sort of thing one usually finds, but he insisted to Mr Wallis that it was the case. It had been lying, doing nothing, in the middle of nowhere, wanted by no one. 'It could have gone rusty,' he said. He'd managed to find a ball as well, which was remarkably lucky, and he'd decided to become a golf pro. He made a large hole in the garden lawn for the purpose and he practised swiping the ball for hours, generally knocking it into the next garden, from which Tom or I would have to retrieve it.

Golf interested me, since I'd never seen it performed before, and I stood behind Terry, watching him line up his shots, and showing great enthusiasm, in the hope that one day he'd let me have a go. I was resting my hands on my thighs, looking intently along the line of putting towards the great crater in the lawn – which grew in size the more he missed it – when Terry made a particularly professional swing. However, before the club hit the ball it hit me, with great force, just above the eye. I was sent reeling backwards. The blood gushed from the cut, running down my face, filling my nostrils and blinding me.

'You've ruined my putt!' shouted Terry. Tom ran indoors to get Mrs Wallis, who nearly fainted when she saw me sprawled on the grass, with a blood-filled face. Terry was furiously protesting his innocence, but he couldn't believe his luck: he'd succeeded in injuring me quite badly and it was all my own fault. He couldn't have planned it better.

A wet towel was wrapped around my head and I was carried like a length of burst pipe, fainting, to the Wallises' car and driven to the hospital. While I was being stitched up in casualty the news was related to our mother. By the time it reached her, via several porters and a student nurse, I had been clubbed half to death at a golf tournament and had lost the sight in both my eyes. Ellen nearly died then and there. She had undergone a further operation on her spine only a few days before and could not be put into a wheelchair but she insisted that she be lifted from her bed and laid flat on a trolley. They wheeled her into casualty where I was lying, waiting for a bed. Her trolley and all her drips were pushed next to my bed.

'Oh my poor baby,' she said, 'whatever's happened to you?' and she stretched out her hand to hold mine, and began to weep. I was so pleased to be in the hospital with her, and to hear her voice at this moment, that, with my one good eye, I wept too. It had a great effect on all the casualty department who witnessed it. It was the kind of scene which generally only accompanied major disasters or family car crashes.

Luckily I was diagnosed as having sustained concussion as well and, since I wouldn't be able to see out of my left eye for a week, it was decided that I should be kept in for the duration. Every afternoon a nurse pushed me in a wheelchair, which I thoroughly enjoyed, from the children's ward to join my mother for tea in Surgical A. She seemed so different from the time when Tom and I had seen her and she refused the black grapes. She seemed more like my mother again and there was no mention of how we had disgraced ourselves by having to go into a home. Our teatimes lasted for hours, and as far as we could, without bursting our stitches, we laughed a great deal. She told me all about her last operation in great detail. I was very interested in all aspects of the hospital, it was such a nice, warm place, albeit only a collection of old First World War huts linked by outside corridors.

'Well . . .' she said, referring to her op', 'they wheeled me down at nine in the morning last Wednesday and sister says I wasn't back until four!' and then her eyes lit up and with a mixture of pathos and relish she said, 'Seven hours under the knife!' A chill ran through me and I wheeled my chair closer to her bed.

'The first thing I said when I came round was "where's my éclair?" ' Ellen laughed at this so loudly that she had to stop herself all of a sudden, because of the pain. 'Oh, I can't laugh too much or I'll come apart like Norman Spanish's suit' – at this she laughed even louder, and had to check herself even more quickly. I was worried that there'd be the most terrific rip and that would be the end of my mother.

'Well, of course . . .' she continued when we had both recovered from the reference to Norman Spanish, '. . . we have éclairs for tea on Tuesdays but the nurse said to me "don't you dare eat one, what with your op' in the morning", so I'd taken one and put it in my locker – so it was on my mind.' We laughed at this as well.

Ellen explained some of the more technical details of her operation, and I described the finer points of the treatment for my bang on the head. She told me all about the length of the cut, the number of stitches and the helicopter that arrived. 'It was waiting for me outside on the grass because should anything have gone wrong I would have been flown straight to Stoke Mandeville.'

'Did anything go wrong?' I asked enthusiastically.

'No.'

'Oh,' I said in disappointment, 'I bet you wished it had.'

'Well, I don't, no, Mr Trifle is a marvellous man.'

'When will you be getting out then, Mum, soon?'

'Not yet,' she said. 'Mr Trifle wants to keep me under observation; they've not done many of these operations and I'm what you would call a guinea pig.' I wondered if she'd be kept in a hutch. 'Then, of course, I shall have to learn to walk again. I've been on my back a year,' she said, and then she turned dramatic and serious and looked me in the eye. 'You realize I may never walk again,' she said.

'Never mind,' I said, 'you can have my wheelchair and Tom and me will push you along.'

'You're a thoughtful boy,' she said. I beamed with happiness all over my face and my good eye, and added to this it was Tuesday and the chocolate éclairs arrived on a trolley.

At the end of this marvellous week the doctor came to see me, the bandage was removed from my eye, and I was declared to be one hundred per cent fit. I protested. I canvassed all the nurses and told anyone who would listen that I still felt giddy. When I pleaded to be kept in for observation I was told that I'd been observed quite enough already. I offered myself up as a guinea pig but all to no avail. They packed up my fruit, the remainder of my orange juice and marshmallows and gave them to me in a paper bag, and pointed me, cruelly, to the door.

I was quite the hero when I got back to the Home, which took some of the pain out of leaving my mother. Everyone wanted to see the gory mess under my plaster, for which I charged a penny. I described the whole process of the putting in of the stitches and the taking out of the stitches in terms that would have been overblown for a sail-maker. So I am quite confident that they got their penny's worth.

Mrs Wallis may have tired of me a little when every time I cut my finger or grazed my knee I insisted that I had sustained concussion and would have to go back. Tom was, naturally, a little jealous. As well as this we were no longer identical twins, of course, as people were now able to tell us apart by the scar above my eye. When strangers foolishly commented on how we were like peas in a pod I'd quickly reply, 'No we're not, I've had a bang on the head,' which always had the most peculiar effect on them.

From this point on, the Sunday visits that Tom and I made to the hospital were much happier occasions but, at the same time, we had begun to miss our mother more and wish we were all back together again. I had tasted something in the hospital which I hadn't known in a long time.

CHAPTER XXVIII

In which we sit our eleven-plus but the results change the course of our lives yet again and my fortunes in particular

Tom and I arrived at our final year at the brightly painted junior school where the classroom furniture had grown ridiculously too small for us all; we loomed over the little red chairs and the short-legged nature table like awkward bean poles. In direct relation to the shrinking of the legs of our desks our own legs had grown long. At the very top of them our short trousers flapped like flags on a post. This served to back up the declaration that we had got to 'the gawky age' and that pretty soon we would be given over to fits of reasonless giggling. We dreaded this, but at the same time looked forward to the new school where we would be allowed to wear long trousers to cover up the yellow stains of iodine which indelibly marked our knees. We were at the top of the school, we knew teachers by their first names, could beat up nearly anyone in the lower forms, and were about to sit our eleven-plus. This marked our form out from the rest because we were being 'prepared' for the ordeal; the younger children, when they passed by our door, were commanded by a prefect, standing sentry, to maintain a perfect silence. We were eagerly watched for signs of stress. All this watching and all this silence only increased our fear of the examination.

I had to stay behind two evenings a week to brush up my mathematics, which was one of my weaker subjects. My only truly strong subject was the nature table. I was an enthusiastic 'bringer in' – ever since the teacher had asked me to stand up and show the class the half of a martin's egg which had fallen from the roof of the Home. The success of this, and the general admiration of my peers, prompted me to fill the nature table almost single-handed. I brought in fungus, leaves, interesting stones, interesting rock formations – which were generally bits of old piping thrown up by the sewage system, and any dead animals that Tom and I did not want to boil down for the bones. Once the classroom had to be cleared because of a rotting blackbird I'd found. Another time it was a circular, flattened, tabby cat that I'd picked up in the road. Lindsey Williams recognized it and burst into tears.

Tom made her feel worse by suggesting that she took it home and gave it to her father for a drinks tray.

Apart from the pending examination it was a happier summer than I'd had for many years. I'd begun to learn how to amuse myself, and fall back on my own resources, and to live in a world of my own which was far preferable to the one I was actually in. In the garden of the Home there was a buddleia bush which the Red Admirals, the Peacocks and the Tortoiseshells loved. I watched them for hours and Mr Wallis bought me a book about British butterflies so that I could learn about their flights and habits. I liked the Peacocks and the Orange Tips especially and I only killed them and pinned them down after they had mated and laid their eggs and were at the end of the season. When I took them in for the nature table Miss Graterex was astonished by the delicate way I had displayed them on the lid of an old shoe box. She made the class queue up to see them and I was terribly, terribly proud.

We sat our examination and on the morning when the two buff envelopes dropped through the door of The Crab Apple Road Home Mrs Wallis shouted up to us, 'They're here, the envelopes have arrived.' We ran down the stairs and stared at them. 'Aren't you going to open them?' she asked.

'No,' we said, 'you open them for us.'

Mrs Wallis closed her eyes to make it fair and by feeling around for a while on the doormat picked up Tom's. She tore the envelope open and read out the single sentence:

'Thomas Stone. PASS. St Saviour's Technical High School for Boys.'

We all cheered and jumped up and down, and Mrs Wallis hugged Tom saying, 'Well done, well done, you're the first boy from the Home to pass.' She could hardly believe it as she thought back over the last eighteen months to the two broody, disturbed children who had arrived one rainy night and had promptly tried to run away. She picked up my envelope and opened it, 'and let's see if you're the first as well' – she was a master at being fair. 'Richard Stone . . .' she began, and then stopped.

'Come on,' I said, 'don't muck about.' She handed me the envelope. In neat, rounded type were the words:

'Richard Stone. FAIL. Broadfield Secondary.'

I dropped to the floor like a dead weight, fiddling with bits of torn envelope.

'I don't understand,' muttered Mrs Wallis. Tom ran into the lounge to continue with his cheering on his own. 'Never mind, never mind,' said Mrs Wallis.

'But I do mind,' I said. 'It's not fair. I stayed behind for extra maths.' Tom came back from the lounge and asked if he could use the telephone. Mrs Wallis gave him permission and he went to telephone Charlie Rubbidge and Barry Foster. His pass had put him on an even footing with them again. After the call he came running up to us shouting, 'Barry's passed for the Tech' too, so has Joey, and Charlie Rubbidge has passed for the Grammar, he's the first ever from our school, but he says he might not go there, he might come to St Saviour's with us because he says it's better to be a big fish in a small pond than a big fish in a big pond . . .' Tom paused for breath and continued '. . . we're all going to have a celebration tea at Charlie's this afternoon.'

I went upstairs and lay on my bed. After lunch Tom

asked if he could go to the hospital to give the news to
Mum. Mrs Wallis said that we would all go to see her,
myself included. At first I refused, and made quite a
scene but then I felt that I wanted to see her, mainly to
curb the praise that would be lavished on Tom.

Tom ran down the ward towards her as I walked slowly
behind. When I got there he was already in full flight
'. . . Barry's mum is buying him a new bike, Joey is
getting Scalextrics and Charlie's already got his micro-
scope this morning, what am I going to get?'

'Here,' she said, 'take some money from my purse and
go and get two ice-creams from the cafe, anything you
fancy.'

'What, both for me?' asked Tom.

'No!' said Mum, 'of course not, one each.' Tom looked
a little disgruntled and marched off.

'Hello Richard,' said Mum. 'I'm sorry, love. If anyone
was to pass I thought it would have been you. You must
be so upset.'

I lay my head down on her blanket and buried my
face.

'When are you getting out, Mum?' I asked, in a muffled
voice.

'I'm sorry, love, I know it's been a long time, but the
last op' didn't go as well as Mr Trifle thought. It looks
like I'm going downhill again, so we've both had bad
news today . . .'

'Will you have another operation?' I asked.

'We don't know. If it's possible I will.' I looked up at
her; she looked so much older and beneath her small
woollen hat I could see that she had lost her hair.

CHAPTER XXIX

*In which we get our new uniforms and I have a problem with
a briefcase, and the headmaster of Broadfield is found to be
a man of great investigative abilities and pomposity*

That summer holiday, with my customary *élan*, I
developed nervous eczema; the first time that I'd achieved
this independently of Tom, who seemed to spend the
whole time talking to Charlie and Barry about their new
school.

At the beginning of the holiday Mrs Wallis got a letter
from St Saviour's listing all the things that Tom would
need. The list was impressive: blazer, flannel trousers,
school jumper, white shirts, cap, black shoes and grey
socks. He needed gym kit, rugger kit, cricket whites,
tennis shoes, rulers, compasses, a briefcase and a fountain
pen. It wasn't until the last week of the summer holiday
that my list, from Broadfield, arrived, with apologies for
the duplicator having broken down. This amused Tom
greatly. He had hung his outfit up on our dormitory door
so that he could see it last thing at night. When we next
visited Mum he put it on to show her. He looked splendid
and heroic in it: a mauve blazer with green and gold cord
running around the cuffs and lapels, the badge on his cap
and pocket magnificently embroidered like the curtain in
the Opera House. Broadfield's letter said that tie and
blazer only were required and they recommended that
the elbows be reinforced. This last part, of course, made
Tom laugh when he read it out.

My blazer was black with a simple brown badge. Tom

was particularly proud of his Latin inscription. Mine had
no caption at all, the governors probably thinking, quite
rightly, that nothing could be said that hadn't already
been reported in the local paper. Discretion was the
better part of disgrace. The design itself was some kind
of wild boar, though the sewing wasn't very good, so
possibly it was a pig. Its symbolism was never referred to
at the school so I didn't ever find out exactly what stamp
of beast was emblazoned on my quivering breast.

Mrs Wallis felt bad about the way I gazed enviously at
Tom's new clothes so she applied to the Welfare for a
special order to buy me as much of the same as she
could: the shoes, the shirts, the socks, the rugger kit, the
fountain pen and the briefcase.

The folly of Auntie's egalitarianism hit me as soon as I
looked around the playground on the morning of my first
day. Not only was I the only boy in full dress uniform but
my briefcase was an item of much amusement to everyone, especially when used for a football. When I walked
into my first class even the teacher remarked, 'Who are
you. The man from the Inland Revenue?'

The fountain pen was a disaster, too; in my hands it
tended to carve the paper and I had the habit of putting
it in my mouth, as if it were a pencil, and dyeing my
tongue blue. I began working on ways of getting rid
of the briefcase. It was a big brown thing with brass
reinforcements on the bottom corners which made it
sound like a skinhead's blakeys every time I put it
down. The handle was made of fawnish plastic which the
manufacturers believed simulated leather. Despite this
the case was still posh for Broadfield, and after one
particularly harrowing day with it by my side I heaved it
over a hedge. 'That's that,' I thought, and then I began
to think, 'What'll I tell Mrs Wallis, when it was bought

especially for me by the Welfare?' 'I'll tell her it's been stolen,' I thought, but then I had visions of Mrs Wallis telephoning the police or, worse still, coming up to the school and telling the headmaster. I had already experienced one of his investigations in which every boy in the school was searched and questioned after money had gone missing from the changing-rooms. I went back, dashed into the garden and retrieved the case.

The next morning I hit on the idea of hiding it under the hedge in our own garden. This meant that Mrs Wallis would see me leave with it in the morning and return with it in the evening. I transferred my things for the day into a plastic bag, and was much happier at school with that. It said 'Dewhursts the butcher's' on the side in rather grand writing. As I walked through the school I felt a great sense of liberation being like everyone else. There were some comments of course, things like 'Oi, briefcase, where's your bag?' I worried about it a bit, sitting under the hedge – what if Auntie were to find it, what if a dog were to pee on it?

Everything went well for the first two days until I came home and found that it had gone. A great weight pounded in my chest. Had they found it? Had a dog run off with it? Had it actually been stolen? I thought it best not to say anything. I went into the Home and straight upstairs whereas normally I would have gone into the kitchen and slammed it down so that there should be no doubt that I still had it. I knew that if Mrs Wallis had found it she would come up and I would have to cobble together some appropriate story. She did not come up. It was an hour later when she said, 'Where's your briefcase?'

I flushed. 'I haven't got it,' I said, quite simply and enigmatically.

'Has someone stolen it?' she asked. 'Did they beat you up and take it off you?'

'Yes, that's what happened,' I said. I knew that I was getting into a very deep trench, and that having compounded my disdemeanour, not only by lying to her but also by making an accusation of theft, I was going to be living with the crisis for some few weeks, maybe the rest of my life.

'You must be so upset,' she said, 'you loved that briefcase.'

'Yeah,' I said.

'Right. Uncle will take you down to the school first thing in the morning.'

'No, please, they might give it back.'

'It's theft!' she said. 'I'm not having you being intimidated at that school.'

I didn't sleep much that night, I went through my story line by line, checking over what I had said during the further interrogation that the evening had brought, to prepare myself for the meeting with the headmaster.

Uncle took me in to see him before assembly. He was a large moustachioed man and his canes stood erect in an umbrella stand in the corner. He'd boasted that he had a cane to suit every boy's bum. I looked among them for mine and recognized it. He was an imperious man entirely unsuited to his post in Prospect; he had previously been beaten somewhere else and had come here to lick his wounds. Perhaps he had entered the profession late and if he hadn't have taken Broadfield would never have risen above senior teacher. Perhaps, on the other hand, he was a genuine philanthropist and had come to give his best to Prospect. Perhaps he'd molested a child at his last school. Whatever it was, there was definitely a reason for his being here with his long circumlocutions deliberately

chosen to be incomprehensible to us. He had, when he
first arrived, attempted to wear his academic gown, but
his great authority and noble nose could not deter the
boys from singing, as he flapped towards his podium: 'da
da da da da da batman!' He could not bear his own
indignity, of which we were the reflection, and he sat in
his study surrounded by pictures of his college XI. His
suit was shiny, worn and wet-looking as if he'd been
wrecked on some rocks and pummelled by a surf of chalk
dust. He would stand before us like a workhouse cook,
ladleing out the gruel of Secondary English Education.
To announce the school song was to invite the universal
shout of 'Come on you Millwall!' His leaving advice to
the older boys was: 'Don't keep dogs in flats,' which was
the only humane lesson ever taught at the school.

Uncle told him that I had been robbed. He looked deeply
shocked as if nothing like that had ever happened in his
school before. He turned to me. 'Now, Richard, I am greatly distressed that such a circumstance should occasion our
first meeting. Can you describe this briefcase?'

'Yes sir, it's brown,' I said.

He waited for me to continue. I looked at the carpet.
At length he said, 'There are many and various shades of
brown. There is the muddy brown of terrafirma, the dark
brown of the tree, there is the brown of bricks. Which?'

'Mud,' I said.

'And what other details can you furnish us with? Did it
have straps as a satchel does or the cords, perhaps, of a
dufflebag?'

'It had a handle,' I said, and added a fuller definition,
'on top.'

'A handle, with which you carried it beside you?'

'Yes, sir.'

'And picked it up by, and put it down again, and swung it by your side?'

'Sometimes, sir,' I said.

'So it's a briefcase we're talking about?'

'Yes,' I said, 'it is.'

He registered some surprise that a boy in his school, and a terribly small boy at that, should have such a thing as a briefcase. He had presumed we had been speaking about a holdall in rather grand terms. 'Now,' he said, thinking how he could imaginatively prise out of me a better description, 'let's say that your briefcase wanted to go abroad, which, heaven hope it hasn't, but let's say you wanted to fill out a passport application for it, how would you particularize it?' He sat back in his chair and looked at Mr Wallis, satisfied that he had displayed his clever way with children to a fellow professional on the same road to correction.

'I don't know,' I said.

'What would be its height?'

'About thirteen inches,' I said.

'Or?' he asked, and turned again to Mr Wallis saying, 'We will soon have the decimal standard upon us. I am keen that my boys begin to think, in all things, with a double standard.' Mr Wallis looked terribly impressed.

'Or seventeen centimetres,' he said with satisfaction. 'Fetch my ruler from the desk.' I fetched it. 'Am I right?'

'Yes, sir, exactly,' I said. He nodded to Mr Wallis who smiled at his success.

'Exactly!' he repeated. 'But do not be deceived by the simplicity of this example, Mr Wallis, for not all inches meet their centimetrical equivalents so neatly. One inch, for example, Richard?' He pointed to the ruler.

I looked at it closely and said: 'Two centimetres and five little bits.'

'Absolutely, and by your reckoning that would make three inches equal to seven centimetres and six little bits, which we term millimetres so that they should not be overlooked, being, as they are, so much smaller than the most familiar parts of an inch.'

He rocked back in his captain's chair and opened his mouth with salivarous deliberation. 'So! a mud-colour briefcase seventeen centimetres high! Does it have any distinguishing marks?'

'It's got his initials on it,' said Uncle, throwing himself into the investigation.

'Ah! and they are?'

'RS, sir,' I said.

'So we're looking for the letters R and S; is there anything else you can recall to separate your case from the common herd?'

'Um . . . yes, it's got some writing on it, sir.'

'Writing!' Uncle looked surprised but not as surprised as the headmaster; he sat up in his chair and said, 'Literacy has broken out and none of my departments has informed me! And which particularly illustrious members of our alphabet are inscribed?' I didn't understand so he had to repeat himself. 'What letters?' he shouted. It annoyed him more than anything else to have to explain that which he'd set out to make perfectly unintelligible.

'An A and an E, sir.'

'And why should someone thus inscribe it?'

'I don't know, sir.'

'Unless, of course,' he said, 'the A precedes the R and the E succeeds the S?'

'Yes, sir,' I said, not really understanding but guessing that he'd worked out what it read.

'Was the mother conscious, Mr Wallis, that this would

occur when she named the boy?' Mr Wallis laughed to the headmaster's satisfaction.

'Were you robbed within the precincts of the school,' he asked in a suddenly more serious tone.

'No sir, on my way here yesterday morning I was attacked.'

'Attacked? By bandits, or your peers?'

'I don't know, I didn't see them.'

'You didn't see your assailants?'

'No sir, they came from behind and blindfolded me.'

'Ingenious,' he said, slapping his hands together, 'and they ran off with their booty before the poor victim had a chance to remove the blindfold.'

'Yes, sir, that's right.' I was very glad of the experience I'd had, being a twin, of improvising a tale under very difficult circumstances.

He pressed on. 'So, by my computation, you still have the blindfold in your possession which can be used in evidence?'

'Um, no, sir.'

'You lost the vital clue as well as your briefcase. Isn't that a little unlucky? Are you telling us the truth in this matter?' He stared at me hard and then he stared at Mr Wallis and he in turn, stared at me, the pair of them trying to burn the lie out of me with their eyes.

'They used my own tie for the blindfold, sir!' I said.

'Oh!' he exclaimed in horror. 'Oh! Fiendish – there's none more inventive than the common thief,' and he got up from his chair. 'I have prayers and detention to read but rest assured, rest assured, Mr Wallis, that this case will be tracked down if I have to lash the last drop of blood from every master and every boy in this school!' And he turned with a flourish at the door shouting, 'The case shall be solved!' I was dismissed with a suspicious sideglance. He didn't really care whether the case was stolen or not. It was a minor detail, the important thing was the investigation.

I joined my class in the assembly hall. He threatened the whole school on my account.

'Someone!' he boomed, 'someone in our midst has lifted an article to which he had no just claim in law! And this someone . . .' he peered over his lectern in a way which suggested that he knew our every sin '. . . this someone has perpetrated this felony in l e a g u e with yet more of you!'

After this *buffo* beginning he paused for a moment to fill in the details, which were of course to him not as interesting as the fact that a crime had been committed. 'A brown briefcase on which someone has written arse,' he said and the whole school laughed. He nodded towards the English master in full enjoyment of his success. He liked to swear because it was the only thing that most of the boys understood and every now and then it pleased him to be understood.

'Now, culprits,' he said, 'I address you. I have in my hand a piece of paper . . .' (he had no such thing) '. . . and on this paper, naturally, are the names of the culprits, which I already know. As it is my custom, I shall be turning this document over to the constabulary at four-thirty. If the briefcase is back on my desk by then I shall deprive the nick of your company.'

One of the boys in my class, Patrick Manley, pulled at my jacket. 'But you haven't had your case for days,' he said. I knew this was my big flaw.

'I know,' I whispered. 'It's been nicked.'

'Oh,' said Patrick, surprised, as if he hadn't understood anything of what the headmaster had said. I kept a low profile all day. The next morning I was called back into his office. My briefcase was sitting on his desk.

'Well,' he said, leaping around the room animatedly, 'I hovered by the staff room until the culprit considered the coast to be clear, then I espied Feathers of 4B nipping in with the case. I lunged and caught him; he attempted to wriggle free but it was a hopeless and impossible task. "Feathers!" I bellowed. "Feathers! Heel!" I said. He capitulated. He fell to pieces in my hands. It was pathetic to see. I have just this moment concluded my interview with him. He claimed, the wretch, that he *found* the case – found it tossed into a hedge! He claimed that he removed it so that he might be a means of its restoration to its owner. Now, I know Feathers to be a timid boy and a novice at crime so was I surprised by such a story? No. Nevertheless I am inclined to believe the part about the hedge, for there were indeed marks of privet mould and a caterpillar resting in the folds.'

I shuddered; he had found me out. What would my punishment be?

'Shall I tell you the details of this mystery?'

'Yes sir,' I said meekly.

'Well,' he said and sat down, picking up a pencil to illustrate his points. 'Feathers retrieved the article from the hedgerow. This I believe. I realized it while I was caning him. How did the case get there? Feathers had retrieved it after your assailants had tossed it there realizing the enormity of their crime.'

'Really, sir?'

'Yes,' he said. 'So I think we'll leave it there. We'll never catch them now, not now we've got the case back.' He handed it to me and a great smile came across his face. 'Well,' he said, 'I suppose you didn't imagine in your wildest dreams that you'd ever be reunited?'

'No, sir,' I said.

'It is a briefcase of character. I can see why you couldn't bear to be parted from it for a moment.'

'Yes, sir,' I said.

I walked back down the corridor, clutching the bugger by my side.

CHAPTER XXX

In which we are split up and I begin to plot against my brother, and in which several boys in white polyester suits perform on the trampoline, and also in which I conduct a campaign against the Education Authority

Broadfield was dull and enormous with many of its classrooms lying empty, without even any desks, because the planners had built it to meet the needs of 'projected children' and these children hadn't turned up on account of the fact that many of them had maliciously refused to be projected into the world in the first place. All the boys in my class were intimidated by the place, no matter how rough and ready they were. Tom and I were now quite adequately institutionalized but Broadfield was more regimented, and colder, than anything I had yet encountered. None of us could adapt to the simple change of now being called by our surnames, and the absence of the little bottles of milk at playtime, however much we had disliked them. There was no chart on the wall with gold stars for merit, there was merely a banner showing a succession of apes walking up a ladder and gradually turning into rather hairy men. It was a depressing image and from what I saw of the older boys it seemed only to be scientifically accurate in the reverse.

When we wrote stories we weren't allowed to draw a picture at the end, the part I most enjoyed, and the stories themselves were now referred to as 'compositions'. This was to distinguish them from comprehension – a discipline by which arid samples of prose were rendered still more arid by our miscomprehension. Worst of all for me was the absence of a nature table – how was I to excel among my peers? All of these sound like silly childish things to complain about, but it was the total effect that disturbed me; the suddenness of the transition from being a child to being a secondary school student.

Broadfield had a single expanse of tarmac, on the far side of which was a high fence separating us from the Broadfield girls. Their school was built to the same design but was set asymmetrically to ours and with fancy flourishes slapped up at the corner. It was on this tarmac that we had to endure break – so named because it was the time when, traditionally, things were broken: anything from rulers to femurs would suffice, generally finding an average in metacarpals and teeth. Boys would set fire to the litter bins and set them rolling on their sides. The senior boys had a separate playground, set next to ours but higher up. During break they would descend on us in raiding parties, carry one of us off to their square of tarmac and then throw us back over the wall that divided the two. To discourage this practice the headmaster had put a fence up, on top of the dividing wall, but this meant that they would throw you up higher, thus increasing the descent on the other side. I was no safer from my peers, several of whom delighted in dead legs or a knee swiftly applied to the groin and other horrible and degrading acts, generally involving the lavatory pan and the loss of one's trousers.

The only way to be safe was to become good at sport or good at fighting. I was good at neither. The only way I could endure the boredom of the football field was to imagine that I was on the field of some great battle, mounted on a charger, and protected by armour. Where other boys ran, and tackled, and did fancy footwork, I would gallop up to the ball whinnying like a horse. On one occasion I was standing by our goal, ostensibly defending, paying little attention to the action which was all taking place at the far end of the field, and scraping my boot in the mud in the manner of a horse, when the ball shot past me and into our goal. The sportsmaster ran up to me. 'Where were you, boy?' he demanded.

'Agincourt, sir,' I said.

At the end of Tom's first term at St Saviour's Mrs Wallis took Tom and me to his school speech day. I wasn't entirely sure what to expect. Broadfield held no such occasion, quite wisely, because if any speeches were made it was unlikely that the pupils, or even the parents, would be able to endure it without turning their attention to the destruction of the seats in which they sat. Never having been to a speech day before, then, I hoped only that I wouldn't be required to make a speech myself, but if I was, I decided, I'd speak very well of Tom and his school despite everything. Mrs Wallis made me wear my school uniform, because it doubled up as Sunday best, and I felt very out of place in it. It was the first major public engagement at which Tom and I did not appear together as identical twins.

St Saviour's did not have a playground, it had a quad. We strolled around it before going into the hall for the speeches. It was a grassy square, so carefully mown that I believed it had been made from two separate strains of grass seed, sown alternately, and the whole quad was surrounded by an arched cloister. St Saviour's was, of course, outside the Prospect boundary and much older than the estate.

'Where do you go at break?' I asked Tom.

'I go to chess club, but you can go to the debate, or tuck, or the library,' he said. Broadfield had none of these things. Boys were not allowed into the library because they tore pages from the old thin paper editions of Dickens and rolled them into cigarettes. Tom pointed out the greenhouses which extended from the science laboratories. Where at Broadfield we were lucky if, in the fourth form, we got a course on bricklaying or car maintenance, here, in the greenhouses, the boys were breeding a new strain of high-yield wheat. Tom showed us the grass tennis courts and, in a clearing, the memorial to old boys who had fallen. I was quite sick.

The school orchestra played before Tom's headmaster rose to congratulate a long line of boys who had achieved excellence in the arts, the sciences and physical fitness. A boy sitting to the side of me looked at my blazer and sniggered. When Tom had spoken to his friends he had not introduced me. During a demonstration of gymnastics, in which boys clad in white polyester suits leaped from one trampoline to another, I began plotting the overthrow of my brother. I wondered if I might drug him, steal his uniform, and take his place at St Saviour's; I would look just like him. Then I felt the scar above my eye and cursed the day I got my bang on the head. 'Perhaps it was the bang on the head that made me fail the exam?' I thought. I felt hopeless, and worse than that, trapped.

The next day I spoke to Mr Wallis in his office. 'Are

you sure they didn't make a mistake with my results?' I asked.

'Richard,' he said, 'I think you're just going to have to accept it.'

'Can't you write a letter to the Education Authority and say I ought to be in the same school as my brother because we're twins and we're the same egg?'

'Same egg or not,' said Uncle, 'you're still going to have to accept it.'

'But I won't, I know I won't,' I shouted. 'I won't accept it.'

'Well, I think you should.'

'Well, I think I shouldn't,' I said.

'Well then, we'll just have to agree to differ,' he said, finally.

'But I don't agree,' I said. 'I differ.'

I did not go to school the next day. I gave the impression that I was going to school; I packed my sports bag and put my homework in my briefcase and headed off out of the door saying that I was going to school, but I did not. I had decided instead to walk the three miles to the Education Offices. I felt sure that when they heard my full story they would move me to Tom's school. The offices of the Education Authority were situated in a large house just outside the Prospect boundary. I went into the reception where a woman was working a Gestetner machine. 'Could I see the man in charge of schools?' I asked.

'Any particular school?' said the woman, facetiously.

'Yes, St Saviour's,' I said, undaunted. 'I'd like to go there.'

The woman was rather taken aback. 'Well, I'm sorry,'

she said, 'you can't just walk in here and say you'd like to go to such and such a school.'

'But I would,' I said.

'There's nothing we can do about that, and there's nobody here you can see, so you can just take yourself out by the door you came in by.'

I turned toward the door and she returned to her duplicating. As I approached the door I saw a chair and decided to sit on it. After a while I said. 'I'm at Broadfield,' hoping it would make her feel sorry for me.

'Really,' said the woman, paying no attention at all.

'It's awful,' I said, after a pause, 'and I refuse to go there any more.'

'Well, you can't play truant, it's against the law,' said the woman.

'I am playing truant,' I said. She stopped duplicating.

'You're doing what?!' she asked.

'I'm playing truant. I'm on strike.'

'What, here in the Education Office?'

'Yes,' I said. A man in a grey overall who was cleaning the windows laughed.

The woman looked at him sternly. 'If you don't leave I shall telephone your school.'

I shrugged my shoulders.

At this point a man came out of an office. 'Have you finished running those letters off yet, Miss Purnell?' he said.

'No, I'm afraid I haven't, Mr Broadhurst, I keep getting interrupted.' She nodded towards me.

'What's he doing sitting there?' he asked.

'He's on strike,' said the man who was cleaning the windows.

'He's playing truant,' said Miss Purnell, as I now knew her to be.

'Young man!' said Mr Broadhurst, and I walked over to him. 'Are you playing truant?' he asked.

'Yes, sir,' I said.

'Do you really think this is the best place to do it?'

'No, sir,' I said, 'but I've come to see about changing schools.'

'About what?' he asked. I always seemed to be having to repeat myself to adults.

'I want to leave my school and go to St Saviour's instead.'

'Which school are you at now?' he asked.

'Broadfield, sir.'

'Oh blimey,' said the old man cleaning the windows, 'no wonder he wants to go to St Saviour's!' He received a reproving glance from Mr Broadhurst.

'Did you pass your eleven-plus?' he asked me, rhetorically.

'No, not completely,' I said.

'Well then, you will know as well as I that St Saviour's is a selective school and you have not been selected.'

'But my brother's there.'

'I can't help that. He's obviously more suited to it than you.'

'But we're identical twins, how can he be?' I said, and I emphasized the point, 'we're the same egg! He's not brainier than me, we've always been the same.'

'Well he obviously did better in his eleven-plus.'

'But he's not brainier than me and I'm not brainier than him,' I repeated.

Mr Broadhurst was getting exasperated. He couldn't think of any way to justify the examination to me. 'There's nothing that can be done about it now. Everyone takes the exam, everyone has the same chance.'

'But I had a bang on the head just before it,' I said.

'I can well believe it,' he said.

'But it's not fair.'

'It's no use your coming here and complaining. Go back to school, and if you work hard you'll get on just as well as if you went to any other school.'

'No I won't,' I said.

'Yes you will,' he insisted.

'Won't,' I repeated.

'You obviously don't even have any intention of trying,' he said.

'I'll end up turning to a life of crime,' I said.

'No you won't. Broadfield is a very good new school.'

'I'm in The Crab Apple Road Home already,' I said.

Mr Broadhurst shook his head at this. He'd met some exasperating children in his time, and more than enough exasperating parents, but I was about to take the biscuit.

'And I wouldn't mind being transferred from their either,' I added for good measure.

'Get out of this office,' he shouted, 'and go back to your school! Miss Purnell, get that duplicating finished and bring it in to me.' With this he about turned, walked into his office, and slammed the door. Thus was concluded my first interview with the Education Authority.

I walked through the woods for several hours, quite downhearted, and then when it would have been time for me to get in from school I returned to the home. There was no one in the lounge so I knelt down in front of the three-dimensional picture of Jesus and prayed:

> 'Dear Lord Jesus of heaven,
> you know I want to go to your school.
> Please help me to get accepted.
> Amen, Richard Stone.'

As I stood up the picture winked at me. Without any reservations at all I took this as a direct sign from God that my course of action was right, and embarked upon a programme of non-co-operation with the adult world. I returned to the Education Authority offices every day that week, sometimes with a banner made from cardboard, like those I'd seen on television saying 'End the War in Vietnam'. Mine, of course, read 'Send me to St Saverers' – spelt wrong. The routine would be the same each day. I would turn up at the office at nine-thirty, they would let me sit there for a while to teach me that it'd do no good, and then, at ten o'clock, they'd telephone Mr Wallis. By ten-fifteen he had returned me to Broadfield where I would be assigned my punishment by the form master. It was generally having to write out, in triplicate, the first four chapters of the Bible.

On the Friday of that week I was returned to Broadfield and taken in to see the headmaster. It was obvious to me that no one knew how to deal with the problem I had created.

'I don't understand it, Stone,' he said. 'What is it about Broadfield that you don't like?'

'The school,' I said.

'Can you be more specific?' he asked, just as he had done when I threw my briefcase into the hedge. 'Is it the architecture that offends your sensibilities? Is it the location? Is the playing-field not close enough to the changing-rooms? Or is it perhaps, that infernal scraping of the chalk on the blackboard which can so set one's teeth on edge? If so, speak up. I'll have the whole school rebuilt for you. Nothing is too much.'

It was a very kind offer but I had to say that it was none of these things.

'Then what exactly can it be?' he asked.

'I don't like the lessons, I don't like the teachers, I don't like the boys, and I don't think I should be here.'

The headmaster reeled back and gripped the arms of his captain's chair, casting his eyes heavenward for strength. 'I don't suppose you're prepared to negotiate?' he asked.

'No,' I said.

He shook his head.

'It may seem unbearably hard to you, I know, but do you think I should really allow a pupil of this school to lay siege to the Education Authority offices? You are a bad apple, it seems, in this respect and I have no doubt that you will rot the whole barrel, since it's a barrel ready to turn. How do you think it would be if every boy who was disenchanted here turned up waving placards at the Authority?'

'I don't think there'd be much room in the forecourt, sir,' I said.

'Would you like to visit me every evening for a caning?' he asked.

I shrugged my shoulders.

'The proper answer is "no sir",' he said.

I shrugged my shoulders a second time. He sent me to stand in the corridor outside his office where he could observe me for the rest of the morning.

When Tom and I visited our mother the next Sunday we found her lying amid her machines, faintly blipping, very pale and unable to speak to us. We sat with her for half an hour but it was hopeless trying to talk to her. I had wanted to enlist her support in my campaign, and Tom wanted money for a school trip, but it was as much as we could do to get a slight movement of her fingers when we held her hand.

As Mrs Wallis was leading us away the ward sister appeared from her office. 'Which one of you is Richard?' she asked. I said that I was and she led me into the office. 'Do you know why your mother is so ill today?' she asked me.

'Because she needs another operation?' I said.

'No,' she said. 'It's something that she doesn't need, she doesn't need a certain young man who won't go to school. Ever since the lady from the social services told her what you've been up to she has worried so much that it has brought on a relapse. Now what do you say to that?' I hung my head down. 'Ellen, your mother, has been fighting bravely for almost two years – do you want to throw that all away?'

'No,' I said.

'Then let me tell your mother that you are going to stop the way you are behaving.'

'I didn't mean to make her ill. I only meant to go to the same school as Tom to please her.'

'But now you'll go to school like a good boy.'

'Yes,' I said. 'I'll go to school like a good boy.'

I felt awful and very guilty. I blamed myself for the whole of my mother's illness. I gave up my campaign.

CHAPTER XXXI

In which Prospect is changing and the houses are improved and a most unexpected turn of events turns the events

It was the early seventies and everything was changing on Prospect. Floral wallpaper was out and Mr Wallis painted the walls of the lounge alternate purple and chocolate.

He thought it looked terrific and terribly modern. The new furniture was less hard-edged and shaped from inside; everything aspired to the form of foam rubber. All across Prospect people were falling in love with expanded rubber. We had pillows stuffed with little brightly coloured pieces of it and when they caught fire you were gassed in a matter of seconds by the fumes.

The roads were changing too. The planners hadn't foreseen that working people would own so many cars so quickly. Some families, where the older boys were of an age to tinker with wrecks, had two or three, blocking the street or in the front garden. The roads of Prospect had been intended for nothing more demanding than council access to their properties, and for the milkfloat. The driving schools of nearby Orpington and Sidcup liked the toy-town nature of our roads and for years squadrons of learner cars had been coming to potter, hiccup and stall their way around the estate. Now, every road was packed tight with cars, they broke up the pavements and spoiled the verges. Groups of men stood around dismembered vehicles in the evenings, fiddling and tapping, interfering with the reception on the TV sets, telling each other that they were tuning the engines. For eleven pounds the council would lay you a driveway and these driveways began appearing all over Prospect with polished Ford Anglias perched upon them.

With the rougher families, and those who were earning a big wage, the Ford Zephyr was the most popular car. It was big and fat and American-looking with a saloon body and the Anglia's rear wings grown out of all reasonable proportion to the rest of the car. They were like great lazy fallen angels, slouching around the estate with their radios blaring country music.

In this atmosphere of improvement and greater wealth,

Tom and I felt increasingly shabby in the Home. Tom was finding it difficult at St Saviour's because of where he lived. The other boys ragged him. The government had passed a piece of legislation whereby council houses could be bought by their tenants. Charlie and Barry's parents had bought theirs, they'd even bought the verges in front, and this, they decided, made them a cut above Tom.

When we told Mum that the Pascoes had bought their house she was perplexed by it. 'It's ridiculous,' she said. 'If you're going to pay a mortgage every week you may as well pay the rent!' This contained a logic with which we earnestly agreed. The idea of owning the place in which you lived was so contrary to expectations that we found the idea ludicrous. 'I mean, what would you do if the immersion heater went?' said Ellen.

The selling off of the houses caused many arguments on the estate, especially when people had bought the verges and wouldn't allow other people to walk on them any more. It looked very strange to see the places where the children had always played being fenced in. Prospect had been moving on apace in the two years that we had all been in the care of the state, and it had left us behind. Ellen began to worry that our house, which had stood empty for so long, would be sold off by the new Tory council.

One night, after school, Tom was depressed by something Charlie had said that day, and Terry was in a particularly foul mood, so we took ourselves out for a long walk across Prospect. We walked past the changing houses. It wasn't enough for these people simply to own them, they had to be seen to own them. The privet hedges were torn out and replaced with brick walls. Porches were built over the doorways and the lawns cemented over, and the windows changed to leaded lights.

Although the whole of this programme was attempted, not all the parts always reached completion, especially where first experiments in glass and mortar were involved. All the parts were attempted simultaneously, and, simultaneously all the parts would be abandoned. Prospect was beginning to look like the chalet and caravan park on the south coast where many working people had formerly expressed themselves in wood, brick, and bits from old cars.

The porches were little chapels dedicated to the patron saint of portals. People put in wrought-iron gates, and gateposts were surmounted by badly cast cement lions. Several houses, on our walk, had French-style shutters and frilly canopies; it was getting difficult to tell them apart from the shops and I fear we upset one woman by knocking on her door thinking that we could buy some sweets. We walked to Clover Gardens and saw the Pascoes' house. Danny had bought shares in a glazier and DIY business and he seemed to have involved the entire stock in his edifice. There was a reproduction Victorian lamp-post at a slight angle, set in concrete, in the garden, and a large plate-glass window, like that of a car showroom. He had painted the exterior of the house red, and the mortar between the bricks he'd painted black as far up as the base of the bedroom windows. Two large bright burglar alarms, affixed to the wall, stood as a warning to any who might wish to divest them of their new wealth and property

Standing next to the Pascoes' our house looked time-locked and sad. The council had kept it in repair but the garden was overgrown and filled with crisp packets and Coke tins that people had thrown over. It upset us to see it like this, and we decided to go into the garden to tidy up a bit, and to remove the leaflets stuffed into the letter-box.

We opened the gate and walked up the path. As I bent down to pick up some litter something caught my eye, moving, inside the house. 'Tom!' I said, 'look, there's someone in there.' Our hearts began beating faster.

'Do you think it's a burglar?' said Tom.

'I don't know,' I whispered, 'but if it is we've got to do something.'

Tom agreed and so we ducked down and began moving nearer to the window to look in. The hydrangea, into which our father had frequently fallen, had grown so large that it covered the lower part of the window. We gradually eased ourselves up from behind it. We saw that there was a fire alight in the grate. A woman in a blue uniform was crossing the room with a cup of tea in her hand. Our eyes followed her until we saw the figure of our mother, wrapped in a blue blanket, huddled by the fire. We didn't wait to knock on the door but immediately leapt up, cheering, to rap on the window. The nurse looked towards us and went to shoo us away, but we saw our mother stop her, say something, and then wave us to go to the door. As soon as the door opened we almost knocked the nurse over in our excitement to get inside.

'Mum, Mum, you've got out!' shouted Tom.

'Now don't go too mad the pair of you,' said Ellen. 'I've had a terrible ride in the ambulance and I'm whacked out. Mr Trifle says no jumping up and down on trampolines until the end of the week.'

'These are your lovely boys you've been telling me about then, Mrs Stone?' said the nurse.

'Yes, these are them,' said Ellen, and we buried our heads in the blue blanket while she stroked our hair. Every now and then we turned our heads to check with the nurse that she really had been let out and that she wasn't going to have to go back.

When we had all been in the house together for an hour, Miss Barnes arrived and we were sent to open the door.

'Oh,' she said, surprised, 'I was just coming to discuss with your mother the arrangements for your return from the Home.' We invited her in. She told Ellen how pleased she was that she had recovered from her long illness.

'And now we can start thinking about re-forming you all as a family,' she said. We were all a little worried by this. As far as we were concerned we had been re-formed as a family the moment the nurse had opened the door. 'I am thinking in terms of the end of next month, when you are fully convalesced at one of our rest homes on the south coast, for Richard and Tom to leave Crab Apple Road.' We couldn't believe what we were hearing and we moved nearer to our mother. Even the nurse looked as if she thought it harsh.

'But I'm having the nurse in every day,' said Ellen.

'Yes, but I'm sure that the last thing you need at the moment is two boisterous boys rampaging around the house making demands upon you.'

'That,' said our mother, with as much courage as she could muster, 'is exactly what I need. Mr Trifle says that the most important thing is the will to live, and they are all I have to live for, all together in this house.'

Ellen stuck to her guns in this matter and we backed her up vociferously, and within the hour Miss Barnes and her feather capitulated and drove us to the Home to collect our things. Everyone there already knew what had happened and the other children looked at us coldly as if we had already left and as if they had never known us. It was the strangest sensation, and not entirely unwelcome.

We spent the rest of the evening getting the house in order, clearing mouldy food from the cupboards, dusting everything, and making the beds with clean sheets. We went to bed very late that night, tired, emotional and, naturally, very happy.

CHAPTER XXXII

In which Mr Bannister is found to be a very great man and his influence changes the course of my life yet again, and in which a great scandal is uncovered by him and great steps are taken

On the second evening of our return Mr Bannister came to call. 'I heard,' he said, 'through my position at the council, that you had been released from the infirmary and . . .' here he blushed with embarrassment '. . . and I had to come and say, after all you've been through, how happy I am for you.'

'Oh, thank you,' said Ellen, 'I'm pleased as well, I can tell you. I shall be in a wheelchair for a few months, but it's so marvellous to be back in the house again. I thought it would have been taken away from me.'

'Oh no,' said Edwin Bannister, 'I wouldn't allow it to happen. Whenever any plans were mooted to turf you all out, I marched into the Housing Office and I put my foot down, I can tell you, I put my foot right down. "If it isn't enough with all the trouble that poor little family have had," I said, "we have to cast them out into the darkness!" I put my foot well and firmly down.'

'Oh, thank you, Mr Bannister. I can't tell you how pleased I will be to see you again every Monday.'

Mr Bannister's face fell. 'Well, I'm afraid you won't actually. I don't do my rounds any more.'

'Oh no!' said Ellen, 'you're not ill yourself are you?'

'Oh, my goodness, no,' he said, 'I'm in fine fettle. You can't walk ten miles a day in the fresh open air – sewers permitting – for twelve years and not to be in fine fettle. No, I'm being done away with.'

'Done away with?' asked Ellen.

'I've been replaced by a book of giros.'

'Oh no, how could they?' said Ellen. Mr Bannister looked down at the boots, one of which contained the foot which he had so firmly put down in her defence and yet which was of no help on his own account. That he had been replaced by a small blue and green printed tear-off cheque was a bitter pill.

Mr Bannister explained to her how she would have to fill in her giros and hand them in at the post office. 'I felt I had to explain it to you myself. I couldn't let a leaflet do it. It's only right,' he said.

Ellen thanked him. 'But surely you're not out of a job?' she asked him.

'Oh no,' he said, 'I have a position in the office. A very good position. It's promotion of course, but I miss direct contact with the tenants.'

'I'm sure you do. What position have they given you?'

'Well, we're not really supposed to disclose details of the way the council operates. It's all very hush-hush. Like God the council moves in mysterious ways, sometimes it doesn't move at all . . .' Ellen nodded knowingly '. . . all I can tell you is that it's a position of great responsibility involving the maintenance of cracked paving slabs.'

'Oh,' said Ellen, impressed, 'I'm sure they must think very highly of you.'

'Well,' said Mr Bannister modestly, 'I'm informed by my sources that I'm not entirely unthought of at the very top.'

'I'm sure you are,' said Ellen. We all agreed that he had indeed done very well to have risen to such dizzy heights in government.

'And this subject,' he said, 'brings me to the second reason for my visit.' Mr Bannister raised his eyebrows and rose up on the balls of his feet in a way which suggested a great mystery.

'You may or may not know that I've not been entirely unthought of by the community at large . . .' he said and we listened intently '. . . and a matter of a few weeks ago I was appointed a governor of Broadfield School.' My ears pricked up. 'In my capacity as governor of Broadfield Secondary School for Boys you will probably be aware that I have access to certain information which would, otherwise, be inaccessible, and I think I have a bit of a shock for you . . .' With this he crossed the room resolutely until he got to the sideboard where he rested his hand. He took off his beret. Ellen took it from him and held it. Mr Bannister drew a deep breath.

'Well,' he said, and we all moved a pace nearer. 'Well . . .' he said a second time, to increase the impact of the shock '. . . you probably realize that detailed files are kept on every human being.' We nodded our heads. We didn't realize this but we were very glad to hear it.

'A file is kept on every boy at Broadfield, not only in the safe at the school but also at the Education Office. These files, naturally, are not to be perused by the public.'

'Oh no, I wouldn't suppose they were,' said Ellen.

'No,' said Mr Bannister, 'a file is confidential – it's not a newspaper, is it? Sometimes a file can work against you, sometimes it can work for you. Sometimes it is so confidential that oftentimes the person to whom it refers is unaware of its existence.' Mr Edwin Bannister was delivering himself of the truly incredible. This was his natural element, that of files and decisions taken along lengthy corridors.

'Having arrived early for the board of governors' meeting, and having debated Richard previously, while I was perusing the files in my capacity I availed myself of the opportunity to have a look at yours, Richard, and do you know what I did?'

'No?' I gasped with the greatest interest I'd ever taken in anything.

'I did exactly that,' said Mr Bannister. He looked at each of us in turn. 'I read your file.' We all waited to find out what he had discovered that was so important that he had to rest his hand on the sideboard.

He treated himself to another deep breath and jangled the change in his pocket (in his exalted position as Governor and Head of Cracked Slabs he missed the everyday jangling of money). 'Education, as you probably realize, has been in a state of flux over the last four years. Since my appointment I've tried, in my own way, to apply myself to the debate. Boiled down you've always got those who are for it and those who ain't. There's the Tories on the one side standing in principle for grammar and then abolishing them all over the show, and then there's the socialists on the other standing for comprehensive and then dilly dallying with it. For the life of me don't ask which is which. As you can imagine, those of us actively involved in the education of the future generation, those of us out there on the front line, don't know whether we're standing on the one leg or the other.'

Ellen and I looked at Edwin Bannister with great sympathy for his plight, but all the same we did wish he'd get on to the contents of the file, having waved the subject around the air so much.

'Setting up a school for Prospect, such as Broadfield, has had its teething troubles. As any bouncing baby does. When we first built it we were working entirely in projections and forecasts. None of us at the council knew for sure quite what was landing in our laps. As far as the academic capabilities of the pupils we had to cater for were concerned we were like Turks on a banana boat. With a system in such turmoil then, what are there bound to be? There are bound to be mix-ups, bound to be casualties, just as with any beach-head operation. Sometimes a sacrifice has to be made for the good of all. Now I've been around top decision-makers all my life, and quite frankly, I can't make my mind up about them. They're a funny breed. A decision will be taken at a low level and it will be overturned at a higher level, and then when the lowest level appeals to an even higher level, the decision of the high level will be overturned and so it's back to square one.'

Ellen nodded in assent to Bannister's analysis.

'Then,' he continued, 'those at the low level who are responsible for the actual implementation of the decision find that, in practice, they were wrong, it's unworkable. It's always people like me, in the middle, who are right. What do the low people do?' We didn't know. The situation seemed so complicated as to be impossible. 'Well, they overturn the decision piece by piece until you wouldn't know that any thought had been given to the matter at all, nor any decisions taken. It is the man in the middle who has the best view of the top and the bottom of the ladder.'

By the end of this hypothesis I felt I had been over-turned several times myself. Mr Bannister paused, and suspected that he had, perhaps, entirely digressed from his point. So much so that he was in danger of never finding his way back. 'I suppose you want to know what was in the file?' he said at last.

Since the whole of my future prospects, let alone the alleviation of the misery I was in at Broadfield, obviously depended on the contents of this file, we all answered in the affirmative, rather loudly. Mr Bannister smiled at his captive audience and rose up on the balls of his feet.

'Naturally I can't disclose the details,' he said. We were immediately deflated by this, but knew that it was only a matter of time and patience before Bannister let it all out. 'Whatever was in the mind of the powers that be, we don't know, we are in the dark. We can only guess. My guess is this, that at the time when Richard sat his eleven-plus, the powers that be were expecting the comprehen-sive system to take effect at any moment. Idealists. Hindsight shows that this was not the case, but then, most things hindsight shows are not the case. So they took the decision that they took, what else could they do?'

We didn't know. He began to relate the actual events. 'The level of grade of teacher that a school may elicit from the general pool is determined by the average intelligence quota, or "IQ" as we in the business call it, of the pupils in the school.' Mr Bannister paused for effect, and seeing that there wasn't one, he continued, adding a few more gesticulations here and there. 'In the year before Richard was admitted to the school there was a bit of a ding dong at the Authority; they were worried that the intelligence quota of Prospect's school had slipped irrevocably, damaging the grade of the teachers they might obtain. So what steps did they take? They took steps at the highest level. They decided to pump a random selection of higher-grade pupils into the Broadfield system.'

It sounded as if he were describing the sewage system again, which seemed to be the form for everything in Prospect. It wasn't until he put his hand on my shoulder and said, 'And you, Richard, were one of those boys,' that all he had been saying became real. 'Whether or not all these psychological people had a hand in it or not who knows. They might have wanted to see how you did in one place and Tom did in the other. I wouldn't put anything past them.' Mr Bannister had obviously greatly enjoyed his investigations and rather wanted to bathe in the glory of his success, but we were full of questions.

'So did I pass my eleven-plus?' I asked.

'Will he be transferred?' asked Ellen.

'Will he come to St Saviour's?' asked Tom.

Mr Bannister beamed. 'I've already had a brainstorming session with the headmaster about how we resolve the situation now the news is out and I can tell you that the answers are "yes, yes, and yes". All we can do now is to try and make it up to the boy.'

We were all very happy with the result.

CHAPTER XXXIII

In which we are reunited and arrive at a happy conclusion, and in which the sewage explodes, and in which Prospect is preserved in a very unusual way

We had an appointment to see the headmaster of St Saviour's at the start of school on the next day. Tom took one handle of Ellen's wheelchair and I took the other and together we pushed her to the school in Chislehurst. It was a wonderful, bright morning with the happy atmosphere of an English Indian summer. Chislehurst seemed the perfect place for a school to me: a pretty church with a tall spire, a common, quiet houses, oaks planted to commemorate coronations, a sweet shop by the bus stop, and a second-hand shop called '*Nouvelle à vous*'.

Tom left us in the corridor and I pushed our mother into the headmaster's office. The room was small and plain, with a view of the school cedar tree. There were easy chairs for his guests and a microphone on his desk through which he could address the school at any time on whatever subject took his fancy. Mr W. C. Gill rose from his chair as soon as we entered the room. He had a nice smile and shook my hand warmly. He invited us to join him for morning coffee. He came from Whitby, he told us, where his grandfather had harpooned whales. He had none of the overbearing pretentiousness of the Broadfield head.

'We're very happy to have Richard join his brother at the school,' he told us, 'and I'll do my best, Mrs Stone, to make sure he's happy and successful here, just as I hope Tom is.' Ellen thanked him and we all chatted a little more about our mother's illness, about Tom, about the cedar tree outside the window and about harpooning whales. At the end he said, 'But you must expect, after Broadfield, Richard, to be at the very bottom of the class.'

'Yes,' I said, 'but I ain't going to stay there.'

From the way he spoke and from the way he smiled I felt as if the slate of the last few years had been wiped clean and forgotten for ever. Very happily I went to my first class.

Mr Harvey, my form master and head of the science department, was himself like a one-man nature table. His pockets were stuffed with little containers full of the pupae of silk moths and there was a colony of termites sealed between glass. All manner of insects hibernated and hatched and spun about his person: little grubby ladybirds before their shells and wings had grown; mosquitoes in phials of water; wood pigs in cork; earwigs in straw; silverfish in little bits of bathroom rug; maggots in cow dung. When he leaned over his Bunsen burner, to point something out, his white lab coat caught fire. He was entirely unaware of the fact until someone put their hand up to tell him.

'Excuse me, sir.'

'Yes Richard, what do you want to know?'

'I think you're on fire, sir.'

'Oh yes, thank you, so I am.' And he'd beat out the flames with one of our exercise books and then check his pockets to see if any of his creatures had been roasted.

On my first afternoon we were sitting on our high stools at the long benches with the sun streaming in through the window. We were growing crystals from tiny slithers of copper sulphate tied with cotton and suspended in a solution, when a butterfly came flapping at the window.

'Right,' said Mr Harvey. 'It's too nice to be inside, let's all go on a trek.'

He led us out across the school fields and into the woods, commenting as we went on the variety of the grasses and worm-casts. He fell upon a puff-ball with great delight, plucked it up from where it grew beside the path, laid it down and stamped on it by throwing himself up into the air and coming down with both feet on the fungus. He was engulfed in a great white cloud. 'There!' he said. 'Seed dispersal! And great fun too! Mother Nature made the puff-ball in full knowledge that we'd enjoy jumping on it.'

After this I walked along beside him in the hope that he'd find one that Mother Nature would like me to jump on. He paused and looked closely into a leaf which was folded like an envelope and bound by a silk thread. He popped it open and pulled a fat green caterpillar from it.

'You see this little chap?' he said to me. I screwed up my face as it wriggled fiercely from side to side, trying to find a soft patch on his finger to bite. 'He's not much good for the trees but he's very nutritious.' Saying this he put it into his mouth and ate it. Everyone screamed and watched in horror.

I looked among the leaves of the tree and found another little envelope, took the caterpillar out and put it in my mouth. It wriggled on my tongue and I could feel its feet, the four pairs of chubby abdominal legs and the three pairs of spikey thoracic legs, scrabbling with their hairs on my tongue. I shut my eyes and swallowed it, just managing to mash it up a bit with my back molars before it went down. It tasted sweet, which surprised me.

Mr Harvey laid his hand on my shoulder. 'Like nature, do you?' he asked me.

'Yes, sir, I do,' I said. 'I collect butterflies.'

'What's your collection like, any good?'

'It's all right, but I've got no fritillaries because I can't get down to the coast.'

'So many species are in decline,' said Mr Harvey, shaking his head sadly. 'People say it's the collectors but it's not. There are many roads to the extinction of colonies: Mother Nature herself turns on them, then there's chemicals, drainage, man's unbalancing of the natural economy . . .' his voice trailed off.

'Science masters who eat the pupae,' I said, smiling and presuming a level of understanding between us already.

Mr Harvey considered what I'd said for a moment and then replied, quite seriously, 'No, I don't think that accounts for a major dent in population.' I laughed and, seeing this, he smiled.

At the end of the afternoon's lesson, when we were back in the classroom, he called me to stay behind. 'Come into my store-room,' he said and I followed him in.

'Now,' he said, 'don't dare let the headmaster know, or anyone in the class, but here, take this and put it up your jumper.' He handed me a butterfly display box.

'It's beautiful,' I said, 'thank you, thank you.'

'When you've got them pinned out bring them in and show the class. Show them what can be done.'

'Oh yes, sir,' I said and stuffed it up my jumper.

As I was leaving the school the headmaster caught me up. 'What kind of day have you had?' he asked.

'Very nice, thank you, sir,' I said. He looked at me quizzically.

'What on earth have you got under your sweater?' he asked. I produced the box, meekly. 'Whatever you do,' said the headmaster, 'don't let Mr Harvey know I've seen it, he'll think he's done something wrong. Good night, Richard.'

'Good night, Mr Gill.'

When I got to the school gate Tom was waiting for me. He looked so elegant in his uniform, languidly leaning against the ivy-covered brick, that I got a tingle up the back of my neck when I realized that if I were to lean against the wall, which I was perfectly at liberty to do, then I would look exactly the same. If anything I may look even better, my uniform being newer, and my face glowing with education. If I wanted to I could loiter against the ivy for as long as I liked displaying my definite air of knowledge and hearing the comments of the passers-by: '*I bet that's a boy who knows a thing or two*', '*I bet that's a boy with Prospects*.' I was in possession of a sure insurance: an understanding of tropical precipitation and a knowledge of the inner organs of caterpillars. Here was a boy, I felt, who would shortly be able to comment on the current political situation, to quote the gross national product of Malaysia, and to name the longest river in the world, and all this, no doubt, by the end of the week.

As it happened I didn't join Tom hanging about by the gate on this occasion, but walked with him across the common to catch our bus. Just to stand at the bus-stop was an excitement; there seemed to be hundreds of us, all with our briefcases and kit-bags, leaping on to buses and departing to locations all over south Bromley. Tom and I sat ourselves on the top deck and I was introduced to Tom's friends. They were full of questions for me like:'Do you both know when the other has been hurt?' and 'Do you have the same dreams at night?'

'Of course,' we replied, and they were all amazed.

There was not a child in the school, I had heard, who

could not read, a fact that greatly impressed me when I considered that for many of Broadfield's young gentlemen reading remained a mystery until the day that they left and confronted their first, over-simplified, form in the dole office.

We got off the bus and walked toward Prospect, occasionally jeered at by the skinheads who sat up in the trees feeding on bags of solvent. It was a windy autumn afternoon and when we came to Blake's Mill we stopped to watch its demolition, joining a small group of men who had worked there. The whole mill had been gutted, the machinery sold to Pakistan, and the ground divided into lots, all to become carpet and furniture warehouses which when built would be staffed by half a dozen or so unskilled humpers where once hundreds had been employed. Large sheets of paper, and lumps of rag and pulp swirled in tornado-like columns in the air around us, and a fake snowstorm of the vellum laid a premature winter on the remaining trees. Other buildings too, on Prospect itself, had more happily been demolished, amid cheers from their former occupants. These were the new places that had gone up in the mid-sixties, of the cram-them-in-like-bottles-in-a-crate variety, constructed from sub-standard cement, and the 'deck developments', which were the same old high rises simply laid on their sides. Only the worst families would take them and within five years they were rat-riddled and cockroach-infested, and the kids sprayed the walls and merged with the vermin in the concrete-pillared basements. The whole lot, only half the age of our house, had to come down again, and hopefully more like them would follow.

When we got to our garden gate we were greeted by the most astonishing surprise. Ellen was in the garden.

'What are you doing, Mum?' I asked.

'I'm cutting these hydrangeas back, the whole garden's overrun with them,' she said proudly.

'But what about your wheelchair?' asked Tom. Ellen smiled. Her wheelchair sat abandoned in the middle of the lawn, one wheel stuck into the soil, and the track marks of a furious struggle behind it.

'Blinking thing,' said Ellen, 'it's no good for going around the garden in.'

'But you can't walk,' I said.

'I know that, but I thought I'd go mad and stand up.'

We ran over to where she proudly and defiantly stood, surrounded by deadheads, and we walked with her through the front door and into the kitchen. In the kitchen, and still standing, Ellen performed the great miracle for which we had waited. She brewed a refreshing cup of tea: her power had returned.

Outside, in the fading autumn sun, Mr Bannister passed, inspecting his fabric, and nodding happily towards the newly tidied garden. He saw the lights and heard the laughter and rounds of applause from inside our house. He smiled upon the success of Prospect which had ably served these people. As he turned the corner there was a slight rumble from beneath the pavement from the innovatory sewage system. The rumble grew to a shake and a Vesuvian blast lifted several of the drain covers in his path. Edwin Bannister grabbed on to a lamp-post as a sudden vision passed before his mind: great explosions and a great shower of effluent raining down upon the people and the property of Prospect, preserving all that it covered in suspended animation, the dogs and the cats, the man tinkering with his car, the woman pegging out, the child in its Davy Crockett outfit, like a modern Pompeii, to be discovered and cherished by future generations, so that they could see what he, and people like him, had achieved in our times.

Outstanding fiction in paperback from Grafton
Books

Nicholas Salaman
The Frights   £2.50 ☐
Dangerous Pursuits   £2.50 ☐

Salman Rushdie
Grimus   £2.50 ☐

Denise Gess
Good Deeds   £2.50 ☐

Lisa Zeidner
Alexandra Freed   £2.50 ☐

Ronald Frame
Winter Journey   £2.50 ☐

Torey Hayden
The Sunflower Forest   £2.95 ☐

Cathleen Schine
Alice in Bed   £2.50 ☐

Doris Grumbach
The Ladies   £2.50 ☐

C J Koch
The Year of Living Dangerously   £2.95 ☐
The Doubleman   £2.95 ☐

John Treherne
The Trap   £2.50 ☐

Outstanding fiction in paperback from Grafton Books

Muriel Spark

The Abbess of Crewe	£1.95 ☐
The Only Problem	£2.50 ☐
Territorial Rights	£1.25 ☐
Not To Disturb	£1.25 ☐
Loitering with Intent	£1.25 ☐
Bang-Bang You're Dead	£1.25 ☐
The Hothouse by the East River	£1.25 ☐
Going up to Sotheby's	£1.25 ☐
The Takeover	£1.95 ☐

Toni Morrison

Song of Solomon	£2.50 ☐
The Bluest Eye	£2.50 ☐
Sula	£2.50 ☐
Tar Baby	£1.95 ☐

Erica Jong

Parachutes and Kisses	£2.95 ☐
Fear of Flying	£2.95 ☐
How to Save Your Own Life	£2.50 ☐
Fanny	£2.95 ☐
Selected Poems II	£1.25 ☐
At the Edge of the Body	£1.25 ☐

Anita Brookner

Family and Friends	£2.50 ☐
A Start in Life	£2.50 ☐
Providence	£2.50 ☐
Look at Me	£2.50 ☐
Hotel du Lac	£2.50 ☐

To order direct from the publisher just tick the titles you want
and fill in the order form.   GF1381

All these books are available at your local bookshop or newsagent, or can be ordered direct from the publisher.

To order direct from the publishers just tick the titles you want and fill in the form below.

Name _____

Address _____

Send to:
Grafton Cash Sales
PO Box 11, Falmouth, Cornwall TR10 9EN.

Please enclose remittance to the value of the cover price plus:

UK 60p for the first book, 25p for the second book plus 15p per copy for each additional book ordered to a maximum charge of £1.90.

BFPO 60p for the first book, 25p for the second book plus 15p per copy for the next 7 books, thereafter 9p per book.

Overseas including Eire £1.25 for the first book, 75p for second book and 28p for each additional book.

Grafton Books reserve the right to show new retail prices on covers, which may differ from those previously advertised in the text or elsewhere.